A SPLASH OF RED . . .

Jessica opened the door into the bedroom . . . and stood absolutely still. She could not stop staring. Through her head ran idiotically the continuation of the same thought. Oh God, the mess, the terrible red mess, all over Chloe's white bed. But this time she did not think that Chloe would be furious about it. Chloe would never be furious about anything again.

For Chloe, little white Chloe, one high-heel dangling from a foot which had fallen over the side of the bed, was lying with her eyes open and an enormous red gaping wound across her throat.

Bantam Crime Line Books offer the finest in classic and modern British murder mysteries.
Ask your bookseller for the books you have missed.

Agatha Christie

Death on the Nile
A Holiday for Murder
The Mousetrap and Other Plays
The Mysterious Affair at Styles
Poirot Investigates
Postern of Fate
The Secret Adversary
The Seven Dials Mystery
Sleeping Murder

Dorothy Simpson

Last Seen Alive
The Night She Died
Puppet for a Corpse
Six Feet Under
Close Her Eyes
Element of Doubt
Dead on Arrival

Elizabeth George

A Great Deliverance
Payment in Blood

Colin Dexter

Last Bus to Woodstock
The Riddle of the Third Mile
The Silent World of Nicholas
  Quinn
Service of All the Dead
The Dead of Jericho
The Secret of Annexe 3
Last Seen Wearing

Michael Dibdin

Ratking

Liza Cody

Head Case

John Greenwood

The Mind of Mr. Mosley
The Missing Mr. Mosley
Mosley by Moonlight
Murder, Mr. Mosley
Mists Over Mosley
What, Me, Mr. Mosley?

Ruth Rendell

A Dark-Adapted Eye
  (writing as Barbara Vine)
A Fatal Inversion
  (writing as Barbara Vine)

Marian Babson

Death in Fashion
Reel Murder
Murder, Murder Little Star
Murder on a Mystery Tour
Murder Sails at Midnight

Dorothy Cannell

The Widows Club
Down the Garden Path
coming soon: Mum's the Word

Antonia Fraser

Jemima Shore's First Case
Your Royal Hostage
Oxford Blood
A Splash of Red
Quiet as a Nun
coming soon:
Cool Repentance
The Wild Island

A Splash of Red

Antonia Fraser

BANTAM BOOKS

NEW YORK · TORONTO · LONDON · SYDNEY · AUCKLAND

A SPLASH OF RED

A Bantam Book / published by arrangement with
W.W. Norton & Company, Inc.

PRINTING HISTORY
W.W. Norton edition published 1981
Bantam edition / February 1990

ISBN 0-553-28071-6

Bantam Books are published by Bantam Books, a division of Bantam
Doubleday Dell Publishing Group, Inc. Its trademark, consisting of the
words "Bantam Books" and the portrayal of a rooster, is Registered in
U.S. Patent and Trademark Office and in other countries. Marca
Registrada. Bantam Books, 666 Fifth Avenue, New York, New York
10103.

For Damian
*and other family voices
heard at Praia de Luz*

Contents

Author's Note

Adelaide Square, either designed by Adam or ruined by Sir Richard Lionnel, does not exist. For the purposes of this story, I have placed it to the west of the British Museum, sandwiched between Bedford Square and Tottenham Court Road.

Chapter One

"No Noise"

"At least you'll be very quiet up here," said Chloe. "All on your own. Except for Tiger, of course. And in his own way he's very quiet too."

"Like all cats. Part of what I love about them. The silent comings and goings." Jemima Shore spoke comfortingly, and gave a long hard rub to Tiger's back as she did so. Tiger arched and his tail went up; he was not to be won so easily. Jemima stopped and Tiger shot away. His departure was soundless on the thick beige furry carpet which covered Chloe Fontaine's flat.

"All the same, you're sure you won't be lonely?" Chloe asked anxiously, putting down her mug of coffee on the wide glass table. The mug was the colour of oatmeal, like most of the furnishings in the flat; the milky coffee blended with the other subdued colours. Even Tiger, a long-haired golden cat, fitted in with the décor—or perhaps, reflected Jemima, it had been chosen round him. Everything in the flat was not only very light but also very clean. Of course Chloe had only just moved in; nevertheless Jemima knew from previous experience of Chloe's houses and flats that the cleanliness was something spiritual in her—a protest of the soul, she sometimes felt, against the disorder of her private life. Mind against Body.

Meanwhile Chloe was looking round her, still anxious, as though, unexpectedly, the flat might reveal some hidden source of either noise or comfort—it was not quite clear which.

"I want to be lonely," thought Jemima Shore. "That's why I'm here. Pure selfishness. Not really to help you out at all." Aloud she said in the kind of bracing voice she had been using to Chloe since they were at Cambridge together: "I'm never lonely, Clo. You know me. I shall love it here. It's so tranquil. And looking

1

after Tiger will cheer me up." Jemima's beautiful and beloved tabby Colette had had to be put down six weeks earlier. Jemima still found the return to her own flat, now empty, intolerable. It was one of the reasons she was happy to move away from it for the time being. "It's so tranquil here," she repeated.

As she spoke, Jemima Shore's eye was caught by a splash of colour through the open door of the pale bedroom. For a moment it looked as if red paint—or even blood—had been dashed on the wall. Then she realized that she was looking at an enormous canvas slurred with red. A woman's figure was involved. The picture gave Jemima a momentary sense of discomfort, the first since she had entered Chloe's cloistered off-white apartment.

Chloe followed the direction of her eyes and smiled.

"You're surprised to see it?"

"Well, everything else is so—"

"I decided to keep just one. And that was the right one to keep. The most violent one of all. To remind me. Never ever again. 'A Splash of Red.' No, that's its title. No matter how many calls, how many evening threats, midnight pleas, how many early-morning demands . . ." Jemima realized that the red-splashed picture was by Chloe's lover—or rather her former lover—Kevin John Athlone. This fact did not make her feel any warmer towards the picture. Besides, Chloe's reason for hanging it was not totally convincing, in view of her famous fastidiousness. Jemima wondered, rather wearily, whether somewhere in her soft heart, Chloe was still in love with the appalling Kevin John.

Yet Chloe's whole reason for leaving her pretty little house in Fulham to live in this new block of history-less flats in Bloomsbury had been as she phrased it tearfully on the telephone "to put the past behind me. I've had it, Jem, absolutely *had* it. I can't stand it any more, the noise, the shouting, the rows, the *blows*—yes, of course there were blows, can't you see it just by looking at him?—no of course I didn't call the police, Jemima, no point, in any case the noise of it was almost worse than the blows. Anyway I'm just off, off to a new flat, just Tiger and me, somewhere where there's no Kevin John and above all *No Noise*." This conversation had ended on a note of rising hysteria.

Chloe Fontaine's new flat was in a large Georgian square near the British Museum. It was certainly an extremely quiet area. Most of the other houses contained offices; but they were offices belonging to solicitors, architects, publishers and other sober professional people. During the day the bustle of business was subdued and scarcely likely to disturb. Even nearby Tottenham Court Road provided little more than a dull reverberation. At night, Chloe told Jemima, there was really nothing to be heard at all. The flats below Chloe's were still empty.

"At least he doesn't have your address. Or I very much hope not!" exclaimed Jemima, stretching out her long legs, tanned from the hot summer, across the carpet. Happily they toned with it. Unlike the picture.

"No, of course he doesn't," Chloe said quickly. "I believe he's gone back to Cornwall, to that studio he used to have. And he's living with a Vietnamese girl. Vietnamese? No, probably not. Balinese? Siamese? Something oriental and"—a pause—"no doubt submissive." There was a small silence.

"Listen," Chloe went on in a much brisker voice. "I've always liked that picture. For itself alone, believe it or not. I think I was rather exaggerating its significance in my life. Now the main point is, will *you* be lonely? I'm sorry about Rosina packing up, by the way, although you may not be. Rosina is a good sort but she's a compulsive talker. In the six weeks since I moved here most of my work has been in a vain attempt to ward off her conversation. She said she'd be away about a fortnight—but she's not a very accurate prophet about her own movements; I suppose she has to be back before I am. Depends on the wretched child's progress. How long do you take to recover from tonsils, darling? Little Enrico is not even a good sort like his mother, but he has inherited the art of conversation from her, so whatever you do—for your own peace, don't let her bring him."

"As usual it's all immaculate," began Jemima. "There would be nothing for Rosina to do."

But Chloe was rattling on, and jangling some keys at the same time. "One thing, whatever you do don't forget your keys. The separate flat buzzers which open the front door aren't ready yet, so it's left open in the day, locked in the evening. And there really is no one within earshot at night. Believe it or not, I did that last week—forgot my keys—and had to spend the night out in Adelaide Square, after climbing over the railings. I know it's a fabulous summer. Even so—but what could I do?"

Chloe sighed, laughed, and continued. "Still it was an interesting experience in its own way. Rather a surprise altogether. Might have altered the course of my life if I didn't already have a new angel, the most divine angel in *heaven*. As it was, it was just a little, a very little, adventure. A casual encounter you might say. A carnal encounter, perhaps. Rather naughty of me under the circumstances. But I couldn't resist it."

Jemima felt relieved. All was explained, including the slightly frenetic quality in Chloe's conversation. A new lover. Not an old fear. No, this was not at all the distraught neurotic Chloe of months back, but the mercurial creature whose changing romances were the wonder of her friends. Like the ordered décor of her houses, Chloe's fragile appearance was belied by the tempestuous nature of her private life. Since Cambridge, when Jemima Shore had been drawn to Chloe's delicate Marie Laurencin looks—sloe eyes in a pale child's face—she had wondered at this contradiction.

What was more, no hint of it appeared in Chloe's work. In her writing Chloe was the reverse of tempestuous: on the contrary, she gave the impression of one wittily in command both of herself and her characters.

"Even Tiger's life is not as crammed with incident as Chloe's," Guthrie Carlyle had once remarked rather crossly to Jemima. "And he's a tom cat. What's more, Tiger is a lot more discreet. Is it possible that Chloe's cat actually wrote *Fallen Child*, do you suppose? When I think of that exquisitely honed prose and those finely judged characters, and then this latest scrape of Chloe's . . ." They were discussing Chloe's decision to leave her husband for Kevin John Athlone at the time—"I know it only adds to the fascination," he added hastily.

Guthrie Carlyle was Jemima's devoted assistant at Megalith Television. He had once been more than that—Jemima's devoted lover, but the affair had come to an end after Jemima's involvement in certain events, both passionate and strange, in Scotland. The tragic outcome of it all had killed in Jemima any desire for anything except work—work and oblivion. Guthrie had accepted this tacit dismissal from one of his two roles in Jemima's life with that air of whimsical sadness which he used to cover up his deepest feelings; however, Guthrie and Jemima remained close friends as well as colleagues.

Jemima Shore was the writer and presenter of one of the more popular serious television programmes. She was billed as Jemima Shore, Investigator, and the title had appealed to the popular imagination as though she were some kind of amateur detective.

In fact the title was merely a catchphrase and the kind of thing Jemima investigated on television was more likely to be slum housing or the fate of unmarried mothers or some combination of the two with perhaps the medical risks of the Pill thrown in for good measure. Nevertheless the title had caught on in the minds of the public and in recent years a number of people had appealed to Jemima Shore to solve their problems—with success. Curiosity was a habit of mind to her. It was tempting even now to try and work out the identity of Chloe's lovers by considering the clues. But she must restrain herself. She had a purpose in coming to Bloomsbury. Distractions were to be avoided.

She concentrated on Chloe's future plans.

"Do I take it then that you're not after all going on this famous holiday alone?" she asked. "I'd rather imagined that since Kevin John there hadn't been anyone, well, serious . . ."

"Oh, darling, it's absolutely not a holiday, not in that sense." Chloe was busy scribbling down a list of local shops ("I advise plunging down into Soho for anything decent: cross Tottenham Court Road, down the Charing Cross Road, avoid the dirty bookshops and it's nearer than you think"). "No darling, I would hardly ask you to come over here, all of a sudden, just like that," she continued, "if I was off on a spree. No, it's work, and God knows I need it. Do you know that my last book sold exactly four thousand copies, in spite of Valentine's gallantly pornographic jacket. And Jamie Grand's angelic review; no, not him personally—though he *is* an angel—but his deeply pompous and deeply powerful paper. So loyal to give it to Marigold Milton, who absolutely adores my work, when you think what some of his other lovely ladies might have made of it."

Jemima recalled the jacket of *Fallen Child* and shuddered: some kind of naked bathing scene had been depicted, a sort of *déjeuner sur l'herbe* including all the family. It crossed her mind that Valentine Brighton was not to blame, and that the artist had not penetrated Chloe's elegant prose beyond the first twenty-five pages . . . still, as publisher, Valentine should have known better. Or perhaps he did and considered the end (sales) justified the jacket.

Jemima murmured sympathetically but without committal on the subject of the jacket. She herself felt on strong ground on the subject of Chloe's work since she genuinely admired it, and had done so since Chloe's first novel was published shortly after they both left Cambridge. She liked the mixture of precision and sensibility; the particular sly humour which regularly inspired critics to compare Chloe to Jane Austen. They generally added: "And I do not use the comparison lightly." To which Chloe would regularly respond: "No, they undoubtedly use it very heavily." But Jemima suspected that in her heart of hearts Chloe was not quite so displeased.

Comparisons to contemporary female writers, however distinguished, on the other hand maddened her. "Another Olivia Manning" was one comment which had provided weeks of irritation; nor was Chloe more satisfied when reviewers in the United States mentioned the name of the ironic and brilliant Alison Lurie, and suggested ·that the latter had provided an inspiration.

"Anyway I found the round figure highly suspicious," Chloe was rattling on in her attractive breathless voice, an attribute which underlined further the childlike quality of her appearance. "And I told Valentine as much, but he swore, in that utterly convincing honour-of-the-regiment way of his which always makes one even *more* suspicious—he swore it was exactly four thousand. In the meantime I'm in a load of trouble over my new book—believe it or not, *libel*, quite ridiculous how sensitive people are, of course there's nothing in it—but he, Valentine that is, is hanging on to the advance. He says the best he can do to tide me over is to pay me a flat sum if I edit an anthology of women's letters down the ages. *The Quiet Art*—no, not heart, art, don't laugh, I know it's pretty desperate, but I'm trying to make something of it. Even I have been investigating the Reading Room of the British Library in my own quiet and, we hope, artful way . . . However, as usual I need more."

"So this is good old *Taffeta* in the ample shape of Isabelle Mancini, commissioning me. *Taffeta* Schmaffeta. But at least it never lets you down. Off to France. I think Isabelle has in mind rippling tensions between a woman and a horse, with her usual optimism, whereas I see it as a lonely woman rides in Camargue. Pictures by Snowdon if we're lucky, the insufferable Binnie Rapallo if we're not. 'Thoughts suggested by white chargers,' cried Isabelle: she never learns. And she always adds: 'Do something about the *food*, darling, don't forget.' It's a hangover from her days as a cookery writer. What do horses eat in the Camargue? If I found out, would that satisfy her? Still, I'm going ahead for ten days to sit alone and perhaps wander and get new ideas. The photographer—Binnie, I have no doubt—follows."

"Alone, Clo?" Jemima jumped up to pace round the apartment.

"Absolutely alone. I am definitely *not* taking my new angel with me. The news of my romance, by the way, is a heavy secret till I come back. I haven't broken it to the last angel, who was of all things—well, perhaps that had better be a secret too till I get back. Why give you a quick blurb on my life when a full-length novel is so much more fun? It might spoil it. A married man—no more for the present."

Chloe was certainly right back in her old form. Two new men at least in her life—or rather new to Jemima's list of Chloe's involvements—two new men and something catalogued as an adventure. Jemima could not quite resist running through a few possible names in her head. Then she was distracted by the majestic view from the vast picture window which ran the length of the room.

Jemima could see across the tops of the great trees of Adelaide Square to the elegant eighteenth-century houses on the opposite side. Chloe's new residence was in a concrete balconied block. To Jemima's mind its style was somewhere between the Mappin Terraces at Regent's Park Zoo and the National Theatre, less charming than the former, more appealing than the latter. Its position turned its architecture into an affront.

It also seemed peculiarly unfair that the occupant of this horror would have the advantage of looking at its beautiful neighbours, whereas they in turn had to contemplate the monstrosity. Unfair indeed—she suddenly remembered the furious protests at the building of the new landmark, or rather the demolition of the great house which had preceded it. Very understandable, but somehow the protests had either been got round or muffled.

That was, perhaps, because Sir Richard Lionnel was involved: an exotic saturnine gentleman whose tweeded figure—he did not affect the normal dark suit of a tycoon—was to be glimpsed in as many government corridors as boardrooms.

"So I shall be quite out of touch and alone, as lonely as you will be here, in a different way. No angel and no telephone calls," Chloe was saying.

"What happened to those protesters, Clo?" Jemima interrupted. "I'm looking into Adelaide Square. The ones who threatened this building—it was this one, wasn't it? I do see their point—if it doesn't sound ungrateful, living in your luxurious eyrie."

"Oh, I believe the original house was riddled with dry rot, in a terrible state. I know for a fact that squatters and what-have-you were imminent. No way it could be preserved. The façade perhaps—but that would have cost the earth."

"So the protest just died down?"

"Oddly enough it hasn't quite. I meant to warn you, except that it's not very serious and certainly won't bother you at night. They still feel strongly about Lionnel himself. That's because they're frightened he'll do the same thing elsewhere. Notably next door. You saw the scaffolding? The battle's lost but you know what demonstrators are. You may get the odd rude note downstairs, but it will just be addressed 'The Occupant,' so pay no attention. There are sometimes people with placards—'The Lion of Blooms-bury, seeking whom he may devour.' 'Don't let the Lion eat Bloomsbury,' that sort of thing. I see them there most days. But they won't bother you. Some of them are quite attractive, if you like that sort of thing. Long hair, beards and very narrow hips, if you know what I mean." Jemima did. It was not an attraction she had ever felt. Involuntarily she frowned.

"They don't make any noise, I'm glad to say. As a matter of fact, with some rather picturesque lions on their placards, they rather cheer up the pavement." Chloe gave a little smile, rather sly, at Jemima's disapproval. "I adore lions, don't you? I always want to hug them at the zoo. Ever one for danger in love."

"'The Lion of Bloomsbury'—quite a title for a programme," muttered Jemima, adding swiftly: "But I'm having a holiday from all that. The series is resting and so am I." Then she couldn't resist asking: "Always the same lot? Of demonstrators, I mean?"

"To tell you the truth, I don't think I look very closely."

"I would get rather fascinated by them if I saw them every day," Jemima admitted.

"You would, darling, you would!" cried Chloe. Now it was her turn to abandon the vast sofa and gaze into the darkening square across the trees. Jemima noticed her slight body instinctively fall into a graceful attitude, almost that of an actress or a dancer, so that the window framed her, and her faintly leaning head. Chloe did have exceptionally long legs for such a tiny woman—a dancer's legs. Looking at her, Jemima considered that she hardly looked any older than when they were at Cambridge together; she was perhaps just a little fatter with a certain roundness of the bosom absent in extreme youth, which only added to her femininity. But her face, if anything, was thinner.

"But then you are Jemima Shore, Investigator. And I'm Chloe Fontaine, with my limited range, my domestic palette with its few and unexperimental colours as my critics frequently tell me."

"I never underrate your range," said Jemima. "Not since our first day at Cambridge when I discovered to my chagrin that the prettiest girl at the Freshers' meeting was also the top scholar of the year. Your heart is another matter, but you have an excellent head, Clo, so long as you manage to keep it somewhere not to far from your shoulders."

"No, I haven't always done that, have I?" For a moment Chloe sounded quite melancholy. The graceful head in question sank still further. She looked quite white for a moment, or perhaps it was a trick of the light. "Memo: keep my head, lose my heart. This new romance, Jem, it's so perfect, or rather it's going to be perfect, so long as I do keep my head. Sorry to sound so mysterious but for once that's all I can say. I'll tell you all when I get back from the Camargue." Chloe wheeled round, facing the open bedroom door.

"I lost my head and my heart over him, didn't I? You see what a warning that painting is. No more splashes of red for me. No, don't turn on the lights. I love the dusk falling over the square. Do it when I've gone. Let me enjoy my flight from responsibility. I've shown you where they all are. Dimmers and everything for a late night rendezvous. Have a good time, a very good time, darling."

"I'm going to be working in the Reading Room of the British Library by day," protested Jemima, "and trying to write at night. It's my chance, while the programme's not on and before we start gathering material in the autumn. No high life at all. I promised Valentine that I would let him have an outline at least and the first chapters of my famous book by September."

"Ah, Valentine. If we kept all our promises to him!" cried Chloe slightly petulantly. "Anyway he doesn't expect it. So long as one is frank about it. I always tell the truth to Valentine, however awful. He can't resist that."

It crossed Jemima's mind that in the nicest possible way Chloe might be slightly jealous of her own more recent relationship with the publisher. Jemima did not flatter herself that Valentine Brighton had commissioned her book entirely for its own sake: the image of Jemima Shore, Investigator, was a strong one in the public's eye. Jemima's name would look good on a book jacket, particularly as television books so often headed the bestseller lists.

Chloe on the other hand had supported herself by writing alone, all her working life, none of her books having been made into plays, films, or even serialized for television. It did not matter that Jemima's projected *opus* was not in fact a spin-off from her television series, but a serious study of Edwardian women philanthropists. It was possible to argue that even with her first book Jemima Shore, Investigator, would start with an unnatural advantage over Chloe Fontaine, lady novelist of some years' standing.

"Well, you could always have Valentine over here," said Chloe with a slightly mischievous smile. "That would be work. His office is in Bedford Square, almost opposite Cape's and his *pied à terre*, his foot on the earth as he insists on calling it, is over there, on the other side of this square. The elegant bit, behind the trees. Very handy for keeping an eye on me—that's *another* story I shall tell you on my return from the Camargue. Quite interesting. We shall make an evening of it—I shall be Scheherazade."

"Like Garbo, I want to be alone," replied Jemima firmly.

Jemima watched while Chloe locked the discreet white cupboard in the corner of the sitting room.

"Sorry—locking habit. You know me. Anyway I've moved most of my London clothes in there, leaving room for yours in the bedroom. I'm taking virtually nothing on holiday." She popped the key in her pocket.

Light and charming as a fairy in her movements, Chloe was even now gathering up her bag, and in a moment was flitting down the staircase. It was a beautiful staircase, broad, even to the penultimate flight where it twisted neatly upwards to the penthouse like a piece of barley-sugar. There at least his architect had done Sir Richard Lionnel proud. The lift did not yet work however: "Don't go near it. You don't want to take that kind of risk," Chloe had said, quite unnecessarily. "And I advise you not to venture into the basement either—unless you have to plunge after Tiger who adores it. Dark and unfinished."

Jemima stood at the door and listened to Chloe clattering down the stairs in the very high heels she always wore. Chloe was six inches shorter than Jemima; even in the Camargue, Jemima imagined that her riding boots would have very high heels.

Down to the bottom went Chloe's tapping heels, gradually

growing fainter. It sounded a very long way down. Jemima continued to listen, deciding, for some reason she could not quite analyse, to wait until she heard the front door bang. After a while she thought she heard a noise—that must be the door. It all took longer than she had expected. It was like listening for a stone dropped into a well: the splash was surprisingly long in coming.

Finally, Jemima turned away and went back into the flat. Still she did not put on the lights. The sky was extremely beautiful, a Tiepolo-like sky, with turquoise and gold and areas of mauve and pink. Going to the window, she thought to watch Chloe passing across the square to the other side where she had left her car. Jemima could see the car—or thought she could. It was a bright green Renault with a hatchback, and Chloe was driving to Dover that night, before taking the ferry the next day.

However, she had evidently missed her. There were a few people about, odd passers-by, foreigners mainly; a few Japanese tourists but the tourist crowds were diminishing in the fine August evening. It was more surprising to see that Chloe's car remained untouched. For a moment she was quite puzzled. Then she gave a brief laugh and turned away. Jemima suddenly remembered that she had no idea of the colour of Chloe's new car. She was thinking of the old one, and she knew that Chloe had acquired a new car recently—"bought out of the royalties Valentine assures me I haven't earned, the pig!" Someone quite different got into the green car and drove away in the direction of Tottenham Court Road.

It was time to turn on the lights. Something soft and furry rubbed at her knees. It was Tiger returned. His tail was up, but in friendly fashion. He must have come in through the balcony window which, Chloe had informed her, must always be left open at least five inches ("you would hardly have intruders at this height—cats are more likely than cat burglars").

Chloe had already installed some tubs, filled with grey foliage—senecio, artemisia—and trailing white geraniums with silver-green leaves shaped like ivy. The cool tones of the plants completed the feeling of serenity. Jemima drew the French window back to its fullest extent. It was hot. She stepped out onto the balcony. The sight of the ugly concrete parapet jarred upon her once again, after the harmony of the plants; perhaps it was just as well that the Lionnel architect, preferring his artistic design to

11

safety, had made it slightly lower than might have been expected, in order not to interfere with the view.

She inspected the rest of the area. She had not realized before that the next-door house was not yet completed, the scaffolding still present. It was to be another Lionnel enterprise. There the balcony was still in embryo. To her right was one of the great houses of Adelaide Square. Here the top floor, in its original state, was not graced with a balcony.

It was immensely quiet.

Her peace was disturbed by the sound of the telephone in the flat. Jemima stepped back in, noticing once more with irritation how the picture—"A Splash of Red"—disturbed the harmony. She, after all, did not need reminding of the value of avoiding Kevin John Athlone. She might even take it down . . . Tiger would hardly object. So far as she could remember, Tiger had shown a cat's good sense in regularly ramming his claws into the wretched Kevin John.

The telephone rang persistently. Jemima picked it up. According to Chloe, most of the calls would be wrong numbers. She had not yet sent out her new telephone number to her friends.

At first, therefore, Jemima assumed that she was listening to a misdirected call. She stepped back all the same and handled the instrument gingerly. It was a mean little white object, giving a rather shrill "pip-pip," as opposed to a full-blooded ring.

Jemima intended to give the correct number in a cold and reproving voice, but did not have time to do so.

"You whore," said the voice quite distinctly. Jemima, urban born and accustomed if not indifferent to such things, began to put the receiver back hastily, when the voice said, equally distinctly:

"Supposing there was a real splash of red on the carpet. Or would you prefer it on the bed?"

Chapter Two

Disappearing in London

Automatically, Jemima replaced the telephone receiver. She stood in the white flat, quiet again after the persistent odious ringing, and looked at the miniature instrument. She considered whether to leave the receiver off the hook.

It was now nearly nine o'clock. She had deliberately not left Chloe's number with the American girl to whom she had lent her own flat in a very different area of London. Jemima had told her tenant rather vaguely that she was "going away" and to get in touch with Megalith Television if there were any crises. She had told Guthrie Carlyle that she was "going somewhere to have some peace" without mentioning that this peace was to be found in Bloomsbury. Her secretary, the nubile Cherry, the toast of Megalithic House, was herself on holiday in Corfu. There were no family demands likely to be made upon Jemima, no sorrowing widowed mother, no helpless bachelor father, no sister in the process of leaving an intolerable husband who might wish to call her.

Jemima Shore had many close friends, many admirers and numerous acquaintances, quite apart from the vast public who assumed they were her intimates from seeing her image on the television screen. But she was one of those rare people who, as far as she knew, had no living blood relations or, at any rate, no close ones. She was herself an only child. Both her parents had been only children and they had died together in a car crash when she was eighteen. Since then a couple of elderly spinster cousins, living together in the New Forest, who had briefly attempted to

13

supply a family for her—without success, for she had not wanted another family—had also died. Jemima Shore was alone in the world. She preferred it that way. She had the freedom, as she saw it, to choose her own friends.

A London holiday had struck her at the time as a brilliant idea for escaping into peace. There was the Reading Room of the British Library, waiting like the belly of a whale to swallow her up during the day. Then there was none of the commitment and disruption of country life; to say nothing of the problems of reaching the country on a summer's day. Her own holiday journey had taken twenty minutes on the Underground from Holland Park station. She deliberately left her precious new Citroen behind— that too was a kind of freedom—and travelled with one piece of highly expensive, highly efficiently packed Lark luggage, navy blue piped in red, sitting at her feet. Her two other Jean Muir dresses in the thin silk jersey she loved, would emerge from it as immaculately as they had gone in—and would scarcely need the long white bedroom cupboard allotted to them by Chloe.

Jemima loved to travel light. Watching the impassive faces opposite her in the Tube, lit up occasionally by the sort of recognition she had learnt to accept without enjoying, she had thought with delight: "You're going to work. I'm going on holiday. I'm disappearing in London."

Jemima Shore, with no ties, thought that yes, she would take the telephone off the hook.

She certainly saw no necessity to receive the threatening calls of Kevin John Athlone. For such, she had realized, the identity of the caller must inevitably be. Who else would have made such unpleasant play with the title of the picture? And there was something quite nastily sexual about the last innuendo—"Or would you prefer it on the bed"—which put her in mind, uncomfortably, of Chloe's last remarks, her hints of violence, her use of the word "submissive." A moment's crossness against the careless Chloe swept through her. To have deliberately stated that he did not have the number—and then to be caught out almost immediately after she had left the flat!

Nevertheless Jemima was surprised. For one thing it was quite unlike Chloe to lie. Eighteen years of friendship—yes, it had to be nearly as long—had included numerous intrigues, mysteries. Jemima had also provided a good many alibis in the course of Chloe's two marriages; one lasting eight years and one a bare twelve months before Chloe had been swept off her feet by Kevin John. Naturally lies had been told in that period. Yet Jemima was convinced that fundamentally Chloe was not a liar. In most ways—except where adultery had been, briefly, concerned—she was abnormally candid and truthful. "Scheherazade"—Jemima remembered Chloe's words—"I'll tell you all." Jemima had had experience of Chloe's frank confessions before; they justified the title.

It was true that Chloe had been holding something back, to be revealed hereafter; but it was hardly something as trivial yet irritating as the fact that Kevin John Athlone had recently discovered her new telephone number. The mystery tantalized Jemima for a moment, and then she dismissed it.

On the glass table in front of the white sofa lay two books. Jemima glanced at the publisher's colophon on the spines. A golden helmet with a B set in it: Brighthelmet Press, Valentine Brighton's publishing house, the name a combination of his own and that of his home in Sussex, Helmet Manor. She looked inside the top book: a quick note was scribbled on the publisher's slip inside, where the golden helmet was repeated. She read: "Tuesday. To the marriage of true minds. Love V."

Jemima was surprised for the second time that evening. Valentine Brighton, that famously polite young man, was fond of sending round books to his authors or people he sought to *become* his authors. Whimsical notes beneath the sign of the golden helmet generally accompanied these gifts, which had begun to arrive on Jemima's desk as soon as Valentine Brighton realized that she might possibly be persuaded to write a book for him. The symbol of the golden helmet always reminded Jemima of Valentine Brighton himself with his sleek poll of thick fair hair. It was hair which always looked neat and clean and brushed, even when fashion dictated that it would sweep the shoulders of his polonecked jersey; and, despite its length, it irresistibly reminded her of the kind of hair possessed by the young officers who went out to die in the trenches in the First World War.

Jemima's book parcels arrived at Megalithic House conveyed by Lord Brighton's chauffeur, driving the Brighton Rolls-Royce. "Old as the hills," said its owner airily. But it was not in fact all that old. It was just that, like all Valentine Brighton's possessions, it looked rather old—and rather good. The chauffeur also figured in Valentine Brighton's airy *dicta*.

"Used to be a gamekeeper at Helmet. But it turned out that he loathed everything to do with potting birds and loved machines. So, a wave of the Brighton fairy wand—and lo and behold, the best chauffeur in London. What luck it is to be a feudal landlord, particularly in these difficult days of staff problems."

Jemima was never quite sure how serious that kind of remark was meant to be. It certainly *was* lucky to have inherited as a child an Elizabethan manor house, both famous and inhabitable, in a fold of the Sussex downs near the sea; plus a great deal of rich farming land surrounding it. Yet, given such a "lucky" deal from life, why had Valentine Brighton elected to work extremely hard in Bloomsbury building up a publishing firm? Presumably, like his chauffeur, he had winced from a life of "potting birds." Yet at the same time Lord Brighton showed no desire to throw off his background. Jemima had never detected in him the faintest gleam of fashionable guilt at his—considerable—inherited wealth. On the contrary, the remark concerning the chauffeur was merely typical of a whole host of such allusions.

Jemima wrenched her mind from Valentine to his note. Marriage. Valentine and Chloe. Was it possible? Anything was possible with Chloe, that she had long ago learned. But Valentine? He could hardly be Chloe's new lover—already a married man by her own account. Or was it her former lover who had been married? Her last words had been ambiguous.

"Tuesday"—and today was Friday. The position of the books suggested that they had not been there very long. Was Chloe really contemplating marrying Valentine Brighton? It was odd, if so, that Chloe's remarks about Valentine, her sales, and the likely problem of her new book had had a genuinely cross rather than a romantic tinge. For that matter, the note itself was ambiguous. "The marriage of true minds" did not necessarily refer to holy matrimony.

Yet there had been something to the relationship. "Quite riveting," Chloe's words. Scheherazade would inform her on her return. Still, Chloe might perhaps cast some light on the topic which had troubled the gossip-mongers in literary London of the past. Exactly what if any were Valentine's sexual proclivities? On that subject, Valentine himself generally took refuge in a cloud of what Jemima privately termed his "feudal" references: "Mummy simply won't *let* me marry the sort of girl who can tell one end of a book from the other." On another occasion: "Mummy says the library at Helmet was full up at the end of the eighteenth century and a bookish girl would only ruin it, by rearranging things, or worse still *reading* the books." It was easy to put all this together, the allegedly dominating figure of "Mummy," Valentine's bachelor state and the pseudo-comic references, to make of him a homosexual. If so, Valentine was an exceptionally discreet one, surprisingly and surely unnecessarily so for the times in which he lived.

On the other hand there was the question of his health. "This weak but well-bred heart beats for you" had been his characteristic way of proposing a publisher's contract to Jemima. It was common knowledge that Valentine's father had died young of a heart condition and that his mother dreaded the same fate overtaking her only child. "Mummy positively panics when I play the third set at tennis." That at least was a modest smoke-screen, for Valentine Brighton, far from being the effete performer his appearance might promise, was an exceptional athlete, at least by the standards of the set in which he moved.

Perhaps "waiting for Lady Right"—another of his teasing phrases—was indeed what he had been doing. And Chloe Fontaine, twice married already, had turned out to be the chosen she. The picture of Chloe queening it at Helmet was indeed a seductive one—even if her reign might prove short-lived. How long would she stand it? A year? Two years? There was still something odd about the whole business. At this point Jemima decided that she had spent enough time in one evening on Chloe and her amours. Resolutely, she ignored both Brighthelmet Press books. They belonged to an elaborate History of Taste, whose main object was to induce feelings of guilt in the purchaser, pangs to be assuaged by buying (but not necessarily reading) the books.

Jemima picked up her own Nadine Gordimer novel, and went to the wide balcony, hoping that there would be light enough to read in the comparative cool of the summer's evening. However, she found an outside switch and turned it on. Suddenly the balcony was flooded with light: for a moment she had the impression of being on a stage in a darkened theatre when the lights are switched on. The dark balcony to the right and the equally dark scaffolding to the left gave the irresistible effect of theatrical wings.

Jemima felt totally vulnerable, even at that great height over the square. She was exposed to whatever strange malignant forces were out there in the darkness. Moreover, an extraordinary fear

seized her—she, not given to such things—that there was someone waiting in the wings. Someone perhaps in the obscurity of the
scaffolding to her left.

As a result, an unexpected soft thump very close to her made
her give a light scream until she realized it was Tiger, returning
from some nocturnal prowl. The ghost of the dead Colette, who
had so often glided into her flat at night through the cat flap, a
small unmistakeable sound, called to her. But she had not come
here to listen to the mew of Colette's ghost.

Resolutely Jemima gave herself up to concentrate on Nadine
Gordimer. She was immediately carried into another far-off and
sombre world. When she next squinted at the elegant little gold
bracelet watch she always wore, it was 11:30.

Time to sleep and be fresh for the Reading Room of the British
Library tomorrow. The intoxication of having disappeared in
London overwhelmed Jemima with childish delight. She would
read—or perhaps she would not read—in bed. She would read,
but she would abandon Nadine Gordimer for the night and read
John Le Carré; she had spotted one by Chloe's bed. It was a great
help that Jemima had read this Le Carré before, and would thus,
in her sleepy state, have a head start with the plot. It was, in its
own way, delightful that she was not in her own luxurious but
somehow demanding bed at home, with all its little pleasures and
appurtenances about it, books, photographs, articles to read,
paraphernalia. Last thing, she put the telephone back on the hook
in the sitting room.

Afterwards she was not quite sure whether she had actually
fallen asleep or not over Le Carré (it was in fact no help to her that
she had read it before; the plot remained dazzling but impenetra-
ble) when she was startled by the plaintive peep-peep of the little
telephone by the bed.

"Dollie?" It was a woman's voice, anxious and quite elderly.
"Dollie? Is that you, dear?"

"I'm afraid that you have the wrong number," began Jemima.
"There's no Dollie here."

"Is that 636 8471?" quavered the voice. Jemima glanced at the
dial.

"Yes, but this is a new flat: the number must have been
reallocated."

Jemima had just said again: "There's no Dollie here," when she
suddenly remembered, feeling rather remorseful, that Chloe

Fontaine's mother always called her Dollie. Jemima, having been at Cambridge with Chloe, was dimly aware of this fact. As far as she could remember Chloe, formerly Dorothy or Dollie, had changed her name on arrival at Cambridge but, as she occasionally complained, had never succeeded in getting her somewhat elderly mother to acknowledge the fact.

"I see, dear. I'll just go on calling you Dollie, if you don't mind," was the most her mother could be persuaded to comment.

"Is that you, Mrs. Fontaine?" said Jemima hastily. "I'm afraid Chloe's gone away." She did not feel like entering the Dollie charade herself; considering Chloe's ancient annoyance at her mother's obstinacy, it seemed somewhat disloyal to her friend. Chloe had after all lived as long under her new name as her old, and had written a great many books under it (for which reason she had never adopted either of her two married names).

"I'm her friend, Jemima Shore," she threw in. "You may remember: we met once at Cambridge. I'm borrowing her flat while she's on holiday."

There was a moment's silence. Jemima had a picture of an old person at the other end of the telephone, grappling with unexpected information. And Mrs. Fontaine, having, as far as she could remember, borne Chloe when she was something like forty, must be in her seventies by now.

"Not Mrs. Fontaine, dear. Mrs. Stover," said the voice at last. It was less plaintive, much firmer. Further Cambridge memories came back to Jemima. The trouble with Chloe's change of name was that she had changed both her Christian name *and* her surname on arrival at university. Fontaine was the name of her real father who had been killed early in the war, and Stover the name of her stepfather who had adopted her. Presumably the reversion represented some kind of protest; at this distance Jemima hardly remembered. Where "Chloe" came from, Jemima had absolutely no idea; it was an unlikely middle name for Dorothy Stover. At all events, Mrs. Stover had persisted in addressing letters to Miss Dorothy Stover at first, until Chloe defeated her by sending them back unopened: "Not known at this College."

"Jemima Shore. Well," went on Mrs. Stover, as though digesting this information in its turn. Jemima heard her say to someone quite loudly: "Dad. Did you hear that? Jemima Shore Investigator is in Dollie's flat. I'm talking to her on the telephone." A strong and very angry man's voice could be heard saying: "I don't care who you're talking to on the telephone, not even if it's Michael Parkinson himself or the Queen of England. I want to know where Dollie is, that's what I want to know."

"You see, Dollie said she would come down here and spend the night with us." Mrs. Stover was now speaking directly into the telephone again: "And she hasn't come. And Dad's worried."

"Worried!" came a shout from the background. "Tell her I'm not *worried*. I'm bloody fed up, that's what I am. She rings up her mother the other day, out of the blue, haven't seen her for ages, too busy, that's what she says, busy with what, says I, she rings us up, says she'll be late, so we sit up for her, Mrs. Stover prepares a meal, and now her royal highness doesn't even turn up before midnight. Worried. I should bloody well think I am worried."

"Whereabouts do you live, Mrs. Stover?" enquired Jemima cautiously, when this tirade appeared to have stopped.

"In Folkestone—'Finches,' Bartleby Road. Near the park if you know Folkestone. She was going to spend the night here and take the ferry to the Continent tomorrow morning. She did say she would be late. But now it's nearly twelve o'clock."

"It *is* twelve o'clock," came the voice of Mr. Stover in the background. "It's tomorrow already, that's what it is."

Jemima gave Mrs. Stover her most soothing television voice. "How very worrying for you—both," she said diplomatically. "Chloe left here about nine so she certainly should have reached Folkestone by now. There wouldn't be much traffic. She didn't however mention that you were expecting her. She told me she was driving to Dover. I just wonder if she could have forgotten." As she spoke Jemima—rather wearily, for she agreed with Mr. Stover that it was tomorrow already—was rehearsing the familiar routine of checking for the non-arrival of a person. She would, she supposed, have to telephone the hospitals and the police, in case Chloe had had an accident or breakdown on the way.

There was another silence. Jemima half expected a roar from Mr. Stover: "Forgotten! She'd bloody well better not forget." Slightly to her surprise there was silence from both Stovers. Then she realized that Mrs. Stover was whispering to her husband. A moment later she heard Mr. Stover himself take the receiver before speaking in a more conciliatory tone.

"Well you see, Miss Shore, it's like this. It is just possible that she, Dollie, as Mrs. Stover and I are in the habit of calling her, has overlooked the appointment. The reason being—" another brief silence of hesitation—"I may as well say, to save your time and ours, that I indicated to Dollie that she had better be here by six o'clock in the evening or not come at all. And she said she couldn't, why I don't quite know, but still we'll leave that one. So I said, I indicated to her, that if she couldn't be here at six in the evening to eat supper with Mrs. Stover and myself, she had better not come at all, under the circumstances, if you understand me. It's true that she still said to her mother that she *would* come—"

"I understand." Jemima felt relief. Chloe had quite clearly not gone to Folkestone, but had driven directly to Dover. It made no sense to leave so late, to spend her time in Bloomsbury chatting to Jemima, if she had been intending to have supper in Folkestone. Why not mention casually to Jemima that she had to visit her parents?

"Look, I think she probably decided in the end not to come," Jemima went on. "Not wishing to keep you up late." That was a diplomatic way of putting it. "Will you ring me in the morning if you have any further problems?"

The Stovers, both of them, rang off. Jemima turned off her light. But sleep did not come. She lay for an hour, rather irritated by the whole affair. In the end she decided that it was because she was not quite convinced that Chloe had not set off for Folkestone. A responsible person would ring the police.

Jemima Shore rang the police, and after being put through to the various exchanges, established that there had been no road accidents involving a Miss Chloe Fontaine in central London or on the Folkestone or Dover roads that night. A call to the hospitals? No, at this point; that was really going too far. It was quite the wrong way to spend her "disappearing in London" holiday, trying to track down Chloe Fontaine. She drifted into sleep.

The next time she was woken by the telephone, she was aware that it was morning. The next thing she was aware of was that the anonymous caller was back again.

At eight-thirty in the morning, to her amazement, Jemima Shore found herself listening to words which began something like: "Shall I come and give it to you in that great bed? I could, you know. Or shall I just watch you through the walls, my private view? I haven't made up my mind. Have you made up your mind? How do you want it, Jemima Shore?" The mention of her own name broke the spell and Jemima slammed down the telephone.

It rang again instantly, as though the slamming action had set off the ringing. Trembling more with annoyance than anything else, she picked it up ready to swear at her anonymous friend.

"Look here—" she began in a loud and furious voice. Then she stopped.

"Miss Shore?" someone was saying at the other end. "This is Mrs. Stover, Dollie's mother. Miss Shore, we don't know what to think now. We had a letter from Dollie this morning. You know what the posts are—it was posted three days ago. First class too. She left out the road number, of course, she always does, although I've written to her about it over and over again, and sent her the Post Office's communication that the name is no longer sufficient, you need the number, and you have to put in Lethermere Road as well as Bartleby Road. Still, as she writes so seldom, I suppose—anyway 'Finches' ought to be enough after seventeen years. There's really no call for marking it 'Insufficient Postal Address'."

Jemima thought she distinguished a cry of "Bloody ridiculous" from the background. Mrs. Stover continued hurriedly.

"Anyway, she said she was sorry she had to be so late, to tell Dad not to be too angry, she was sorry about their words, but she'd definitely be with us by eleven. She said she had something special to tell us. She had to tell it to us personally, couldn't write it. We didn't know what that was, of course. So, Miss Shore, she's not here, her bed's not been slept in, she didn't come in the night. Miss Shore, wherever can Dollie be?"

Chapter Three

"Care for a Visit?"

The next voice on the telephone was more vigorous. Mr. Stover also sounded angry, as though Dollie had deliberately failed to arrive during the brief period of forgiveness he had extended and must now take the consequences. But his actual words were jovial enough, if hardly likely to cheer Jemima herself.

"I've just said to the wife," he half-shouted, "we're dealing with the Press here. This is Miss Jemima Shore we've got on the other end of the telephone. Jemima Shore, Investigator, no less. People round here would be queuing in their thousands to speak to her about the slightest thing, and we have her on the end of our telephone. She'll find Dollie for us, Mother . . ." But Jemima had not, she reminded herself, established a singularly successful career in television without being able to deal with the likes of Mr. Stover.

She interrupted him firmly as he was still relating at some length his dialogue with his wife.

"I advise you to call the police, Mr. Stover. That is, if you're really satisfied that Chloe—" she refused to adapt to Dollie; the persistent use of the name seemed to her part of the Stovers' fantasy about their daughter—"if you're really satisfied that Chloe was intending to visit you and not go straight to the ferry."

Jemima heard Mrs. Stover's more plaintive voice in the background. It was still unfortunately clear.

"Show her the letter, Dad," she was saying. "We must show her the letter." Strangled sounds from Mr. Stover. A pause and an even more plaintive cry. "You're *wearing* your spectacles, Charlie." Mrs. Stover added something which sounded like: "But the telephone is cheaper on Saturday, Charlie. Your cousin Poppy told us."

23

The image of the two old people in Folkestone—"near the park, if you know the town"—worrying over their daughter and their telephone and their spectacles made Jemima feel increasingly desperate. Her holiday, her disappearance in London, was being melted away by the most unwelcome compassionate feelings.

It was not at all difficult for Jemima to imagine the Stovers at home in "Finches" because she had just completed a programme on the special loneliness of elderly parents whose successful offspring had moved up the cultural scale, leaving them financially secure, but desperately, uncomprehendingly, lonely on their lowly rung of the ladder. It had been called *The Unvisited*. Chloe Fontaine had not contributed to it. She was, involuntarily and rather too late, contributing to it now.

"Read it over to me." It was the best she could do. Yes, Chloe's letter sounded positive enough about her arrival as Jemima listened and the clear light of the August morning filtered delicately through Chloe's Japanese blinds. She imagined "Finches," an immaculate little home, breakfast long since finished, crockery washed up, beds made, house garnished. The rooms would be small, unlike Chloe's airy palace. There would be plants in rows in unequal pots on the window sills, all green and rather bushy, with a small red flower or two, all quite unlike the graceful symmetrical white and grey shapes of Chloe's floral décor.

She could imagine photographs. A dark-haired Dollie with plaits winning prizes at her local grammar school. Dollie—now Chloe—in the group photograph of their first year at Cambridge. Dollie/Chloe marrying Lance Strutt? Chloe marrying Igor? Jemima had been to both weddings and not met the Stovers. It was more likely that one of those large romantic photographs of Chloe by Snowdon and Bailey and Lichfield and, best of all Parkinson, which adorned the backs of her novels and almost swamped the paperback versions, causing sardonic grief to reviewers, one of those must surely grace the Stovers' piano. Chloe in a picture hat, nestling on a swing, modern Fragonard, rising out of roses, corrupted Boucher; on one fabulous occasion actually surrounded by a flight of doves—only Binnie Rapallo could have decided to make a pastoral Greuze out of the author of *Old Miss Stevenson*, a wry tale about a spinster and her past.

Piano? A memory of Chloe at Cambridge: "My mother actually wanted to send the piano along with my trunk. A chastity symbol

I can only suppose. Certainly it would keep anything more tactile from entering this fearful room." So the piano waited for Chloe in Folkestone. Like its owners. There would be much waiting done in that house. Waiting for Dollie.

In Chloe Fontaine's new Bloomsbury apartment on the other hand no waiting had been done at all; Chloe had not even waited to tell Jemima that she intended to visit her parents. She had hardly waited to move into the flat itself before setting off for the Camargue. Jemima heard again the light clack-clack of her high heels and her characteristic rather breathy voice: "No, no, down the stairs, there's no lift. I'm in a hurry." A further pang of pity for the unvisited voices on the other end of the telephone seized Jemima; an atavistic pang perhaps for those dead parents of her own, dead before Jemima took her first steps into another world. Might they too have become the unvisited?

"Look, Mrs. Stover—"

"Mr. Stover here. The wife's gone into the kitchen to make us some tea. All this is very upsetting to her, Miss Shore. Her nerves have been all to pieces, I don't mind telling you." He sounded reproachful and on the verge of rehearsing the events of the night before all over again. Jemima was once more engaged in cutting him short when she heard him say:

"One thing directly following upon another if you understand my meaning. First Dollie's call out of the blue, quite unexpected, equally unexpected, and then she doesn't make an appearance—"

Jemima with a sinking feeling heard the story all over again—all this still before her first cup of coffee (a time when Jemima always felt that the whole world should know that she was to be treated with circumspection).

"I'll call the hospitals in London," she proffered. That could no longer be avoided. She did not mention having checked with the police the night before. "You call them in Folkestone and Dover. I'll call Chloe's editor at *Taffeta* if I can find her home number. There's probably a perfectly simple explanation for all this. If not, it's up to you to decide whether you call the police. What with Mrs. Stover's nerves," she added in a slightly less crisp tone.

All this took some time although Jemima, uncombed hair flowing over her navy blue silk kimono, did at least manage to drink a mug of coffee while dealing with the little white telephone. She also took time to feed Tiger. But Tiger's presence, golden and expectant, was not as comforting as it should have been to a confirmed cat-lover. He crouched in the middle of the carpet, haunches raised, paws forward in the attitude of a slightly aggressive sphinx. His eyes were half closed, as if he did not want her to know he was watching her and regarding events of which he did not approve. When he did abandon this stance, it was only in order to stalk through the wide balcony windows, inspect Adelaide Square or perhaps the tops of the giant trees where inviolable pigeons might be expected to lurk, and then return to the same sphinx-like position. Once only he mewed at the front door of the flat.

Tiger did not coil himself or curl up with his paws under his cheek or slumber like a thrown-away toy as Colette would have done at this hour in the morning, dreaming of the night's adventures. Jemima, efficiently telephoning the hospitals—no, no one of that name admitted since yesterday evening—was vaguely disquieted by Tiger and tried to remind herself that the animal was not only new to her but comparatively new to the Bloomsbury flat. All the same, Tiger's restlessness perturbed her. She began to have a feeling of something not altogether explained quite near them both, the woman and the cat.

She went through to the large bathroom with its shadowy flowers on walls and shutters, as though projected imperfectly by an unfocused lens. When she returned to the sitting room she reckoned that it was finally late enough to telephone Isabelle Mancini, the editor of *Taffeta,* without sounding a note of panic.

Isabelle Mancini was a notorious gossip. The trouble was that she liked to spend her night hours in company—when taxed on the subject, she was wont to point out that chic loneliness was hardly becoming or even useful to the editor of *Taffeta*. Gossip was Isabelle's personal contribution to these night marathons. She would certainly regard Jemima's present venture into loneliness as "utter madness, dulling."

This gossip was never intended to be malicious. On the contrary, the creation of legends (living)—that was Isabelle's business, and the business of *Taffeta*. If trouble was the outcome, no one was more distressed and even injured than Isabelle Mancini. But her very loyalty to Chloe might lead her to broadcast in Tasha's or Dizzy's or one of the other ludicrous smart discos for the young that she affected, that Chloe Fontaine was burdened with aged, tiresome parents "to whom she was quite wonderful."

Isabelle would never have heard of Chloe's parents and so

would know nothing of their characters; nevertheless to Isabelle all her geese were swans, and since Chloe had parents, aged parents, apparently poor parents, it must inevitably follow that she was "wonderful to them." Jemima thought that Chloe would probably prefer to be spared Isabelle's loyalty on the subject of her parents.

Isabelle Mancini's private life, or to be more exact, her sexual inclinations, were like those of Valentine Brighton, a subject of occasional amused speculation among her friends. It was generally believed that she had been married, once, long ago, in Paris or possibly Rome, and that Mr. Mancini had been abandoned along with residence in these capitals; nowadays she was resolutely Miss Mancini in public. What Isabelle patently did admire both in the pages of *Taffeta* and her own conversation, was the female sex.

At *Taffeta*, she patronized women writers, particularly talented women writers who were photogenic, with enthusiasm. Chloe, for example, owed a great deal to Isabelle's encouragement, particularly when her finances were low as in the present instance. So for that matter did Binnie Rapallo, a deliciously pretty photographer who had begun a successful career by celebrating these same writers in *Taffeta*. Were Isabelle's "little passions" ever reciprocated? Or did her continuous emphasis on "loyalty"—"All my friends are completely loyal to me and of course I'm so loyal to them"—hide an aching heart because "loyalty" was never equated with love?

It was Saturday. It was while looking for the telephone directory with Isabelle's home number that Jemima first noticed the piece of bright red paper lying on the carpet near the door. It was square, garish, made of card. Tiger had moved and was crouching near it. For one instant Jemima imagined that he had pushed the card to that position with his paws, had somehow delivered it.

She picked up the card rather gingerly and turned it over. "A Splash of Red" was printed in black letters on the other side. Above it the words Aiglon Gallery, directors Crispin Creed, Peter Potter, and below: "Recent pictures by Kevin John Athlone will be shown at the Aiglon Gallery February 1-28." It was now August. With relief Jemima realized that she was merely holding an official—and out of date—announcement of an exhibition. It was printed, formal, innocuous. She turned the card over again and saw for the first time that there was a message scrawled along the bottom in bold handwriting: "Care for a visit?"

It was by now far too late for any London post. Indeed no letters had arrived that morning; the flat was both too new and too cut-off for that. Letters and circulars, if any, were probably mouldering downstairs in the empty hall with its freshly cut marble floor where a "grand porter", Chloe had assured her, was shortly to be installed. The thought of this impending porter was not much consolation now, if in the meantime Kevin John Athlone was to be paying her unsolicited visits as and when he wished.

It struck her that the card must have been delivered while she was in the shadowy bathroom; she could hardly have missed the little red flag on the pale sea of the carpet while she contemplated Tiger's aggressive crouch. The coincidence made her both uncomfortable and angry.

Jemima would endure no more of this. The Stovers struck some chord in her heart; Kevin John Athlone nothing. Grimly, she went to the door to fling it open and if necessary confront him—only to be checked by the second lock. Jemima remembered too late that she needed a key to get out of the flat as well as into it.

Tiger sidled forward and gave a little plaintive mew beside her, something more like the cry of a baby in distress than the conventional cry of a cat. She was reminded unpleasantly of the cautionary tale of Harriet who played with matches: "Miaow, Mioo, we told you so." Perhaps after all it was better to dispose of the Stovers first; undoubtedly they were waiting anxiously by the telephone to hear from her. That meant calling Isabelle Mancini to get some kind of address in the Camargue for Chloe. She only hoped she was in England and not on a Greek island or in the South of France or somewhere else where at this time of year in Isabelle's opinion it was all happening.

The telephone was answered immediately—but not by Isabelle. "Miss Shore, Isabelle would just love to talk with you," said a voice at the other end of the telephone warmly. Either its owner had just visited the United States, or she felt that only this kind of voice was appropriate to one who answered the telephone for the editor of *Taffeta*. The accent was not quite perfect but the expression of impersonal rapture at the mere sound of Jemima's name was well done—that she, Jemima Shore, should somehow have managed to get through to Isabelle Mancini's number without succumbing to the nameless perils which lay in wait for users of the telephone system! So was the sincerity of the disappointment which followed: "But I'm afraid Isabelle is not available right now. May I take a message? This is Laura Barrymore, Isabelle Mancini's personal assistant. As of now, I am also her house guest. I am between apartments. I should be so happy . . ."

"She's in England?" Jemima spoke with relief. It was after all August.

"Why no, Miss Shore, she's not in *England*." For a moment the voice sounded just a little disappointed in Jemima, as though the daring act of telephoning must have slightly blunted her sensitivity. "Isabelle has been in Paris for the Collections. I meant that she's not available to speak with anyone till noon. She's at L'Hôtel, in conference with Princess Wagram, then she would be available to take your call, then she expects to lunch with—" a Japanese name followed. "She plans to return on Sunday."

"Of course," cried Jemima hastily. Then with all her television warmth, "I should so hate to bother Isabelle personally at such a critical moment. In fact, I naturally did not expect to speak to her. It's just that I'm trying to contact Chloe Fontaine rather urgently. Something to do with the autumn series—"

"Chloe Fontaine?" The voice was suddenly raised several tones higher and much sharpened; its native South Kensington origin was audible. "I hardly think that Isabelle would be able to help you with Miss Fontaine's address, Miss Shore." Warmth had also fled, along with transatlantic softness.

As sweetly and as rapidly as possible, Jemima explained her mission. The result was surprising. Coldness in the voice gave way to genuine astonishment.

"A piece on the Camargue? Chloe Fontaine for *Taffeta*, Miss Shore?" The implication of the last remark was clear: have you, Jemima Shore, made the unforgivable mistake of confusing *Taffeta* with *Vogue* or *Harpers & Queen*, or *Cosmopolitan*, or *Woman's Journal* or—beyond that the possibilities were too horrendous for one such as Laura Barrymore to contemplate. But Jemima knew that she had not made a mistake. She had an excellent memory for that kind of thing. She could hear Chloe's breathless voice: "Good old *Taffeta* . . . commissioning me," and then: "*Taffeta* Schmaffeta, but at least it never lets you down . . ." What interested her was the implication in Laura

Barrymore's rapidly rising tone that the very combination in itself of Chloe and *Taffeta* was unthinkable.

Jemima had to concede that a commission to Chloe Fontaine, involving both a handsome sum of money advanced and a subsequent rendezvous abroad with a leading photographer, was hardly likely to be quite unknown to Isabelle's personal assistant, one close enough to the editor to be her "house-guest" while she was "between apartments." However, for the sake of the Stovers, she persevered. Laura Barrymore was adamant.

At the end of Jemima's enquiries, however, Laura clearly felt it necessary to round off the conversation in her warmer manner. "I should just love to take this opportunity to tell you how I adored your last programme, Miss Shore," she murmured. "That twilight home. The old lady and the old gentleman, both knitting, it was his knitting which just reached out to me. Like a Dutch picture sprung to life." Jemima remembered that particular phrase since it had occurred in the *Guardian* review, and the paper had also referred to the programme in the third leader. "A Dutch picture sprung horribly to life, showing the despair masked by an outwardly harmonious composition." That was how it had actually read.

Still, it might just be worth making some use of Miss Barrymore's enthusiasm.

"You've been so kind . . . hardly worth bothering Isabelle with all this . . . quite, quite, so busy at this time of year." She took a breath. "Just one thing . . . I was contemplating, you know, an in-depth profile of Isabelle, allied to the development of *Taffeta*, in my autumn series. You know, the serious side of fashion . . . people never quite realize . . . the part played in the British economy, why exports alone . . . social significance." Jemima murmured on, and ended quite quickly: "The only thing is that I was proposing to invite Chloe Fontaine to write the programme, so much her style in a way, and she brings her own elegance to these things. But if by any chance that would be unacceptable to Isabelle—this conversation is quite between ourselves, naturally."

"Believe me," said Laura Barrymore, "Miss Fontaine would be *quite* unacceptable to Miss Mancini. There are some trusts which if betrayed—" She stopped, aware that she had abandoned the swanlike supremacy of the perfect friend and assistant. My God, thought Jemima, so Chloe had quarrelled with Isabelle—the fool,

and then to suppose that *Taffeta* would give her a commission—
no, wait a minute, had Chloe ever indeed really tackled *Taffeta* for
work?

"Particularly from a writer who had been such a very close
friend. Isabelle had been so *good* to her." Laura Barrymore was
continuing as if her indignation would not quite let her stop,
despite her better judgement. "And a writer of Chloe Fontaine's
stature. Her previous stature, perhaps I should say. Why did she
need to draw on her friends' private lives? Surely her own
provides quite enough . . . It was so terribly *disloyal*. And then
the letters—Isabelle felt she had been nurturing a viper."

My God, thought Jemima again, the novel; the libel which
Chloe had dismissed as petty but which worried Valentine
Brighton. Chloe's new book must in some way have impinged
upon—if that was the right word—the Mancini sensibilities.
Disloyalty. No wonder the ultra-loyal Laura Barrymore, the
faithful assistant, had frozen at the very notion of Isabelle
commissioning Chloe.

"I am of course Chloe Fontaine's house guest," Jemima put in
as diplomatically as possible at the end of this tirade. The
reminder had the desired effect. Laura hesitated.

"You're actually in her flat? Her new flat? I hadn't quite
appreciated—"

"Exactly."

For a moment the honey returned. "In that case, Miss Shore, it
occurs to me that it might be helpful if I came by, maybe I could
talk with you on the subject of Isabelle and Miss Fontaine, put you
in the picture—"

"No, no!" cried Jemima hastily. "Really, it's of no conse-
quence." She had absolutely no wish to be further embroiled in
Isabelle Mancini's row with Chloe. The solution to what she was
rapidly beginning to rate as the Chloe Mystery, certainly did not
lie in the files of *Taffeta* magazine.

Jemima must now put that mystery away from her thoughts.
Easy now to sign off her brief relationship with the Stovers.
Clearly Chloe was in some enigmatic way in control of her own
destiny. She had lied to Jemima about the Camargue, or at any rate
misled her. Undoubtedly for the same strange reason she had also
misled her parents. In fact, Jemima reflected wryly at the end of
her long-drawn-out telephone call to Isabelle's flat, if anyone had
succeeded in disappearing in London without trace, it was Chloe

31

Fontaine rather than Jemima Shore. But that was no longer her concern. It was time to gather a notebook and depart for the British Library.

When she telephoned Mr. Stover and told him that *Taffeta* had no trace of Chloe's whereabouts, and he must use his own judgement whether to summon the police, Jemima made it clear from her tone that she thought the step unnecessary. Mr. Stover too sounded heavier and almost resigned.

"The wife always said I was too fierce to her on the phone," was his first comment. "Thank you, Miss Shore, we'll look out for you on television in the autumn. If she does phone you—" He stopped. "Mrs. Stover, she does worry, in spite of everything, she can't help it. But she's led her own life for too long, Dollie, we don't really know her any more. That's what I tell her mother. Now if we'd had one of our own—"

It seemed an appropriate moment for Jemima to bid them a polite goodbye. She did not expect to hear of or from the Stovers again; she retained a tiny flicker of interest in what would happen to that old, unvisited couple, that worrying old woman, that old man who felt now that he had been too fierce and driven off the golden bird who was their only link with youth. Concentrated study would soon extinguish even that flicker.

But Chloe—that was different. Jemima was full of natural and cross curiosity about her wayward friend's inexplicable behaviour. If she gave full rein to it, she might ruin this whole promised day of earnest research, by mulling, pondering, even making a checking telephone call, when she, Jemima, was supposed to be incommunicado. Time to be gone. Wearing one of her favourite dresses, silk jersey in the beige she loved with its own little splashes of red and navy blue, practical enough for the British Library, elegant enough to give her spirits a lift, she picked up her notebook. It was a pretty Italianate thing which appeared to be covered in wallpaper whose unsuitability for serious research, like the delight of the flowing dress, she found both soothing and cheering.

This time she remembered to use the second key to unlock the flat door. Tiger sidled towards her and rubbed himself against the high-heeled golden sandal which, on the principle of the notebook, Jemima had decided to wear to the British Library. Jemima shooed him away. "Back for dinner. Enjoy your balcony, there's a good cat." And she was still in fact addressing the cat when the door swung open, and she felt both her arms roughly seized. The keys were twisted from her grasp.

"Didn't she get my visiting card?" said Kevin John Athlone. He was so close to her that Jemima could see the slight sweat on his cheeks. She noticed involuntarily that he had not shaved. "Care for a visit?" He was flushed as well as sweating. "Well, now she's getting a visit, whether she likes it or not. And you too, Miss Jemima Shore."

Pushing her back into the flat, he deftly relocked the door. From the wrong side of it, Tiger gave a long unhappy mew.

Chapter Four

Irish Accent

"Where is she?"

Jemima thought Kevin John Athlone had been drinking: drinking all night. His breath smelt sour with a nasty tang of acid in it, mingling with the smell of the sweat which beaded his cheeks and damped his bright blue towelling T-shirt. He wore light blue jeans which did not fit particularly well. They sagged on his hips; the broad leather belt which supported them had given up beneath the curve of his belly; the jeans look more rumpled than creased.

He was still startlingly handsome. He ran rather than lumbered to search the remaining rooms of the flat; his movements were surprisingly light.

"Where's she hiding?" he demanded, grasping both her arms firmly.

The huge circular eyes which gazed into hers like those of a drugged but hostile animal being taken away to market, were of an astonishing blue. The bulging red veins visible in the white only set off their immaculate sky colour. His lashes so close to Jemima's own—for he still held her tight—that she could see them quivering as the sweat ran down the corners of his eyes, were as long as a woman's. His hair, although greasy and falling round his face, far too long for elegance, was dramatically dark and thick.

Kevin John had always looked far more like a young Irish actor than a promising English painter. His father, not half such a handsome man, had in fact been quite well known on the Dublin stage; Jemima fancied that his mother too had been an actress. At this moment he resembled some actor flung out of the Abbey Theatre Company, or perhaps just a member of the company after a hard night.

34

"Where is she, I said." It was quite surprising to find that he spoke without a trace of an Irish accent.

"How the hell do I know?"

By way of reply Kevin John simply twisted her arms sharply. Her bag and notebook dropped.

"Find her then." The stink of his breath was even more offensive than the pain. "Jemima Shore, Investigator." The sneer with which he pronounced her name infuriated her.

"Let go of my arms, you drunken slob." This time Kevin John let go of her arms and gave Jemima a wide swinging blow on the side of her face. The pain of it was so unexpected that tears came into her eyes. Her whole head felt dizzy. As Jemima reeled, he struck her again on the face but harder this time. She staggered. He hit her again and as she felt herself sinking he shouted something which sounded like "harlot." Or perhaps it was "harder."

"It's no good," she heard herself saying faintly. He seemed to go on hitting her. Then she toppled or sank onto the carpet.

The next thing she knew Kevin John was kneeling over her. He appeared to be crying or perhaps it was merely the sweat pouring down his face. His breath still smelt terrible.

"Oh, sweet Jesus," he was saying. "I'm sorry, I'm sorry." Now he was crying in earnest. He sat down beside Jemima on the thick carpet, put his enormous handsome head on his arms and started to blubber. Jemima heard words like: "I love her, I love her," mingled with apologies, louder cries, and confused insults, of which "effing whore" and "tail-wagging bitch" were about the mildest. At any rate the words "whore" and "bitch" were prominent amongst them. Dizzily, Jemima wasn't quite sure whether he meant Chloe or herself.

After a bit Kevin John stopped crying, raised his head and stared at her: "I'm drunk."

Jemima said nothing.

"Could you be a sweetheart and make me some coffee? I must talk to you." Jemima rose unsteadily from the floor and held onto the edge of the sofa. She was glad she had not hit her head on the edge of one of Chloe's smart little glass tables as she fell. All the same she wondered what her face looked like as she walked, still unsteadily, her head aching, into the kitchen. She looked out of the window which was at the back of the building. The kitchen had a small modern fire escape attached to it; the door was merely bolted. Chloe had shown her the key, while recommending her not to use it, except in emergency. But Jemima decided that even if the situation demanded escape, she felt far too dizzy.

She peered into the kitchen mirror (there were mirrors everywhere in Chloe's flat). Although there was a large red mark on one side of her face, as though she had slept on it, otherwise it did not look too bad. But the sting and the ache were fierce.

Jemima made some coffee, the one thing she always boasted of being able to do automatically, even half-conscious. Under the circumstances, that was fortunate.

When she came back into the living room, Kevin John was sitting on the sofa. He did not look at her as she placed the mug of coffee beside him. Jemima went and sat in the big white chair near the window, as far away as possible from the sofa; the roar of the traffic below and the occasional sharp little tooting reached her from far away, as though from some remote shore.

"Don't worry, I'm not going to hit you again." He gulped the freshly made coffee as if it were spirits—he seemed indifferent to its heat. "Have you got a cigarette?"

"I don't smoke. You can look around."

"She never has any cigarettes." But he heaved up his body and started to prowl about the room, disarranging the huge downy cushions as though packets might be disgorged. Then he vanished into the bedroom. The keys of the flat were lying on the table. Jemima wondered rather hazily whether she should grab them and run down and out into the square. She was still contemplating the move when Kevin John returned, smoking a black cigarette. The new harsh smell made Jemima feel nauseous.

"These yours?" He held out a box of Black Sobranies, and a lighter.

"I told you I didn't smoke."

"They're not hers. The——" He added a crude description of Chloe.

Jemima remained silent. She was fairly sure such conspicuous cigarettes had not been visible in the bedroom the night before since her own distaste for cigarettes, above all in a bedroom— even unsmoked—would have caused her to remove them. He must have routed them out from some drawer, exacerbating his own hurt; still it was pointlessly provocative to say so.

"Look at this." The lighter was dumped down in front of her. It was a pretty little object, striped black and white enamel, with an opaque reddish-brown jewel—a beryl or a piece of agate—set in its head. "Recognize it?"

"No." But even as she spoke, a memory stirred; she felt she had seen the lighter or something very like it before. For one thing it was the kind of personal detail Jemima noticed automatically about people whether she was interviewing them or not, a professional habit of observation. Placing the precise person was more difficult because during the last month, both setting up programmes for the autumn series and clearing the decks for her own holiday, Jemima had spoken to, eaten and drunk with an inordinate number of different people, types jumbled together.

It was also possible that she had marked down the lighter at Megalithic House. Cy Fredericks, her boss at MTV, had a fine taste in gold accoutrements, and was fond of throwing any new little bejewelled toy at her as a joke at the expense of what he supposed to be her Puritan streak: "Fancy it, Jem? Gems for Jem? Yours if that programme wins the prize at Amsterdam." The last time Cy Fredericks indulged his taste for that particular pleasantry, he had been referring to *The Unvisited*.

But the lighter was, she had to admit, in rather too good taste for Cy. It was really very attractive, with a feeling of modern Fabergé about it. Where *had* she seen it? Never mind, it would come back to her.

"Where is she, Miss Jezebel Fontaine, the bitch of Bloomsbury, the fuck of Fulham, the harlot of the Brighthelmet Press, the curs' delight—" And Kevin John proceeded to embark upon a string of imprecations in which terms of Biblical denunciation and suggestions of animal congress were mingled. His language had always been appalling—if colourfully so—but what had seemed rather amusingly vivid in the jolly young painter Chloe had run off with, was now merely the gratuitous thrusting of his untrammelled anger on the world.

At the same time, despite his outburst, it was clear that Kevin John was rapidly becoming less drunk. But the expression on his face being no less threatening and his wild round blue eyes still dilating, Jemima had no confidence that temporary sobriety would prevent him beating her up again if he was so minded. It had been a bad mistake not to run while she had the opportunity.

"I tell you again I haven't the slightest idea!" Jemima almost shouted the words. Despair, brought on not only by an aching head but also by a sense of the ludicrous unfairness of his question, to say nothing of his behaviour, made her abandon caution. She proceeded to tell Kevin John, furiously but succinctly, exactly what had happened since Chloe tripped so lightly out of her own flat the previous night, allegedly en route for the Camargue, leaving Jemima as her house-sitter for a month. How the Stovers had telephoned, expecting a visit; as a result of which call, Jemima had investigated the Camargue expedition and found it to be a fabrication; how there was therefore no record of Chloe's present whereabouts.

Jemima left nothing out of the story except for Laura Barrymore's strictures on Chloe's new novel.

She ended: "All this and your calls too!" She wanted to say your "filthy calls" but thought it impolitic.

"It was the picture she liked. It was the only thing of mine she took from the Fulham house. She sent the rest of my work down to Cornwall in a van. I found the card in the pocket of my jeans." He spoke more flatly. "I suppose I kept it for the Aiglon number. When I come to London, I generally try to wrench some of his ill-gotten gains—gotten at my expense—out of Creeping Croesus or his side-kick Pansy Potter. Dropping the card in was the only way I knew how to reach Chloe."

"I meant the telephone calls." An immense weariness was overcoming Jemima. She wished Kevin John would go away, find Chloe or not as fate—Chloe's fate—would have it, and leave her to crawl back into the white bedroom, shutter out the dry blazing Bloomsbury sunlight and sleep.

"How could I call her? She wouldn't give me her number. I only got the address in the first place by charming the pants off that new woman in Fulham. Little Chloe, sweet little Miss Delilah, paws-in-the-air have-me-any-time-you-want, God rot her for the lying scheming Dutch-doll-faced bitch she is, had been oh, oh, so sure that she didn't want anyone to have her address. 'One's public, Mrs. Ramsbotham, how they haunt one, don't they? One is never alone. An artist needs peace . . .'" He gave quite an accurate parody of Chloe's breathless little voice, even if the words were ridiculous, and caressed his untidy black head with exactly the same delicate air as Chloe was apt to pat her own, as though too much pressure might bruise it.

"An Irish accent."

Kevin John gave her his angry red-blue stare.

"Those telephone calls; obscene telephone calls. You had an

Irish accent. *He* had an Irish accent. Not very pronounced but it was there."

"Look, Miss Jemima Shore, Investigator"—he took perverse pleasure in reciting her public title and every time he used it his anger increased—"I don't know what half-arsed Judas you're talking about or what calls either. Christ, I could use a drink. No cigarettes, no drink." A black Sobranie was in his fingers as he spoke; he had been chain-smoking them. The packet was half full; he didn't seem to notice.

"There's some white wine in the fridge."

"Oh, I bet there's some lovely chilled *vino blanco* in the fridge . . . And I'll pour it in long green glasses just for us two." Once again the imitation of Chloe was at least recognizable. "Well, I don't want any of Chloe's delicately scented ladies' piss. I want a whisky."

"Find it. If you can. I've no idea if there's any whisky here or not." Jemima confined her own drinking strictly to wine.

"It's too early. It's much too early for whisky. Quite the Delilah yourself, aren't you? Do you want to make me drunk at his hour in the morning? Want to control me? Bring me down? Well, I can tell you this, Miss Jemima Shore, Investigator, no one brings me down." He glared at her. "So what was that about the telephone?"

Jemima told him about the two calls. It seemed the safer topic of the two. She still wasn't convinced that he hadn't made them himself. She might have imposed an Irish accent because her abiding mental image of Kevin John Athlone was as being Irish—and rough. If he had been drunk enough, he might easily have made the calls and forgotten the next morning.

"But I didn't know her number. How could I do such a terrible thing?" he remarked at the end in an injured voice. His long eyelashes fluttered slightly; there was something mechanically boyish about his manner, something wheedling about his tone. Jemima glimpsed with no particular favour the handsome and indulged young man Kevin John had once been. She still didn't know whether to believe his assurance or not.

Suddenly he leant forward and to her absolute surprise and horror planted a kiss full on her lips. The stubble on his chin grazed her skin and she wriggled backwards in her chair without being able to speak or do more than mutely struggle. His mouth was enormous; it was as if a gigantic fish were trying to gobble her up.

"You're a darling, aren't you? A real sweetheart. You'll forgive me, won't you, sweetheart, because I'm going to say sorry so nicely to you. I'm going to be so utterly, utterly charming and pleasing—"

For a moment Jemima thought he meant—no, surely even he—

"I'm going to have a shower and a shave—I'm sure that"—he paused and then said in his naughty-boyish voice—"that *lady* has a razor somewhere about. Then I'm going out and I shall buy you the biggest bunch of flowers in the whole of London, this bitch of a city, which frightens the daylights out of your poor honest artist even on a fine summer's morn."

"I don't want any flowers." Her voice was low. "I have no idea where Chloe is and now will you please go away and leave me alone."

"Oh, you'll never be quite alone here, sweetheart. Never quite without me. I'm a match for you, darling. Look—there's my picture looking down on you. A great wonderful splash of red for you. Still, if you really don't want me further, I'll leave you. Maybe my old pal Dixie is still in London; I have an idea we were drinking somewhere together last night. I couldn't get an answer from Creeping Croesus." He passed his hand over his head as if the recollection pained him. "He'll give me a razor and a bath. And then I'll buy you the flowers. Splashes and splashes of them. All red. Cheer up this whited sepulchre of hers."

Jemima hated red flowers.

"You really have no need to apologize further," she said coldly. "You were drunk."

"Ah, sweetheart, the flowers won't be an apology. They're to woo you, to please you, and then with your matchless wits, Miss Jemima Shore, Investigator, you'll find Miss Chloe Fontaine for me. I know you will."

"*Please* go away. Unlock the door and go away—"

And then to her further surprise he did. He unlocked the door, deposited the keys carefully on the table, and left. She noticed once again the lightness with which his shambling body could move. Kevin John did not, however, shut the door behind him and she lacked the energy to get up. She heard his footsteps on the uncarpeted stairs, loud, thumping all the way to the front door. It was a long way down. The street door was opened. She did not hear it shut.

Jemima regained her energy and walked unsteadily to the

balcony. She looked over. Amidst the desultory passers-by on the pavement of the huge Bloomsbury square below, Kevin John in his bright blue shirt was easy to pick out. He wove through the traffic and disappeared in the direction of the British Museum. It was not much more than twelve hours since she had looked for Chloe in the same square and missed her.

He was definitely gone. She was alone. Except for—

"Tiger!" she cried aloud. "Tiger!" Oh no! Tiger, last heard mewing with outrage when Kevin John had precipitately pushed her inside the door and relocked it, leaving the cat either by design or mistake on the wrong side of it. She had no clear memory of hearing any further mews, but then the ensuing scene had been sufficiently violent to drown the plaints of an excluded cat. Tiger was certainly nowhere to be seen or heard now. He had not chosen to return by the balcony window. She wondered whether a cat would ascend the scaffolding of Adelaide Square all the way from the street. She must go downstairs and look for him. Perhaps he had vanished into the darkened basement area, the last lap of the long staircase.

Remembering to take the keys, and deciding it was prudent to lock the flat behind her—she wanted no more unscheduled visits—Jemima set forth rather gingerly down the first flight of stairs. After the airy brightness of the penthouse, the light was dim.

"Tiger—Puss, Puss, Puss—" Her voice echoed rather queerly in the well of the stairs, occupied by the lifeless lift cage.

There was no other sound. It was Saturday, and the rest of the building was of course quite empty. Even the noise of the traffic from Adelaide Square and its echo from the Tottenham Court Road was subdued.

It was as Jemima was passing the door of the third-floor flat—a substantial mahogany door, preserved no doubt from the original house, set incongruously into the concrete—that she heard quite distinctly the mew of a cat.

Chapter Five

The Lion's Den

Jemima called and the cat mewed again.

She banged heavily and tried to turn the handle. It was ornamental. The cat began to cry quite plaintively, that odd infant's cry she had remarked as a curiosity before. Now it drove her frantic. She banged harder.

"Is anyone there?" she shouted.

Absolute silence from whatever lay behind the polished darkness of the mahogany. Then further mewing. This was the moment for those powers of reasoning first praised, if warily, by the nuns at her convent school, more enthusiastically by her tutors at Cambridge, finally lavishly admired by her public, as well as treasured by Megalith Television; that logical faculty, in short, incarnated in the title which Kevin John Athlone so much despised—Jemima Shore, Investigator.

But it did not in fact need supreme detective gifts to work it out. The cat could only have passed through the door if the door was open; *ergo* the door had opened. It was unimaginable that such a door should have blown open, flown open, and unlikely that it had been left open (she would certainly have noticed on her way in; Chloe on her way out, and Kevin John, lurking, could hardly have missed it). Therefore some human agency had opened it, and moreover had done so in the comparatively short time since Tiger had been shut out of the top-floor flat.

The only other possibility was that Tiger had after all tried to scale the outside of the house, and miscalculating, had entered an open window on the third floor. That raised the question of why he didn't depart by the same window on finding the flat empty—if indeed he *had* found it empty. In any case, if Tiger had after all already accustomed himself to climbing the heights of Adelaide

Square, during Chloe's short tenancy of the flat, why did he not of his own accord return to his natural home in the top flat?

Nevertheless the point could be quickly established by inspecting the majestic façade of the house for an open window. It might be worth looking at the back of the building, too; the third-floor flat must also be connected with the fire escape.

She called encouragingly: "Puss, Puss, Puss" and decided to give the mahogany door one more bang, partly to keep contact with the cat inside, partly to make quite sure that it had not actually jammed. After that she foresaw a routine with the police—and firemen—if no visible window presented itself.

As a loving cat-owner of many years' standing, Jemima had had her share of such experiences. Blanche, the disdainful white cat who had preceded Colette, had had the capacity of a feckless aristocrat for getting herself into scrapes and then expecting other people to busy themselves rescuing her. Jemima had a vision of Blanche, white and fluffy like some garment which had come to rest high up in a tree, gazing at the firemen hired to rescue her with implacable condescension. Life with Blanche had been an expensive and demanding business; life with Tiger and his mistress Chloe was so far proving equally demanding. Yet unlike the erring Chloe, Tiger could not be consigned to his fate over the weekend.

Jemima gave the door one last bang and almost fell over as it swung open silently at her blow.

As Tiger, a golden streak of fur, dashed between her legs onto the staircase, Jemima found herself faced with a huge cave of a room. It was carpeted in something navy blue or even black which looked like felt, but otherwise contained no furniture whatsoever. Three of the walls were painted a shiny dark cobalt blue, a pretty colour in itself, but one which scarcely relieved the sombre floor. The third wall was in fact a vast window of darkened glass, of the sort generally seen in the windows of discreet cars; it was this smoky area which gave the room its feeling of a cave.

The contrast between the summery textures of Chloe's flat and this vault was remarkable. Even the ceiling here gave the impression of being low, whereas in reality it must be considerably higher than that of the flat above; the effect of the various blues was subterranean. Jemima could see that this flat, like Chloe's, did enjoy some form of concrete balcony, somewhere behind the smoky window. Here too, the feeling of trees and space, if untrammelled by darkened glass, would be spectacular.

Jemima speculated on the weird mentality of someone who would rent a very modern flat on the third floor of a Georgian square and then deliberately exclude the view.

The proportions of this flat in general, whether because of the colours or not, seemed to lack the harmony exhibited by Chloe's above it. Perhaps Sir Richard Lionnel's architect was more accustomed to designing penthouses than third-floor flats which had to be fitted into the site of a former Georgian mansion.

Grotesquely, a marble mantelpiece of classical design was stuck into the middle of the left-hand blue wall although there was no grate within it. It had the air of an old-fashioned oasis in a very modern desert.

"Adam," said a low voice behind her.

Jemima jumped and gave a little scream. Her heart beat loudly and unpleasantly. The word, almost whispered, sounded right in her ear. She wheeled round and found she was gazing straight into the eyes of a young man who had been standing in the angle of the door, neatly concealed by it as it swung open. He was smiling at her.

"Adam," he said again and then with a further grin at her bewilderment pointed at the mantelpiece.

"Adam. Made for the *piano nobile* of this house, I'll be bound. Doesn't it look ghastly hoiked up here? Particularly, stuck in the middle of that hideous wall. They might just as well have papered it with PVC or even cut up some plastic macs to secure the same effect. Why bother with paint?" He was rattling on, but it seemed to be natural garrulity rather than nerves. "Nice cat that, by the way. Matches the colour of your hair. The eyes are different, though. You do have the eyes of a cat, of course, undoubtedly you've been told that before, but it just happens to be a different cat."

During this colloquy, Tiger, as though encouraged by the direction the conversation was taking, had ventured back into the room and was rubbing himself against Jemima's legs and purring. She was touched that their short acquaintance had made such an impression on him—considering the way he had been treated—until she was aware that the stranger was being similarly honoured.

"It wanted to come in, by the way, and as I believe in liberty of the individual I permitted it. I also gave it some milk." He waved towards an open door, presumably the kitchen. "I was worried about letting it out in case the cars would get it. Squeal, whoosh and Goldilocks is no more."

"Tiger. Male."

"Seventeen-eighty, the original house, to speak of loftier matters," continued her interlocutor warmly as though she had not spoken. "One of the finest things Adam ever did. This was named for him originally, you know, Adam Square; they changed it fifty years later for Queen Adelaide on the accession of her old man. I've got all the original drawings, I copied them in the British Museum as a matter of fact. I had the idea of blowing them up and plastering them all over the PVC walls as a kind of reproach when I leave. What do you think?"

"Aah. A squatter."

His smile became even more friendly.

"Certainly. What are you? Though I detest the word, don't you? It has an unfortunate association with the position Indians adopt to perform their natural functions. I prefer to term myself a Friend of the House. Like Friends of the Earth but a bit more upright. Literally. No offence meant to the Friends of the Earth; excellent people; in fact we Friends of the House deliberately copied their title and took it further—upward. Officially we're FROTH—Friends and Revivifiers of the House—but I myself think there's something altogether too bubbly about that title. It hardly expresses the calm and repose which we Friends of the House aim to spread about us."

There was something curiously relaxed about the house's self-styled friend; this, despite his loquacity. His most striking physical characteristic was an aureole of reddish-brown hair. His eyes were exactly the same colour. But the hair itself, although abundant, was not unkempt and the beard which framed his chin was neatly trimmed; the Friend of the House's looks certainly showed more recent signs of care than those of Kevin John Athlone. The Friend was also taller than she had supposed at first sight; about as tall as Jemima herself. Although he was also exceptionally thin—she could have put both hands round his hips in their worn jeans—his shoulders were broad and the arms in the white T-shirt well muscled. With his curly mouth, smiling even in repose, and pointed ears, there was something of Pan or some other sprite, Robin Goodfellow perhaps, about him, not exactly malign, but distinctly mischievous.

Jemima also observed how white and clean the stranger's feet were in their thonged sandals, and indeed his skin generally. She wondered suddenly how old he was. Like his height, his age might be deceptive. For that matter, who *was* he?

"Adam. Adam Adamson." She had the impression that the bright squirrel's eyes had read her thoughts. "May I introduce myself since I take it we are neighbours? Adam Adamson. I know it sounds affected and maybe it is, but maybe equally it is a poor thing but mine own. In this interesting world of make-believe and make-forget in which we live, who knows or cares what I was originally called? My intense admiration for Robert Adam obviously makes my patronymic peculiarly appropriate, although I cannot claim to be descended from him. At least I am descended from Adam, straight descent all the way down, no one can question that particular aspect of my pedigree. So that Adam Adamson, whether my own legal name or not in the opinion of our literal-minded authorities, is at least a name to which I can morally lay claim. I made exactly the same point to the magistrate last time I was arrested," he added conversationally.

"For squatting? Sorry to use that vulgar term but I can't remember exactly what it is you call it."

"Revivifying is what we prefer. I am for example revivifying seventy-three Adelaide Square and so, I fancy, are you. How pleased Adam would be incidentally, to think that you, someone so classically beautiful as you—" He cocked an eyebrow at her. "What is your name by the way?"

"Eve," replied Jemima Shore in the same light tone. To tell the truth, she wasn't quite sure whether or not the request for her name was a further affectation. Jemima was too level-headed to allow her instant recognizability to affect the course of her life. On the whole she regarded her popular fame as a convenient weapon to be wielded when necessary in the cause of her serious work of television reporting. Nevertheless it was rare that she was not recognized by someone of Adam's particular television-watching age group.

"No, no, you're not," replied Adam Adamson. "You're not Eve at all. I know perfectly well who you are. I've known all along. You're a classical goddess. Grey-eyed Athena, found on a pillar perhaps; not nearly solid enough to support one, no caryatid you. Something to be worshipped; or a fifth-century Demeter, perhaps; with your strong straight classical lines—"

"You're talking about me as a building. And I'm generally told my eyes are green." Jemima couldn't help smiling back at him. Something about Adam Adamson appealed to her. Besides she had made at least two major programmes over the years centred round squatters, their various ideals and projects and in most, if not all, cases, had respected them. Nor did she lump all squatters together. The Friends of the House, for example, clearly had a high standard of hygiene—not an attribute possessed by all squatters whatever their idealism—for the echoing modern cobalt blue cavern was very clean. Unless Adam Adamson had only just moved in.

"A few weeks back," said Adam, repeating his uncanny trick of answering questions she had not yet put, "we were demonstrating as usual outside this revolting monument to Sir Richard Lionnel's maniacal vanity, when someone tipped me the wink that a key could be had to the third floor. No questions asked. Perhaps some enlightened human being took the line that I would be a desirable tenant. Or perhaps some fellow son of Adam had conceived a violent hatred for the devouring lion's ornamentation of his own den. Oh, didn't you know?" He waved his hand. Again Jemima observed its whiteness, set off by a few red-gold hairs; the nails were clean and scrubbed-looking. "This was to be Sir Richard Lionnel's own home." Another wave.

"Yes, I'm squatting in the Lion's Den—and for a den I suppose the word squatting might be appropriate for once. I'm revivifying the whole house, but I doubt if much revivifying could go on in this blue hell. Cleansing fire would be more appropriate." A further Pan-like smile.

"Still, it's the principle of the thing, and it's for the principle of bearding the lion in his den—please note the beard specially grown for the occasion—that I have deserted my previous salubrious accommodation in Chelsea. I deserted that to suffer quite dreadfully here. Oh, my aesthetic sensibilities in the excrescence of Adelaide Square!"

He showed no signs of stopping. "The Lion is making us suffer every time we charge round Adelaide Square. Arriving at the demo in the morning causes a true ache in my heart, especially if you look at the sort of thing the Lion has recently devoured, as illustrated on the opposite side of the square. So why should he not suffer a tiny little pang at finding his own personal domain occupied? I suppose the Lion's jackal-in-chief, Judas Turpin, will let him know on Monday morning. Too late to ruin his weekend in Sussex by the sea, but a splendid sobering start to another week of swallowing houses whole in his maw. You know that he intends to devour the corner property as well? Regurgitating it as something similar to this, but worse. He's had the whole structure condemned as rotten. Ah well, he has a surprise coming." Adam took a breath.

"Now tell me about yourself," he continued kindly. "And by the way shall we sit down on the Stygian carpet as we get to know each other better. Or would you prefer to entertain me in whichever corner of Hades you have chosen?"

"No, no, not upstairs," said Jemima hastily. She had had enough of unwanted visitors for one day; even though Adam Adamson might prove an amusing addition to her life. Caution also dictated the minimum of involvement with squatters—even revivifiers.

Chloe Fontaine was after all a legal tenant at 73 Adelaide Square. No revivifier she, as *Time* magazine would put it. Having leased or bought such an expensive flat—Jemima wasn't sure which but if it was a lease presumably it was a long one, acquired with the proceeds of the sale of the Fulham house—Chloe had a vested interest in the maintenance of law and order in the building.

So far Adam Adamson presented on orderly front; but this was on the basis of one day's occupation. Jemima had seen what the most amiable squatters could do to an interior within a very short space of time. Did Adam intend to dwell here alone and if so for how long? A single rather slight man would not be very difficult for Sir Richard Lionnel's minions to eject. Perhaps he envisaged moving in some allies. On the other hand it was possible he contemplated a mere token occupation and would depart, leaving as he had suggested blow-ups of the original Adam designs on Sir Richard's dark blue walls as an artistic reproach.

Jemima's loyalty was towards her old friend. If squatters occupied number 73 in earnest, so that there was a prolonged siege, the value of Chloe's property stood to diminish drastically. Chloe, with all her faults, was a woman alone in the world supporting herself by her own—hard—labours. She probably also contributed to the welfare, if not the happiness, of the Stovers of Folkestone. Since it was not suggested that number 73 was to be left empty—indeed the Lion of Bloomsbury was intending to occupy one portion of it personally—she was not at all sure that a squat was morally justified by her own standards, if it proved financially damaging to Chloe. This was after all an aesthetic protest, not the housing of the homeless.

At the same time the architecture of this latest addition to Adelaide Square *was* brutally displeasing. If Sir Richard proposed further similar intrusions and had somehow bamboozled the powers-that-were into accepting them, there was a case to be made for popular protests. That might secure what lawful authority had failed to protect.

Jemima found herself toying with the problem, despite herself, in professional television terms. "The Lion of Bloomsbury or Sir Richard the Lionnelheart?" (She had read some colour magazine article about the tycoon under the latter heading.) Excellent visual material available; an entertaining interview with Adam Adamson; a cool deliberately low-key one with Sir Richard Lionnel: let him damn himself out of his own mouth if necessary: Jemima Shore, Investigator, knew exactly how to conduct that kind of interview. Guiltily she remembered the claims of the British Library and the Edwardian lady philanthropists.

Gathering Tiger into her arms, Jemima said hastily: "No time for the present to talk about me. But I've much enjoyed hearing about *you*." Tiger wriggled in her arms and his fierce green eyes gazed at her with indignation. "Look, I must be off. I have an appointment." Let her sort out her correct attitude to Adam Adamson and his fellow Friends of the House in peace, rather than under his enquiring squirrel's gaze. She did not, for one thing, like the sound of that future project, whatever it might be, planned by the demonstrators. It might be her duty to Chloe to find out a little more about it.

"Yes, why don't you think it over by yourself?" said Adam with a smile as though she had spoken. "And then, my dear goddess, I am convinced that you will join us in our cause, bringing all the powers of your fellow gods and goddesses to our aid." Was he mocking her and was that a glancing reference to the might of Megalith Television?

"But do tell me before you go, exactly what brought you, you with your archaic smile, to Adelaide Square from Mount Olympus? Or wherever it is you generally inhabit. I sense a mystery here."

"I had better tell you plainly that I am not a squatter—revivifier," Jemima said quickly as she left the flat. "I've been lent the penthouse by a friend as a matter of fact. A straightforward tenant. They do exist."

She did not wait to see Adam Adamson's reaction to this bold announcement. Back in the penthouse she deposited Tiger, fed him and checked that the balcony window was open for his egresses during her absence. How delightful and bleached and open the penthouse seemed! Like a glorious sandy seaside after the murky cavern of the third floor. Not all the works of the Lionnel Estate were bad.

She would have preferred to have eaten a quick meal there, but she had finished all the salad the night before. Jemima decided on a local café instead, somewhere where she could enjoy a glass of wine and read a book. *Fallen Child* might be dipped into again, as tribute to her hostess. She selected a copy from the neat little row of Chloe's novels, stored modestly and inconspicuously at ground level. As usual, she admired the author's photograph which occupied the entire back of the jacket. Chloe really was amazingly photogenic: Valentine was right to take advantage of the fact. All the same, why on earth had a lace parasol seemed an appropriate accessory for this particular picture? No wonder the reviewers sometimes sneered.

Jemima carefully locked the flat behind her with the second Chubb key.

But as she returned down the stairs to re-enter the outside world, she found Adam Adamson waiting for her on the landing of the third floor. He was not smiling quite so broadly, a mere curve of his lips saluted her. He was in fact blocking her way.

"Just one more thing, green-eyed Pallas Athena, oh wisest one. What is the name of the obliging friend who lent you the flat?"

There seemed no point in keeping it from him. For all she knew, there were letters addressed to Chloe in the hall below.

"She's called Chloe Fontaine. The writer. You may have heard of her." She was carrying *Fallen Child*. "Look, you might recognize her, even if you don't know the name. She sometimes appears on television." Chloe's large sloe-like eyes gazed at them, provocative, enigmatic, beneath the white frame of the absurdly pretty parasol.

Adam Adamson gazed down at the photograph. He looked utterly disconcerted. He still smiled but as she analysed it later it was a smile of genuine surprise, even disbelief. In some way she had astonished him.

All he said was: "Chloe: a nymph's name. But for a writer, one of the muses might have been more appropriate. Calliope, perhaps, the muse of tragedy. Still, she's certainly very beautiful." And on that enigmatic and faintly disquieting note, Adam Adamson went back into the flat and closed its heavy mahogany door.

Chapter Six

B for Beware

The Reading Room of the British Library, lying inside the British Museum, was very hot. Not unlike the summer streets of Bloomsbury through which she had passed, the Reading Room exuded an atmosphere of dust; it was also airless being without air-conditioning or open windows, the sun beating on the great glass dome which surmounted it. As a result, an aroma of faint dampness met Jemima as she presented her pass at the entrance. For a moment she was tempted to abandon this humid temple to literature in favour of the cooler halls of the Museum itself, presided over by huge wide-mouthed slant-eyed Egyptian monarchs and eagle-headed Assyrian deities. Other vast feline figures were guarding temples which had long ago disappeared. Here tourists worshipped with wondering eyes.

The Reading Room on the other hand was full of up-to-date activity. No one wandered. People strode. Unlike the tourists, the reader, carrying briefcases and rolled copies of the *Guardian*, gave an unmistakeable air of knowing where they were going. Because the Reading Room constituted its own busy little world in the midst of the great sprawling castle of the Museum, with its staircases and salons and guards, it always seemed to Jemima peculiarly appropriate that it should be built in the shape and design of a spinning-wheel in a fairy story. So one might fancifully imagine its toilers bent over intricate webs.

There were however a great many toilers already present this Saturday afternoon in August, and that particular idle fancy quickly gave way to irritation as Jemima embarked on the notoriously long-drawn-out process of finding an empty seat. Doggedly, she inspected the rows of seats, which radiated out from the central enclosure, forming the spokes of the wheel. After a while she gazed at those fortunate enough to possess them with the hostility of one searching for an empty taxi. The trouble was that the British Library system of sending for a book from the stacks necessitated the possession of a seat before you could fill in a request slip.

In the past, Jemima had enjoyed one concentrated and instructive spell working in the Reading Room. During a temporary lull in her television career, she had supported herself for three months researching in the Reading Room on behalf of an enterprising publisher who wished to launch a series composed of abridged versions of Victorian classics—out of the public mind, and also out of copyright. The series had never appeared and the publisher had disappeared. Jemima had gone back to television. But during the long days, Jemima had surreptitiously begun to study, on her own account, a topic more congenial to her own taste. This was the genesis of the book on the Edwardian lady philanthropists.

She still remembered the curious stifling anonymous freedom of working in the Reading Room every day, as though going to some office where one was at the same time totally unknown and yet expected. She had also, during that original sojourn, learnt the Reading Room rules about looking up books, which had their own logic, not readily assimilable on the first visit, but like riding a bicycle, once learnt never forgotten.

Jemima turned left and began to pace round the semicircle of seats radiating out from the central desk. They were arranged alphabetically, and she found herself beginning at L. The despised little central row of seats between each spoke were marked double L, double M, and so forth. The first three or four sections were too full to be inviting.

From an old girlhood habit, she began to tick off the letters of the alphabet in her own personal superstitious terms—L for Love, M for Marvellous, N for Naughty but Nice, O for Optimism, P for Peace, R for Romance . . . But as she searched for an empty seat, aware of a few people looking up at her with an air of vague disapproval as she passed on her high heels (or perhaps it was recognition or perhaps in the Reading Room the latter quickly turned into the former) she found imperceptibly that her litany was turning into something more macabre. V is for Violence, said the voice inside her head, and double V is for Victim of Violence. But V in Jemima's alphabet had always been for Variety, one of her favourite words, so much more diverting to the curious mind than the certainty of Victory, the bull-headed sound of Valour.

And then as she crossed over the entrance to the corridor which led to the North Library and began the alphabet again—this time at the beginning—she found herself reciting A is for Accident, B is for Beware . . . C is for Chloe . . . she found her mind automatically continuing. But at B for Beware and before C for Chloe was reached, Jemima suddenly found that B9—the first end seat and thus her favourite for its slight extra feeling of space—was empty. Someone must have recently vacated it, for such a desirable position to be available so late in the day, by British Museum standards.

August after all was notorious for an influx of overseas scholars. Valentine Brighton had warned her as much when she announced her intention of using the summer season to work on those ladies inevitably christened by him, with his characteristic penchant for trivialization by nickname, "Goodies of the Golden Age."

"I assure you that you will find a mob of sweating scholars from Minnesota: they run package tours to the Reading Room in August."

"You've never been seen in the British Library in August," retorted Jemima. "You simply sit at Helmet in the world-famous Elizabethan garden, having patrician nightmares about the prole-tarian professors."

"My God, how wrong can you be? And I thought you were supposed to be an acute social observer, Jemima Shore, Investi-gator. I shall think twice about entrusting my Golden Goodies to you, let alone old Aunt Emma Helmet's deeply philanthropic diaries about stamping out sex among the Sussex poor. ['But the book was my idea, Valentine,' thought Jemima.] My dear girl, throughout the whole of August, I just can't wait to leave my world-famous Elizabethan garden for the ordered tranquillity of my Bloomsbury office. Those same sweaty professors from Minnesota also hie themselves inexorably to Helmet. Weekends, when the office isn't functioning, are pure hell. It's not so much them asking questions about the history of Helmet—Mummy always insists on answering them by the light of invention anyway—as *telling* me things about the place. And there I am, at one and the same time a cringing victim and the unworthy possessor. At Helmet in the summer they have me at their mercy; I much prefer the anonymity of Bloomsbury."

It struck Jemima, glancing from her new vantage point of B9, that for the purposes of disappearing in London, the Reading Room would be ideal; for everyone, that is, except the very few physically famous. It was not ideal for Jemima Shore, for example.

As she looked up the press marks of the books she needed in the lumbering leather catalogue, a girl with long brown hair and a sharp nose spoke softly at her elbow.

"Miss Shore, I simply loved *The Unvisited*. It's all true, so true; the artificiality of our geriatric culture . . ."

"Thank you so much," said Jemima hastily, beginning to move away.

"Just one question. It's rather personal I'm afraid; in fact I did think of writing to you—"

Firmly, Jemima filled in SHORE J. on the white book slip, gave the reference number, hoping devoutly she had got it right, and beat a quick retreat, murmuring: "Yes, why don't you?"

The girl stared after her. Her gaze was both annoyed and vulnerable. Jemima posted her slips, six of them, in the little brown tray at the central desk and settled down in the harbour of B9 to await her books. One to two hours was said to be the average delivery time: perhaps on a Saturday she would be luckier. B for Beware—yes, indeed, beware of strangers accosting you in the British Library.

But then it seemed that no place was absolutely ideal for Jemima Shore's planned disappearance. The tomb-like weekend quiet of the concrete Bloomsbury block had been disrupted already by one visitor and one squatter—no, revivifier, but the interruption was the same; what was more the revivifier showed no signs of leaving, and the visitor might be lurking anywhere in the district. There had been that cacophony of telephone calls both from the pathetic Stovers and a so-far-unidentified male of presumed Irish extraction.

Only Chloe Fontaine possessed the magic art of disappearance, eluding a persistent ex-lover, worried elderly parents, and her great friend Jemima Shore with equally maddening grace.

Jemima had a book of her own with which to while away the waiting time—*Fallen Child*, which she had begun to reread with pleasure while in the Pizza Perfecta—but the heat and stickiness made her more inclined to put her head in her hands and rest. As for B for Beware, V for Violence and the rest of it, she put that down at Kevin John Athlone's door. The British Library was, if anywhere, a safe refuge from physical violence; no possibility of assault here (except verbally by importunate strangers).

As a resting-place it was also unparalleled, if you could stand the airless atmosphere. The man—or was it a woman—next to her had already given up the struggle for consciousness. The fair head was bowed onto the desk and the pile of delivered books ignored. Jemima recalled other people sleeping on their hands in the Reading Room in the past, on a hot afternoon, but they had been older; retired professors perhaps, turned out by their wives to graze peacefully in these quiet pastures. But there was something different about the attitude of this slumbering flaxen poll. The figure was utterly slumped, giving the impression of total abandon, even despair. It was almost as if its owner were dead rather than asleep, had found his or her last resting-place in the Reading Room, not merely a convenient situation for a quick kip.

"Hamilton? Your books." A handsome Asian with a cultivated voice deposited five books carefully on the desk beside her, and was whisking out the white slips poked into them. He was wearing a dazzling green T-shirt with the single word BOMB on it. The books were about chemistry.

"B for Bomb," she thought automatically. "Beware the Bomb. Ban the Bomb. Beware the British Library." Why were her thoughts so insatiably morbid today? She said aloud:

"No, I'm Shore, J. Shore. These aren't mine." At that moment the fair head next to her raised itself and a pair of light rather narrow eyes were gazing at her. The long mouth twitched; the lips, like the eyes, were rather narrow but the general effect was not unhandsome in a conventional English fashion.

"Jemima Shore! I do declare!" The Asian glanced at the slips, picked up the books and went away. He seemed unconcerned by the mistake. In that respect the British Library had not changed. Jemima wondered how long it would be before her own books arrived.

"B for Brighton," said Jemima, wondering how she could have mistaken Valentine Brighton's sleek thick fair hair, even recumbent, for anyone else's—let alone a woman's.

"Naturally it's B for Brighton, my dear. Where else should I sit? You know my obsession for my own initial, expressed in so many fascinating ways, not the least of which is the famous colophon of the Brighthelmet Press. But what good fortune that you too should have chosen to honour this humble row. Welcome to B—"

"But, Valentine, what on earth are *you* doing here? It's a Saturday in August. Even the professors in Minnesota can't have driven you this far."

Valentine looked at her. For a moment he did not seem to understand the reference. Jemima saw that he was rather pale and there was perspiration on the fine fair skin of his brow.

"Can't you guess?" he said at length in his usual bantering tone. "Three guesses. You won't need three hundred."

"Hardly. You're the most unlikely sight here I can assure you."

"I'm waiting for Chloe."

"What!" In her amazement, Jemima's voice had risen above the sibylline murmur adopted by Library readers. The woman in the seat next to Valentine looked up crossly and clicked her tongue. "Where is she, then?" Jemima hissed.

"I am hardly the person to ask, my dear girl, since I have been waiting here, pinioned to row B, for longer than I care to remember. Hence the state of torpor, not to say stupor in which you discovered me on arrival."

"We must talk. Can you come outside for a moment?"

"That sounds as if you are challenging me to a duel, or are going to knock me down or something. However if the encounter is to be non-violent, I shall be delighted. What is the time? Can we get a drink or something?"

"It's after two o'clock. No, I don't need—want—a drink. I've just had lunch. Pizza, salad and one glass of white wine. Perfect scholar's meal and as a matter of fact I had it at the aptly named Pizza Perfecta. But as the mystery of Chloe's whereabouts deepens, I can't lose this opportunity of getting one or two things straight."

They both got up.

"Aren't you going to leave a note?"

"Ah. Good thinking." Valentine wrote with a flourish in red pentel on one of the white book request slips: "C. Gone for a good chat with Jemima Shore, Investigator. Hope to iron out your problems to both our satisfaction." He signed it: "V." The red writing sprawled across the printed slip, a splash of red.

"V for Violence" floated through Jemima's mind automatically.

It was an inappropriate thought. Of all the men she knew, Valentine Brighton was the least redolent of violence; he seemed to lack even the smallest trace of that natural aggression which goes with masculinity, hence his oft-discussed lack of sexuality. Not that Valentine was in any way effeminate. Adam Adamson, with his youth and slightness, was the more girlish looking of the two. Yet it occurred to Jemima that oddly enough, he was also the more attractive. Even the odious Kevin John had a kind of forceful demanding sexuality which she could appreciate, while shuddering away from it. Yes, that was it. It was Valentine's polite lack of demand towards either sex, so far as could be made out, which caused the question mark to be raised. Besides, he really did not look at all well, perhaps the rumours of his heart condition were something more than maternal fussiness.

Jemima walked with Valentine out of the Reading Room in the direction of those cool Egyptian and Assyrian halls, the memory of which had originally tempted her. As they left the Reading Room, Jemima's handbag was searched in case she should have slipped out a rare book or two. Valentine was ignored, like all the other men without briefcases.

"So *why* were you meeting?"

They stood amidst the vast deities, one or two sufficiently markedly feline to remind her of Tiger, now prowling perhaps on the roofs of Bloomsbury.

"I intended to give Chloe some good advice."

"An odd choice of venue."

"Not my choice, I can assure you. I needed to catch my wayward author before she set off on her secret trip and this was the only rendezvous she would consider. Don't ask *me* why."

"But I must ask you why. And for that matter—what secret trip? To the Camargue, I take it."

"Ah. You knew then. I thought—" For an instant a look akin to surprise or even possibly apprehension marked Valentine's normally bland face. "I thought she kept it a secret from you," he finished. It caused her to remark once again on his uncharacteristic pallor.

"In a sense she did. She told me she was going on a solitary mission, researching an article for *Taffeta* and it was only when that turned out to be a fabrication—"

"*Taffeta!*" This time there was no mistaking the surprise. "What an extraordinary choice of alibi." Valentine gave a wry laugh. "But how absolutely typical of Chloe, for reasons you probably won't appreciate, and if I get my way, never will."

Jemima reflected that she already had a pretty good idea what those reasons might be, thanks to the ladylike indiscretion of Laura Barrymore, but she felt less interested in boasting of her involuntary detective work than getting to the bottom, once and for all, of Chloe's holiday plans. She also felt no particular need to obtrude on Valentine exactly how her discovery of Chloe's mendacity had come about: the Stovers' vigil was no concern of his. Yet, a vague feeling of hurt possessed her that Chloe had chosen to tell the truth—whatever it might be—to Valentine, a friend of far more recent standing, and concealed it in an elaborate tale about *Taffeta* from her old friend Jemima. It encouraged her to press Valentine further. Her hurt was slowly turning to anger, an anger further fuelled by recollection of the hours of the day already wasted on Chloe's complicated intrigue, to say nothing of Kevin John Athlone's assault.

"Where was she really off to? You'd better let me know. There's been quite enough lying already."

Valentine considered, or appeared to consider. Jemima suspected that in such a deliberate man, the decision to confide in her had probably already been taken. "She's off to the Camargue all right, but not until Monday, I gather. She's spending the weekend in London. Then she's going to the Camargue with her latest lover. You know Chloe. You must have guessed that part of it at least."

"But she specifically swore she wasn't! 'Not my new angel.' Why the lie? Why not tell me? Why the need for the cover-up?"

"Dearest Jemima, you're her alibi, don't you see?"

"Yes, I should bloody well think I am her alibi!" Jemima burst out. "I seem to be her alibi for the whole world this morning. But what's the point of the secrecy to *me*?"

"Jemima Shore, Investigator," said Valentine brightly.

"Investigator nothing. I've been her alibi enough times in the past, I can assure you; all through those two marriages. She could have trusted me. We've been friends for years; nothing about Chloe could shock me now. We're both adults, to put it mildly."

"*She* could have trusted you. It was her lover who couldn't."

"Did he need to know I was in the secret? It would have made things so much easier for her, as it happens, if she had trusted me." And the Stovers, Jemima added mentally. "It's all so unlike Chloe, not the intrigue itself, but the lies surrounding it."

"This whole affair is all very unlike Chloe," Valentine commented. "Besides she—he, if you like—needed your innocence. In case the Press got wind of it. You are Press yourself in a kind of way. You could convince them quite genuinely that you didn't know where she was."

"Oh, Isis and Osiris!" exclaimed Jemima with a groan. "I'm going to sit down." They sat on a stone bench, hard and rather uncomfortable.

"Mind you, I'm still not quite sure you wouldn't have been sufficiently fascinated by her new involvement to investigate it *just* a little," continued Valentine. "I could see quite a programme shaping up there. The intricate ways of love: A Woman's Choice, exquisite lady novelist and—well, no, perhaps I had better not tell you."

"Beware my aroused curiosity," said Jemima coldly. "B for Beware, as well as Brighton. Besides I don't work on that kind of romantic and gossipy trash."

"Beware, beware," repeated Valentine soulfully. "How often did I beg Chloe to beware . . . It was so terribly indiscreet, the whole thing, right *there*, under everyone's nose. But I'd better say no more."

Jemima realized with increasing irritation that not only was he playing a role but he was also enjoying it. "Valentine, I'm not sure if murder has ever been done in the British Museum, but I am convinced that these sinister Assyrians have seen a thing or two in their time. How cruel their expressions are. Gods crossed with birds. A terrible combination. At least those colossal crouched lions remind me of Tiger. Anyway, unless you tell me who Chloe's lover is, and why she was meeting you in the Reading Room, I shall behave like Ninurta armed with a thunderbolt and drive you, for the demon you are, out of my temple." She pointed to the label above their heads.

"There, there. I only did it to annoy. I've every intention of telling you, now that Chloe hasn't turned up. I need your co-operation to get hold of her."

"*Where is she?*" It suddenly seemed more important than anything to know immediately the whereabouts of Chloe Fontaine; more important even than the identity of her lover.

"Seventy-three Adelaide Square, I think the address is. You

60

would know. First-floor flat, I believe. *Piano nobile*, they call it, or did before it was wrapped in concrete. She's shacked up there for the weekend with her love, Sir Richard Lionnel. Do you feel like paying a call?"

Chapter Seven

Scheherazade

"I don't believe it!" That was Jemima's first startled exclamation. Afterwards, as she trailed her way back to Adelaide Square and thought over the whole strange encounter with Valentine, she realized that the words had not really been true, even as she spoke them.

Under the circumstances Jemima felt a certain reluctance to re-enter number 73. The garden in the centre of the square on the contrary looked inviting. The huge trees waved their heads far above her in the sky, level with the penthouse. She remembered that a key to the square was on the ring with the keys of number 73. She entered the garden. It was quite empty, a green enclave; no summer flowers, merely a series of flowerless shrubs planted round the edges of the garden; their function seemed to be those of guardians; to protect the inhabitants of the gardens from prying eyes, rather than anything more elaborate. Here at last was the privacy she craved. A locked garden: no one could get at her here. Where the penthouse and the Reading Room had proved insecure refuges, the square garden would surely remain inviolate.

Of the benches available, all empty, she chose one which faced the block of number 73. That would, she felt, concentrate the mind wonderfully. In fact, her first impression on sitting down was to be struck anew by the full monstrosity of Sir Richard Lionnel's concrete cuckoo in Robert Adam's neo-classical paradise. Renewed sympathy for the twentieth-century Adam and the Friends of the House filled her. Adam Adamson, the revivifier, was presumably still lurking somewhere within the third-floor flat. Was his surprise at the name Chloe Fontaine now more explicable? The memory had teased Jemima ever since, for she hated pieces of a puzzle which refused to be placed. Could it be that Adam actually knew of the romantic tryst taking place two floors beneath his and intended to make some sinister use of that knowledge? If so, it was odd that Adam was at the same time unaware that Chloe was the tenant of the penthouse flat.

As she watched and pondered, she saw the front door of the concrete block open and the figure of Adam Adamson emerge. The evening sun touched his curly head and bright jaunty beard and made it look quite fiery. He looked straight in the direction of the gardens, but showed no signs of having seen Jemima; she was in any case partially concealed by one of the ubiquitous shrubs. Then he walked in a leisurely manner away in the direction of Tottenham Court Road. He gave the appearance of being a man very much at his ease. He might have been the owner of 73 Adelaide Square instead of a squatter—revivifier. Jemima looked at her little gold watch. It was 5:30. She found she felt rather sorry to think that Adam Adamson had abandoned number 73.

She ticked off the remaining inhabitants of number 73 in her mind. Up above, golden Tiger crouched on his balcony. The curtain's of the broad first-floor windows, she noticed, were closed; they had scarlet linings, a series of red bars lit up in the evening sun. Within them Richard Lionnel and Chloe were presumably cosily installed, or at least Chloe was. That left the second floor: no blinds as yet, merely large blank windows. And the basement. Tiger's haunt. Goodness knows who may be hanging about there, thought Jemima crossly. After Chloe's behaviour in that place, anything is possible.

"I don't believe it." But suddenly, startlingly, she did believe it. It was as though Chloe's whole character and exploits, past and present, were lit from a completely new angle, the red evening sun falling upon them. Chloe had lied to her parents at Cambridge about her sex life—well, all my friends did that, thought Jemima, except me who had no parents. But Chloe had lied throughout her adult life, if you chose to analyse her behaviour in that light (up till now Jemima had not done so).

Those alibis, those affairs, those passionate plunges into love, marriage, adultery, divorce, and worst of all emotion—a great source of lies, emotion; the whole involvement with Kevin John, so incomprehensible to Jemima; did it not all add up to a cool capacity for concealment as well as a reckless capacity for love? Adultery in Chloe's case had not been the first step to deception but only one of a number of steps.

There was no doubt, now that her surprise was fading, annoyance was beginning to take over. Jemima Shore had been used and she did not like the feeling. The implication that she, Jemima, had been deliberately *chosen*—out of all the gullible fools available—to occupy the penthouse flat while Chloe cavorted with her prestigious lover on the first floor—no doubt laughing the while at Jemima's ignorance—well, to say the least of it, it was irritating to Jemima Shore, Investigator.

Chloe's anxious phrases floated back: "You're sure you won't be lonely?" "No noise." Chloe so beguilingly helpful when Jemima confided her own distress at the death of Colette. "You need a change of scene. Borrow my new flat while I'm away." Chloe so carefully establishing that Jemima intended to receive no visitors, was not in the mood for company.

Chloe had used Jemima as, to be honest, she had been using people all her life. Jemima began to think of both the Stovers and Kevin John in rather a different light. Chloe had come as an upsetting force—"out of the blue" as Mr. Stover had put it—into the Stovers' neat sad lives last week; that much was clear. Chloe, who had ostentatiously abandoned the name of her youth, thus taking from the couple who had brought her up the consolation of her public fame, had first threatened the unvisited Stovers with a visit and then withheld it for reasons of her own which were doubtless connected with her new romance.

Isabelle Mancini now—the enthusiastic patron of Chloe's work through all the years when Chloe was lovelorn and financially desperate: how had she been repaid except, it seemed, by some fairly ruthless portrait in Chloe's new novel?

For Kevin John, it was possible to argue that he had been a promising young painter, his violent impulses confined to his canvasses where they properly belonged, until Chloe like Pandora had let out his evil spirits of drink and assault.

Taking the thought further, Jemima had to admit that she too had been just a little deceived by the precision and irony of Chloe's work. Yet all Chloe's friends, most recently Guthrie Carlyle, were fond of commenting on the contrast between the work and the woman. There was pride involved too: her own. Only yesterday she had been describing Chloe to herself as fundamentally candid. Jemima, who was a professional judge of character, had made a bad mistake about one of her oldest friends. Jemima thought again of that pale bedroom in which hung the scarlet picture. Symbolic of all the violence she intended to eliminate from her life, had been Chloe's breathless comment. Was that not yet another piece of deception?

"I don't believe it." But Valentine's story did make a kind of bizarre sense. He had recounted it to her in the British Museum with some relish after his original revelation about Chloe's whereabouts. He related how Chloe, caught up in a passionate but secret love affair with Sir Richard Lionnel, had sought his, Valentine's advice.

"Why me?" he had enquired in his airy rhetorical manner. "Simple. Because I found out about it by chance, sloping round to Adelaide Square one day on a publisher's rounds. Chloe needed a confidant of course and I know Lionnel since he lives near Helmet. More to the point I also know the dread Francesca Lionnel, who's a great buddy of Mummy's but also a first-class candidate for the role of Medea. Already she exudes wronged beauty with every pore, without, so far as I know, anything specific to exude it about. So I can advise on *that* score. Besides, Chloe is a story-teller. She positively enjoyed telling me all about it."

"Scheherazade."

"Scheherazade in reverse, since I believe the ambition of that lady, being married, was to hold off the evil day of her own death. Chloe's ambition was, as I shall tell you, to achieve the first stage of the process."

To herself Jemima commented: I suppose that the original Scheherazade told some pretty tall stories too, as the Arabian Nights wore on. Still, that was self-preservation.

"You see, dearest Jemima, our Chloe's decided to settle down. She plans to become the second Lady Lionnel."

"What? She must be mad!" Several tourists jumped.

"There I personally entirely agree with you. Marriage—what a ridiculous aim! Babies, children, an establishment, ugh—you know how resolutely I have avoided the former, babies absolutely horrify me, and the latter, of which I do have first-hand experience, is pure purgatory. Why not *carpe diem*? Accept the free flat and any lolly that's going, the new car—he gave her that, naturally—and enjoy, enjoy . . . I begged her to forget about marriage. But Chloe wilfully didn't agree. A strong sexual attraction—I was assured in terms much stronger than those of Chloe's novels that this is the case. Plus that essential in all

Chloe's plans, novelty. Lionnel offers her the earth—a new earth, as she put it to me. On being informed that it was a marriage of true minds, or intended to be such, I offered my help."

"The marriage of true minds," repeated Jemima. "How on earth did they meet?"

"It was a media romance. They happened to be on the same television programme—"

"Good God!" exclaimed Jemima. "I arranged it. Chloe wanted some publicity for her new book. Some kind of round-table chat to do with industrial sponsorship of the Arts. Isabelle Mancini was the chairman. I knew she would be managing one of her wonderfully poised plugs for *Taffeta*—somehow she always makes that magazine sound far more socially committed than the *New Statesman*. As she adores Chloe"—Jemima hesitated and Valentine said nothing—"I thought she would hardly object if Chloe plugged her new book. I watched most of it to see how she made out. Wait. The lighter. I suppose it was his, Lionnel's. That's where I saw it—on telly."

"Afterwards Lionnel whirled her away for dinner at the Mirabelle. *Coup de foudre* was the expression used; I was far too frightened to enquire any further."

"And not a whisper in the Press. No goggling in the gossip columns. No daring speculations by diarists. Perhaps Lionnel fixes them."

"On the contrary. He's very worried about it. The Press hate him, serious papers as well as muck-rakers. That kind of gentleman-buccaneer always tots up a number of enemies among the less piratically minded. No, he's particularly keen on silence at the moment because he's hoping to go respectable. I mean really respectable. He's being tipped as the new Chairman of the Committee for Arts and Caring Industry. Now that could be *very* big indeed in the respectability stakes. You know how keen the Royal Family are on the CARI. They may not be crazy about the arts or industry separately but they find the combination quite devastating. The mere thought of CARI sends them into ecstasy. Lunch with Prince Philip every other day. The Prince of Wales to breakfast. Jogging with Princess Anne. You know the form."

"Hence the Camargue and that *Taffeta* cover story, I take it. But why the clandestine weekend in London first?"

"At the last minute Lionnel was called for some meetings at number ten; couldn't of course refuse. He suggested a kind of romantic breakaway in his official suite, attached to the office, since Lady L. was hardly likely to rumble him there, so blatant it's actually safe. As for Camargue, Chloe plans that to be a trial honeymoon—Chloe will be doing the trying. She intends trying to persuade Lionnel to commit himself to a divorce after the CARI announcement has been made. Her view is that she's already got her man wriggling on the hook. He says he hasn't felt this way for years, youth returned and all that sort of rot. Now she reckons on landing him in the Camargue. My view," concluded Valentine in a pious voice, "is that for something the size of the Lion of Bloomsbury you need a net and not a fishing-rod. But Chloe never understands anything about the animal kingdom. Her novels are full of mistakes in that respect."

The colossal figure of a winged lion couchant which faced them, so much mightier than the bird-gods, leant picturesque credence to what he had just said. Such creatures were not to be captured lightly, but by stealth and imagination.

"Scheherazade, indeed. I can't help hoping she gets away with it."

"That's just the trouble. At this very moment she's in danger of getting away with nothing. You see Lady Lionnel may well have rumbled the Camargue plan, and it's all my own silly fault." Valentine gave a theatrical gesture of putting his hand to his forehead and smoothing back the fair hair. "Or shall I blame country life in August? Nothing to do. Mischief made. First step: over comes Francesca Lionnel to tea with Mummy. Second step: she tells Mummy that Sir Lionnel's gone to the Camargue to have a real holiday, and as they're opening the gardens to the public, he's taken Tommy McKenna.

" 'The Camargue!' cries Mummy over the teacups, not really interested, but showing a fine natural instinct for making trouble where Chloe's concerned, since she's decided long ago—quite wrongly, alas—that Chloe's After Me. 'What a coincidence. Valentine was just telling me that pretty little writer of his, that one who's always getting divorced, what is her name, darling, Clara, yes, Clara Fontaine, she's off to the Camargue. I wonder if they'll meet,' she adds for good measure.

"As Francesca is beginning to burble most graciously something to do with admiring her books and isn't her name Chloe, I butt in: 'Oh Mummy, the Camargue is not like a restaurant; you don't bump into people there." But the damage has been done. For one moment I've seen the glint in Medea's eye and, my dear, she *knows*. She must already know that Lionnel has met Chloe; he may even have told her about the original jolly dinner at the Mirabelle, in a burst of adulterous put-you-off-the-scent nothing-to-hide-you-see honesty. Possibly she knows about the penthouse flat. My dear, Tommy McKenna's story had better be good, otherwise murder might be done, starting with Chloe and probably going on to include that hapless stooge, Tommy McK. And it was in fact to warn Chloe of just that, that I rang her and arranged to meet her this morning. I couldn't come to seventy-three because of Lionnel, you see, or for that matter you.

"So here I am. And here she isn't," Valentine had ended plaintively. "Jemima, as you're living there, do you think you could—"

"No," Jemima had said very firmly. "Warn her yourself." But in the end of course she had agreed. While finishing her work in the Reading Room, she was rather looking forward to the confrontation with Scheherazade.

When she had thought things through to their logical conclusion, Jemima found her usual calm restored. Valentine's role in Chloe's romance still intrigued her, and one or two aspects of his story struck her oddly, but that might have been the presence of his mother as a character in the tale; never having met the famous Hope Lady Brighton, she was never quite sure whether Valentine romanced about her peculiarities or merely reported them accurately.

Jemima would confront Chloe and of course warn her about Valentine's indiscretion. She felt controlled and tranquil in the sinking light of the evening, heat still rising from the pavements, but something tranquil in the atmosphere, or perhaps in her own attitude, very different from the wild imaginings and images of the Reading Room that morning. It would not do for the marriage of true minds to founder at the outset; and the hackneyed quotation which still never lost its power, suddenly reminded her that Valentine had also used it on the slip of the Brighthelmet Press book in Chloe's flat. Valentine's story gained plausibility.

Jemima unlocked the gate and let herself out. There were hardly any cars about as she crossed the broad road to the western side of the square. Nor did any demonstrators lurk outside the concrete block, for which Jemima was thankful. She was beginning to feel such personal distaste for the architecture that she was honourable enough to be ashamed of being seen to enter the building. The outer door was closed but not locked; she hesitated a moment on the doorstep. A cool collected conversation with Chloe, that was the best policy. But Jemima had already decided that she would not need to leave the penthouse flat in protest—hardly. First of all, to be honest, it would be most inconvenient to her plans; secondly, it would smack of moral protest towards Chloe's romance, which was the last thing she intended. She would merely make it clear that she could not be involved personally in any prolonged deception, be it towards Lady Lionnel (whom she did not know) or the world's Press (which she did).

Thus bolstered up, she opened the front door. It was oddly dark inside the marble hall, after the golden light of the evening. Jemima made for the stairs, and stumbled over something. It was heavy, sacklike, and apparently lying half on the floor and half on a chair. Frantically, Jemima reached for the unfamiliar light switch, and as she did so, the sacklike shape stirred and groaned. Her eyes too were getting accustomed to the twilight. But in the end it was her nose which told her the identity of the person before her.

At last she found the time switch which illumined the hall for a given length of time. She found herself gazing once again at Kevin John Athlone. The smell, that same sour masculine smell of the morning, brought back the events of violence and a sense of her own battering sharply to her. She felt for a moment quite sick. His eyes were shut. He looked more dishevelled than ever. The blue T-shirt was marked with dust; it could even be that he had been in a fight. He was snoring or gasping slightly.

Furiously, Jemima shook his shoulder. Sickness and fear left her. She was aware of nothing but a desperate need to get this intruder out of the house before he somehow suspected the presence of Chloe. Then, indeed, murder might be done. Francesca Lionnel was at least graciously presiding over Parrot Park in Sussex. Kevin John Athlone, packing no mean punch as she herself could testify, was right here in the building. His long eyelashes fluttered and his eyes opened. Immediately Kevin John gave her the most ravishing smile and jumped to his feet. He appeared in no way drunk and, if dirty, indifferent to it.

"My little sweetheart! You're back. And I meant to vanish before you returned, like the good fairy I am, leaving you all to your surprise. It was just that it was all too much for me, the climb, the excitement, the fun, and I probably had a drop or two at lunch with my old mate Dixie, otherwise I wouldn't have done it at all."

"What on earth are you doing back here?" exclaimed Jemima wearily.

"Wait and see. Wait and see. Just wait and see what a splash of red awaits you in Chloe's white heaven. I climbed, I climbed, all the way up the scaffolding, on the inside mind you, didn't feel like attracting attention, although there was no one about, might have been a ghost town, and I've left you the most magnificent present. All because I was something less than a gentleman this morning. I've copied down the telephone number by the way, so I'll be able to be in touch."

"Oh no."

"Oh yes, darling, oh yes. Up the scaffolding, clutching my gift, in through your balcony window, conveniently left open—just for me. In. Deposit. Out. Await you. Fall asleep. Awoken by a maiden's kiss."

"No kiss," said Jemima. "No kiss at all." But then, somewhat to her surprise, Kevin John actually did give her a kiss, not one of his rubbery kisses but a gentle kiss. It was also a kiss which preceded his departure.

"I'm a gentleman at heart," was his parting shot, as he lumbered down the steps. "You see if I'm not."

Jemima closed the front door thoughtfully. She waited for five minutes in the hall in case there should be a spontaneous return of the ebullient artist. Then she climbed the broad stairs to the first floor. She knocked and called gently:

"Chloe. It's me, Jemima." She felt extremely foolish doing so but she had her duty to do. "Chloe. It's me, Jemima. I've got a message from Valentine."

There was a bell. The neat plate beside the door read: Lionnel (Sussex) Offices Ltd. Hesitating, she rang the bell. The sound was extremely loud on the landing and startled her. Was it startling those within? There was no sound at all. She wondered whether this door would suddenly fall open, as had the door of the third-floor flat. Sheer curiosity about her friend's daring plan to storm the heights of marriage to Sir Richard Lionnel had brought with it a modicum of amusement. She was back on Chloe's side. Deception was, once more, forgiven.

After ringing once more and knocking twice, Jemima realized

that Chloe must either be out or asleep; the warning would have to wait for the next day. If Chloe and Richard Lionnel were in bed, they were best left to it, without a visit from Jemima Shore, Investigator. If she suddenly interrupted some highly romantic moment, then another form of murder might be done! Jemima had absolutely no wish to be seen in such a tiresomely prurient light.

She decided to go up to the penthouse and find out what Kevin John had deposited for her, like some huge puppy leaving an unwelcome gift for its master. She gave the door of the third-floor flat a wide berth. There was no sound from there either. Indeed, the whole building had fallen silent since the departure of Kevin John. Its silence oppressed her. Perhaps it was the contrast with the busy low whispering of the Reading Room in which she had spent the afternoon. Still, silence was what she craved. It was odd how worrying it now seemed.

She opened the door quickly and a look of horror crossed her face.

A great scarlet geranium of the most violent hue possible sat in its pot in the middle of the white carpet. Already there were dirty marks round it. Earth, dirty footsteps and some water. The red glared at her. It was revolting. The bedroom door was shut. Jemima's loathing of scarlet flowers came back to her with force. A splash of blood indeed: she was reminded of Sylvia Plath's brilliant blood-stained poem about red tulips in hospital. How on earth the heavily built and debauched Kevin John had managed to scale a scaffold clutching this object was another matter. He did seem to have dropped it once or twice for she saw that the pot was slightly cracked, hence the earth and water which were seeping out. A note next to the pot read:

"A Splash of Red. Red roses would have been better, but this was all I could find in this urban desert."

The mess was distasteful, almost as bad as the garish scarlet colour of the plant. Serve Chloe right, perhaps, for fooling around with Kevin John's affections. Now, thought Jemima, she will have to have her virgin carpet cleaned. Chloe will be utterly furious about that.

She opened the door into the bedroom. Jemima stood absolutely still. She could not stop staring. Through her head ran idiotically the continuation of the same thought. Oh God, the mess, the terrible red mess, all over Chloe's white bed. But this time she did

71

not think that Chloe would be furious about it. Chloe would never be furious about anything again.

For Chloe, little white Chloe, one high-heel dangling from a foot which had fallen over the side of the bed, was lying with her eyes open and an enormous red gaping wound across her throat. There were other red marks on her body. Blood had splashed across her white cotton broderie anglaise petticoat. Blood had formed pools on the bed. Compared to the blood on the bed, the great picture hanging above it now looked quite flat and tame. Chloe had told her last story; this time it had not saved her. Scheherazade was dead.

Chapter Eight

Who, Who?

For several moments Jemima stood quite still in the doorway, burned with pity. Chloe looked so tiny, there on her huge bed, her still face and the terrible gash giving her the air of a murdered child. Jemima moved forward and touched one little white hand where it had fallen on the counterpane. Her foot encountered something sharp and she saw a razor lying on the floor by the side of the lace valance. The hand, though cool, was not stiff and for a moment she thought—but no one could have survived a great gaping gash like that—something so violent, brutal and efficiently executed must have killed her more or less instantly. Besides there were other lesser wounds. Jemima felt automatically for the pulse. There was none.

Her eyes were wide open. From that sad simulacrum of life, Jemima at last accepted that Chloe was dead. She closed them with gentle fingers, knowing with one part of her mind that she should touch nothing. But still she could not bear to leave her friend with her huge eyes gazing blindly at the destruction which death had wrought on her once immaculate bedroom.

Jemima turned away and, ignoring the rise of tears and nausea, both of which were trying to claim her, ran back into the sitting room, knocking over the scarlet geranium as she passed so that more earth spattered over the carpet.

She dialled 999 and within a few seconds, in a voice which surprised her with its calm found herself asking for the police. To Scotland Yard she gave no details other than the fact that it was urgent. All the time through her head was running the question: Why, Why? It was not until Tiger suddenly awoke from the somnolent eyes-shut crouch he had adopted in the sunlight on the pale carpet, that his slow sleepy stretching mew-mew changed the note of the refrain in her head to something quite different: Not Why, Why? but Who, Who? . . .

At that very moment she heard the sound of a police siren in Adelaide Square. While she was still talking to the female voice on the other end of the telephone, a policeman in uniform—no jacket but his bright white shirt looked equally formal—came sharply into the flat. His voice and movements were brisk but not hurried, with that special kind of negative courtesy—an absence of all kind of delaying emotion, good or bad—she associated with the police. He was quite young with very smooth pink cheeks.

"Mrs. Shaw," he began. "You dialled nine-nine-nine? We answered your radio call." Then he recognized her. "Ah, Miss Jemima Shore. It was your call—"

"The body's in there. I found her. I can identify her. This is her flat." Suddenly Jemima felt she could not re-enter the bedroom until she had fought down both her pity and her nausea. "I don't think there's much to be done for her." He went swiftly through. Jemima picked up Tiger. She could not endure the idea of the cat picking its delicate curious way into that sullied chamber. She put him, scrabbling in her arms, onto the balcony and regardless of the heat, shut the window. As Kevin John had reminded her, she had left it unlocked. He had entered the flat by that route. And who else?

Who, Who? . . . was beginning to beat in her head with more force as the cat mewed angrily against the glass.

She heard the policeman talking into the black radio link on his shoulder, the thick black plastic wiring curling out of the machine like a snake. He was talking to Bloomsbury Police Station. In between crackles and other little squeaking sounds, she heard him calling for the CID. And a police surgeon. At that moment, he returned to the sitting room.

"I'm afraid I closed her eyes," Jemima said rather woodenly. "I shouldn't have touched anything."

The policeman was kind.

"The shock. I presume you and the deceased were acquainted. Detective Chief Inspector Portsmouth will be here in a few minutes. In the meantime, Miss Shore, it is Miss Jemima Shore, Investigator, isn't it?" He gave a faint rather embarrassed smile. "No question of *your* identity—I'll leave the questions to him." He was writing in his notebook.

He looked round the flat.

"Excuse me, Miss Shore, is this all there is?"

"And the kitchen." She waved her hand, and he trod in his quick authoritative way towards it, his heavy black shoes making no noise on the carpet. His manner, and his confidence, belied the extreme youth of his appearance. Through the open kitchen door, Jemima saw that the glass kitchen door leading to the fire escape was still shut and bolted.

The police and their work, including that of a murder squad, were familiar to Jemima Shore. In particular she enjoyed good relations with Detective Chief Inspector John Portsmouth (Pompey as he was familiarly dubbed) of the Bloomsbury Police. It was a friendship which had begun several years back when it had suited Pompey's purpose to issue an appeal on television for information concerning a missing child. Later he discussed the case in a brief interview. Jemima had handled both appearances.

Still later, in view of the unusual nature of the case, there had been a discussion group on television in which Pompey had featured. Even the *Guardian*, in rather a dazed way, had described Jemima's organization of this as "fascinatingly fair-minded." Pompey had evidently agreed with the *Guardian*, since with his help, Jemima had been able to make a programme about women detectives, and another about detectives' wives. A friendship had been struck, based on the odd drink, the odd chat, the odd consultation from both sides about each other's work. On at least one occasion these conversations had resulted in the solution of a mystery temporarily baffling to Pompey. No, the arrival of Pompey held no fears, only a kind of reassurance for Jemima.

Nor was death itself a stranger to her. She had seen it in many guises, and helped to track down its begetter in her private investigative capacity. But this time it was her friend who was dead, murdered in that very room where only twenty-four hours before the living, graceful Chloe had moved lightly about in her high-heeled shoes, packing her bag. After so many years of friendship, it was as though something of Jemima's own past had been slain.

Who, Who?—the question was still going through her head when the police surgeon in the shape of a local GP arrived, followed by a police photographer; another policeman, identity and role unknown; a young man in plain clothes, probably a detective; someone she recognized as the fingerprint expert from Bloomsbury Police Station; and presiding over it all, Detective

Chief Inspector John Portsmouth—Pompey—who with great urbanity took over the whole case and, as it seemed, the whole flat.

He shook his head when he saw Jemima, that gently placatory gesture which their various forays on television had made famous. Nothing ever surprised Pompey; his manner suggested that he had all along predicted that one Saturday night Jemima would find her best friend with her throat cut.

The police surgeon, a nice rather weary man, duly pronounced life extinct—to Jemima's view slightly unnecessarily, but she knew the careful ways of the police. However the doctor did summon up some enthusiasm when discussing the cause of death. He also proved to be a connoisseur of modern painting. "Cause of death cut throat. That's clear enough. The first blow killed her, very well done, severed the windpipe immediately, that accounts for all the blood, main arteries you know, must have spouted like an oil well. By the body temperature, about six hours ago. *Rigor mortis* only just beginning to set in—the hot weather. Nothing to do with that razor by the bed of course; clumsy, aren't they? I much prefer the electric sort myself." He smoothed his own chin appreciatively.

"They'll have to look for something else. Good picture over the bed by the way. It's an Athlone, isn't it? I thought so. There's one in the Tate rather similar. I'm very glad to have had an opportunity to see *that*." He might have been visiting an art gallery in a provincial town.

He added in a much brisker voice: "Most unsuitable for a lady's bedroom, I would have thought."

"How about this, sir?" It was the young detective, addressing Pompey. He was holding in a gloved hand one of Chloe's long sharp kitchen knives. It was part of the *batterie de cuisine* which Jemima had admired the night before. According to Chloe—could one believe her?—it had been a housewarming present from Isabelle Mancini. Chloe, the domestic cat, had once been an excellent cook; now her gleaming *batterie* had been literally the death of her. The blade of the large knife looked as if it had been dipped in rust.

Jemima was familiar with the slow grinding of the police methods. She recognized the need for the endless questions and the establishment of apparently obvious facts. Nevertheless she was relieved when Pompey suggested that she should think about taking herself elsewhere—a police car would be provided—where they could continue their essential conversation in some greater comfort.

Powder was now everywhere. Everything in the flat had been dusted and tested for fingerprints. Jemima's own—fingerprints "friendly to the environment" as Pompey put it—had been taken for elimination. It proved quite a jovial procedure, accompanied by some grave shakes of the head from Pompey.

Jemima repeated her basic story. How she had left for the Reading Room at about 12:30, going to the Pizza Perfecta *en route*. How the flat had certainly been empty when she left, since it was very small. She had visited the kitchen just before leaving to see if she could find anything interesting to eat. She was sure the *batterie* was then complete because she had used one of the smaller knives to cut a piece of cheese, before suddenly deciding in favour of the Pizza. She had returned at approximately 5:30.

Finally Chloe's little body, wrapped in hygienic black plastic, was carried away down the stairs, off to the local mortuary, at the orders of the Coroner's office. There, like the rest of London, it would spend a quiet weekend—no noise, no disturbance— awaiting its post-mortem from a pathologist on Monday morning. The efforts of the police photographer, first taking shots of the body, and then general shots of the flat, punctuated the proceedings. He might be an ardent *paparazze* trying to nose out a juicy scandal with his flashing camera, thought Jemima: but then, of course, that's exactly what he *is* trying to do.

It was illogical, but she still minded the desecration of her friend's pale paradise. It was better to concentrate on the notion of scandal, and *that* was a thought which led directly to the subject of Sir Richard Lionnel, a topic temporarily eliminated from her mind by shock. Who, Who? . . . As though on cue, yet another policeman appeared in the doorway and whispered in Pompey's ear.

Pompey left the flat abruptly. His expression was enigmatic, with only the unexpected severity of the shake of his head to give some clue that for once perhaps he was very slightly surprised. Jemima was deciding to organize herself into an hotel—there must be some quiet private room in Bloomsbury of a Saturday night— when the telephone rang. Cocking an eyebrow at the remaining policeman, she answered it. She was greeted by the sound of pip-pips and then a loud voice bellowed in her ear.

"Dollie, is that you? Dollie, this is Dad." But Jemima had already recognized the arbitrary tones of Mr. Stover. Oh God, she thought, have I got to tell him? "I'm at the station," he went on.

"Which station?" said Jemima in a shaky voice.

"Tottenham Court Road tube station," Mr. Stover sounded extremely testy. "That's where. Not Folkestone station I can assure you, which I left some hours ago at your personal request. Awful journey by the way. British Railways ought to be ashamed." Pause for emphasis. "Tottenham Court Road tube station that's where. Where you said you'd meet me at six o'clock. And it's now six-fifteen precisely."

Jemima covered the mouthpiece. "Officer, I think you'd better deal with this. It's the dead woman's father . . . stepfather, I mean. I mentioned earlier that her mother was probably her next of kin. He appears to be here in London."

The police officer began to address Mr. Stover in that same voice of neutral courtesy which had characterized all the proceedings.

"I am a police officer, sir, at your daughter's flat; dealing with a certain matter. No, I am afraid I cannot discuss it with you on the telephone. No, sir, I cannot at the moment give you any information. If you would just stay where you are, sir, a young lady police officer will arrive to look after you."

"He's an old man," Jemima thought dully. "A confused and angry old man. This shouldn't be happening to him."

The man Pompey brought back with him was one to whom she felt confusion was quite unknown. Sir Richard Lionnel immediately dominated the scene by his mere presence. It was partly his physique—the Lion of Bloomsbury was well named.

Lionnel was urbanely dressed in a light tweed suit, so well cut that it did not even look out of place on this summer evening; the colour complemented his tanned skin. He was not in fact particularly tall, a little taller than Jemima herself perhaps, but his shoulders in the tweed suit were broad, giving an air of authority, and he himself, if not exactly heavy, was certainly a substantial man. Beyond that, everything about Lionnel exuded extraordinary life and force, from his black curly hair, tonsured by baldness like a monk, but still black and growing very vigorously, so that the curls seemed to be springing from his head, like a devil's horns, to his bright black eyes, definitely the eyes of some attendant devil at Lucifer's court. As they snapped from side to side, taking in

Jemima, the flat, the policeman, the mess, they created their own energy. Even Lionnel's tan—or perhaps it was merely the native olive of his complexion—added to the air of natural force by making him look vigorously healthy.

The Lion of Bloomsbury, yes, indeed, a powerful animal. Instantly, Jemima understood what had attracted Chloe—not novelty, not sex, not security, although doubtless all these elements had been present, but command. Sir Richard Lionnel, the powerful pirate vessel, would carry along Chloe's frail little craft in his wake, and supply that command which somehow, Chloe, through two marriages and innumerable love affairs, had failed to find. For a moment Jemima, the cool, the collected, the independent, found herself irrationally jealous of her dead friend.

What was further remarkable about Sir Richard Lionnel under the circumstances, was that he was absolutely and totally at his ease. Yet, thought Jemima, taking refuge from her instinctive moment of jealousy in a meaner mood of sardonic satisfaction, when all is said and done, he has a great deal of explaining to do. A mistress in his office flat of an August weekend. How will that be kept from the papers? Or for that matter Lady Lionnel? No question of gossip columnists now or the satiric snipings of *Jolly Joke*—headlines would be the order of the day for the beautiful slain Chloe Fontaine, romantic lady novelist. Sir Richard Lionnel's desire to go respectable had met an untimely end—as had his mistress. The pirate ship would not find a safe port at CARI after this. Of course—she looked down at his strong hands—he may have even more explaining to do. Who, Who? . . . She shuddered.

Lionnel introduced himself to Jemima with perfect gravity. "Richard Lionnel. I own the building. I came back to my office flat downstairs to find the police. You were her tenant, I believe. I understand you found her. This must be terrible for you. Where will you go?" He did not even pause on the second word "her"; nor could Jemima decide whether his avoidance of the name Chloe Fontaine indicated stress or total self-command. Lionnel certainly seemed indifferent to the fact—he could hardly be unaware of it—that it must also be terrible for him. The only conceivable sign of strain he exhibited was the fact that he was smoking as he entered the flat—although he stubbed the cigarette out immediately.

The black stub receded from her view into the pale glazed

pottery ash-tray; it was shortly joined by another. Neither cigarette was fully smoked, a habit Sir Richard had in common with Kevin John Athlone; it was the image of the latter, stubbing out ceaselessly the black Sobranies he had found in Chloe's bedroom, which confirmed to her that this man before her had known her friend well, had from time to time shared that bedroom with her, had stored his cigarettes there, had perhaps stored a razor as well. Now she was dead, murdered.

Jemima did not of course know what had transpired between Lionnel and Pompey downstairs. Had he made a statement or were matters not that advanced? Which did he fear more—the Press or the police? These questions tantalized her as she replied with composure to match his own: "I'm going to an hotel near here, I hope. Then I shall try to find something else. My own flat is let and I need to be in this area to get on with my work in the British Library." She glanced at Pompey, who gave a very gentle shake of his head, and added firmly: "And of course I want to give the police all the help I can."

"Naturally," replied Lionnel, as though she was offering to help him rather than the police. Once again he did not apparently feel it incumbent upon him to express the same helpful attitude. They stared at each other. "Whatever the police know at this point about your relations with Chloe," thought Jemima, refusing to let her own green eyes fall before his black ones, "*I* know. But do you know that I know?"

"Excuse me, sir," said the young policeman, with a deferential cough. "There's the question of this pet." He was holding in his arms the golden bundle of Tiger, whose wild green eyes, rather the colour of Jemima's own but far more baleful, gazing with savage outrage at his imprisonment, made the policeman's description of him seem singularly inappropriate.

"Oh God—Tiger—I'd forgotten. Who will feed him?" began Jemima, just as the infuriated so-called pet eluded his captor's arms. Delivering a vicious scratch to the policeman's shoulder, protected only by a white shirt, he leapt away and to the floor. From this point he then leapt with equal precipitation right up on to Lionnel's tweed-clad shoulder. It was as though in his feline language, he was pointing directly and threateningly to their secret acquaintance. If so, Lionnel's reaction was equally significant. Without any visible annoyance, he simply struck the clinging cat off his shoulder, as one might brush off a beetle or some other flying insect. Tiger let out something closer to a squawk than a mew.

"Cats in their place," said Lionnel pleasantly, but without a trace of apology. This was how Jemima had witnessed the Lion of Bloomsbury coping with television. "Lionnel Estates will definitely be building further high-rise blocks—Lionnel Estates will be demolishing unsafe Adam houses—Lionnel Estates will do this, do that—wherever the permission is granted." And then at the end, an unexpected grin, making him look like a happy satyr. He was not grinning now. "But there's no need for them to starve. Cats, Miss Shore, not the masses. By repute, as you know, I'm less particular about the latter. Besides you might not get into a very salubrious hotel at this hour, and at the height of the tourist season. I'll call my people on Monday and see what we've got on offer to accommodate you. In the meantime, Miss Shore, why don't you stay downstairs? I've an office flat," he went on blandly, "which I'm using till my own flat on the third floor is decorated. Quite comfortable. Yes, really quite comfortable. I take it you're alone." He looked round.

"Yes, quite alone," said Jemima in her most poised voice. "How very kind, Sir Richard. But what about—" she phrased it diplomatically— "your own plans?"

"I'm going back to the country. Now." And to Portsmouth he added: "You have my number there of course, and I'll be available at any time."

"Thank you, Sir Richard. I should like to have a further word with you before you go." Equally noncommittal.

"So why not, Miss Shore?" Why not indeed? It was true that Jemima felt a growing obligation towards Tiger, as though tending him was her own expression of mourning for Chloe. She could not abandon him now to his wildness. Who else would tend him? Adam Adamson? Was he yet back from that mysterious errand? Ah, that was a thought. The whole question of Adam Adamson, to say nothing of Kevin John Athlone, brought her back to the persistent refrain Who, Who? . . .

To deal with it, she needed two things. First of all, time and space for a clear think. And that the first-floor flat would provide. Second, and of this she was quietly optimistic, she needed a good long talk with her friend Detective Chief Inspector John Portsmouth, otherwise known as Pompey. She had after all a great deal of information for Pompey. Jemima, spirits rising as the habitual curiosity quickened in her, thought Pompey, unofficially of course, might have some for her.

One last encounter remained before she could descend to the abstract peace of the first floor. In its own way it was as surprising as anything which had yet confronted her that day.

Mr. Stover was an unexpectedly little man. From his fiercely resonant voice, Jemima had anticipated more physical substance. He stood in the doorway, panting slightly from the climb, felt hat in hand, mackintosh over his arm—careful on even such a blazing day of what sudden rains might lie in wait in the capital. He was quite dwarfed by the policewoman at his side; she was rather pretty, with neat fair hair pinned up under a cap and a pleasantly freckled face; her black and white tie and rolled-up sleeves, revealing freckled arms, gave her the air of a school prefect.

The smallness of Mr. Stover depressed Jemima once more. But then Chloe's so small. No, Chloe *was* small. She tried to put aside the memory of that frail corpse on the bed. And anyway, he's only her stepfather.

But Mr. Stover was still talking quite fiercely and the eyes, in the lined face, under the white hair, were bright and even angry.

"We never came here, you know," he was saying. "Her mother and I were never invited."

He looked round at the wreck of the pale flat, which now, under its police occupation, looked like some kind of abandoned film set.

"Very plush, I must say." It did not seem the right word. "No garden, of course."

"There's a nice balcony, sir," said the policewoman brightly.

Mr. Stover shot her a sardonic glance. "I can see that, my dear, I can see that. Seventy-seven next birthday and still got my own eyes. Can't say the same about my teeth, mind you, but then I don't see with my teeth, do I?"

"No, sir," said the policewoman in a voice of friendly encouragement, as though he might if he tried hard enough.

"Those your teeth, by the way?" Mr. Stover suddenly barked at Jemima, reminding her of the voice on the telephone. His small stature was certainly delusive.

"I believe so."

"Funny. Always thought they ripped them out if you went on television and gave you new ones. That's why I never accepted any of their numerous offers to appear, you see." Then the little spark subsided; there was something automatic about it as though Mr. Stover was comforting himself with his familiar witticism.

"A balcony, yes," he went on in a much less energetic voice. "All very nice. But you couldn't put a baby on a balcony, could you? Not for very long. Her mother said, 'Charlie, I'd like to know about the accommodation.' That's the last thing she said. 'Is it suitable, Charlie? You must tell Dollie to make quite sure she has a little garden.' " Then he choked and Jemima realized that tears were running down his cheeks, had been running down his cheeks while he talked of Dollie and her garden, and twisted his felt hat in his hands.

"She was so happy, the wife, when Dollie telephoned. We quite forgave her all the waiting. The second letter, cancelling the visit, never arrived, you know. Some problem with the address, I suppose. It will come—" He gave a little dry sob. "She was so happy. In spite of the, well, somewhat unusual circumstances, least said soonest mended in that direction. 'A grandchild at my age!' she said. Dollie was her only one, and we never had one of our own."

Mr. Stover turned to Jemima, as though the police were not present and she, and she alone, must hear this news.

"Yes, Miss Shore, Dollie was going to have a baby. That's what she wanted to tell us. And this morning she was so happy."

As Mr. Stover still stood there, having delivered this bombshell, Jemima found the old question coming back in force. Who, Who? Not only the murderer but the father of Chloe's child. One person or two. Who, Who?

Chapter Nine

Fallen Child

"Yes, she was pregnant all right. About three months, according to the police doctor," said Detective Chief Inspector Portsmouth. "We got on to the mortuary immediately in case anything could be done to save the child, which of course it couldn't." He was sitting, nursing a pale whisky and water, in what was designated as the receiving room of Sir Richard Lionnel's office suite.

The décor was quite unlike that of the shocking cobalt blue aquarium upstairs. Here it was most obviously gracious: a great many well-polished surfaces belonging to furniture which could have been photographed as it stood for the pages of *Country Life*. Lamps were huge, marble based with wide shades. The sofa on which Pompey was sitting was discreetly covered in tobacco-coloured material, with appropriately tawny cushions. The flowers, a huge arrangement on the bow-fronted sideboard which otherwise bore only cut-glass decanters containing a variety of rich red liquids, consisted of gladioli and roses. Red and orange predominated. Jemima expected to see *Country Life* itself lying in sheaves on the low table in front of the sofa (such planning, with its lack of any personal element, recalled irresistibly the dentist's waiting-room). Whoever had decorated this suite, it was certainly not the same hand and imagination at work as had been rampant on the third floor. Perhaps the Lionnels merely hired the most fashionable decorator of the time, regardless of style.

Only Jemima herself, still in the rippling beige dress with its tiny splashes of red and navy blue in which she found herself spending this strange day, brought some lightness into the picture. Pompey noted once again Jemima's gift—and the gift of her clothes—of seeming unruffled and elegant even in the most bizarre circumstances. It was something to which his wife had first

84

drawn his attention. Pompey merely thought Jemima an unfairly pretty girl for one who was so markedly—even awkwardly—intelligent. Every time they met he had to adjust to the combination all over again. Shaking his head, he expressed something along these lines.

"I don't believe it!" Jemima burst out. "Oh thank you, Pompey," she added quickly. "No, I meant Chloe and the baby. I can't quite believe it. But then I'm always saying that about Chloe now. I'm beginning to think I never knew her at all." Jemima took a long cool sip of white wine—a Muscadet happily found in Sir Richard's office fridge; but then many people drank white wine as an aperitif nowadays not only Jemima herself—Chloe, for example . . .

"Tell me about her. A rather adventurous young lady, I take it." A gentle shake of the head. "A bit of a slip-up, that about the baby. Didn't she watch your famous programme, then, about the Pill?" Pompey's references to Jemima's programmes were generally jocular; Jemima was glad of this indication that he was in a relaxed—and therefore confidential—mood.

"Adventurous, yes. Young, well, you're always so chivalrous, Pompey. She was exactly my age." Pompey spread his hands expressively. He looked quite roguish. The omens were good for a rather jolly discussion, if any discussion on such a painful subject could be jolly; it was one which involved Pompey's keen wits and Jemima's devouring curiosity.

Jemima had already described what she knew of the last twenty-four hours of Chloe's life. She had kept nothing of importance back, relating quite straightforwardly the various episodes of the telephone calls (including those of the Stovers), and the morning intrusion of Kevin John Athlone as she was about to leave for the Reading Room. Her description of her encounter with Adam Adamson had incurred quite a fierce headshake from Pompey but he did not interrupt her. She passed on to her unexpected meeting with Valentine Brighton in the Reading Room and her subsequent return first to the square gardens where she had spied Adamson leaving, and then to the house in Adelaide Square itself, where she had found Kevin John Athlone.

Jemima left nothing material out. She knew that if she was to pursue her enquiries successfully, she had much to gain from being very frank with Pompey in the hope that he would to some extent pool information. Only with regard to Valentine Brighton's mission to London did she tread somewhat circumspectly. This was for two reasons. First, Jemima had her own reservations about Valentine's story, told amidst the Assyrian gods. His whole presence in Bloomsbury needed further explanation so far as she was concerned; the image of that slumped figure—like a dead man as she had thought at the time—in the seat so providentially next to hers, remained to tantalize and disturb. Second, Chloe's alleged ambition to marry Lionnel was, by the rules of evidence, merely hearsay.

Jemima therefore contented herself for the time being with telling Pompey that Valentine had had a rendezvous with Chloe, and that Chloe had not kept it. On the subject of Lionnel generally, she kept her peace. Here was an area where Pompey possibly had something to tell her.

He did. Or rather, he was able to confirm a substantial part of the Brighton story out of Sir Richard Lionnel's own statement.

"She was his mistress. Oh, yes." Doleful shake. "*And* he didn't know she was pregnant, so he says. He also swore, by the way, that *she* didn't know; he thought the old man was making it up, had got the wrong end of the stick." Pompey coughed. "This is before the report from the mortuary confirmed that she *was* pregnant, of course!" Another cough and a shake. "Yes, a very adventurous young lady. Because you see, Jemima, if Sir Richard Lionnel's statement is to be believed, and we have no reason at this point to doubt his word, he could not be the father of her child."

"I've just been working that out for myself," Jemima said slowly. "Three months pregnant. And the programme on which they met was at the beginning of June—I'll fill you in on that if Lionnel hasn't. Certainly not earlier, because I was in Japan until the second week of May, and Chloe's book—*Fallen Child*—must have been published at the end of the month. The programme came after that. She only moved here in June. She was already pregnant then. It wasn't visible, even the night she died, except— yes, maybe the figure just a little fuller."

"*Fallen Child*, eh?" The title seemed to confirm Pompey's gloomiest supposition about the late Chloe Fontaine. "Well, she was certainly fallen, poor lady. In the old-fashioned sense of the word," he added gallantly, as if Jemima were far too young to have heard the expression.

"And to the last I always found something rather childlike about her—" Jemima hesitated, recalling their last conversation. Chloe framed in the window, the waif-like face and the newly rounded bosom, which at the time had seemed to indicate increased voluptuousness, but was now revealed as something far more vulnerable.

"You've called her adventurous, Pompey. She was, obviously. But she was also greedy, greedy like a child. Grabbing at things, people, experiences. I see it much more clearly now, now that she's no longer here to charm and woo me—Chloe wooed everyone, you know. This last grab, at Lionnel I mean, it must have been terrible for her when she found out she was pregnant. A child with child. Perhaps that's why she panicked."

"Someone panicked, not necessarily the deceased. She didn't cut her own throat with a kitchen knife, you know. No question of that. This was a swift and quite expert piece of work. The stabs came after and were extra to requirements. Sign of a lover, more likely than not, all that frenzy."

"I was referring to her future. Did Lionnel give any indication—"

"Said they were off to France. Taking the ferry and driving down to the South. Quite open about it. That they were spending the weekend in London because he had to be at number ten—quite open about that, too. Still, it's a very good alibi. The second best alibi in the world you might call it, the best being only half a mile away up the road."

"D'you think the Queen's actually at home on a Saturday?"

Dubious shake and Pompey continued: "He left this flat at ten o'clock and returned at six-fifteen according to his statement. It will be checked, of course. Unexpectedly free at lunch so telephoned Miss Fontaine at twelve-thirty. No answer. Rather surprised. Still it was a lovely day—she might have been in the gardens. The first-floor flat, as you see, does have a balcony, but she would have heard the telephone from there. Went to a restaurant in Soho. Ate his lunch. Telephoned again at two. No answer—by that time of course she was probably dead. We think she was killed between one and two o'clock. Shortly after you left the house. Back to his meeting and arrived here soon after six to find the police. That's all except he doesn't remember the name of the restaurant, something Greek was all he gave us, but that's no problem. We shall find it."

"He's certainly highly recognizable." There was something

confusing to Jemima about her own relief that Lionnel was in the clear; was it for his own or for Chloe's sake—her last love not her killer—that she was pleased?

"But did Lionnel make any statement about their future?" Jemima ventured. "I know this sounds a trifling question, Pompey, but it might be relevant in piecing together Chloe's past if I knew when she was telling the truth and when she wasn't." It was also relevant to the past of her friend and publisher Valentine Brighton.

"He gave us as much as he had to, and he knew he had to, sooner or later. No more, no less. Quite straight. He's a man of the world. No point in fooling around with the police, now, is there? Not for a man in Sir Richard Lionnel's position. Too much to lose. He needs us, doesn't he, to keep the Press off his back—"

"Ah." Jemima was wondering about the Press, so far—mercifully from her own point of view as well as that of Lionnel—absent. She knew it could hardly last.

Pompey sipped his whisky appreciatively; his whole attitude was one of melancholy but unsurprised regret at the perpetual foolishness of human nature.

Her own 999 call had been sufficiently uninformative to elude the interest of some stray listener-in to the police radio link. Saturday night was a dead time in Fleet Street, with the Sunday papers not only printed but already despatched to the provinces; it needed an emergency to alter the leading stories of the London editions. But on Sunday Scotland Yard would be notified of what had occurred and that notification would reach the Press Bureau. Then the second tornado, that of the Press following that of the police team, would strike. Chloe's murder would certainly be announced on the Sunday evening television news and splashed across the morning papers.

"In so far as that can be done," continued Pompey, "and in so far as we want to co-operate, which for the time being, in view of the connection with number ten, and the incomplete nature of our enquiries, perhaps we do. Of course they'll be right on to the fact that he owns the building, particularly as there's been all this fuss about it, but he didn't own her flat, the flat where she was killed. As to the relationship, well, they may suspect, may have heard rumours, but they've got to be very careful about what they print. This is a murder case, Jemima, not your average juicy scandal of adultery in high places." From Pompey's prim tone, you might have thought that Pompey actually preferred murder to adultery. He added: "He's made his statement and he's gone back to Sussex."

"To Lady Lionnel. I wonder what *her* reaction will be?"

Pompey rose to his feet. For all his natural authority he was not a man you would pick out in a crowd—a fact in which he took some pride—and even after Jemima's original television interview, people had not immediately recognized him in the street. Even his age was mysterious; for all his paternal manner, he was probably not so many years older than Jemima herself. Indeed she sometimes darkly suspected that his paternalism—and his chivalry—was a professional ruse to instil confidence, and thus elicit it. Yet when one studied his face closely it had at least one highly memorable feature: a pair of curiously bushy eyebrows rising to tufted points over bright rather small eyes which together gave him the look of an inquisitive fox. Jemima could only suppose that because Pompey did not want to become instantly recognizable in television terms, he had somehow willed himself to remain anonymous. Talking to him face to face she was instantly aware of his presence. Certainly of all the men Jemima had interviewed in depth for television Pompey had adapted most naturally and unselfconsciously to the medium. Television to him had been merely another problem to be solved and he was certainly not going to be surprised or fazed by it.

"Now *that* you can tell me, Jemima, better than I can tell you. You know the old saying—Hell hath no fury like a woman scorned. Not, I am sure," he added with another gallant nod, "that you have ever been scorned."

"But *was* she scorned?" murmured Jemima. "Was Lionnel really intending to divorce her and marry Chloe?"

"Ah, now how about a woman's intuition to solve that one?" Pompey's expression was positively humorous. "Me, as a mere man I shall take myself down to the station to see about the more mundane matter of fingerprints, eliminating those friendly to the environment. That's my next job. Then there's the question of the cleaner; the woman Rosina Whatnot, you say you never met her. My boys will interview her in the morning and take *her* prints. We'll be contacting Lord Brighton in Sussex or at his Bloomsbury flat, and we'll pick up that squatter fellow when he returns, if he returns. Myself, I want to see if my men have raised that bruiser of an artist for me yet."

So, shaking his head in a fatherly manner, Pompey departed, taking care to leave Jemima the number of his direct line "in case of need." The need was unspecified. Jemima guessed that Pompey had chivalrous doubts about leaving her in the gaunt building, with only Tiger, now in a highly restless mood, as company. She herself had no such fears.

It was only after Pompey had gone that something extraordinary and on the face of it quite illogical about her own attitude to the case struck Jemima. Regardless of what Pompey might discover, why was it that she herself had not immediately concluded that Kevin John Athlone was responsible for the murder?

He was the obvious suspect. And Pompey had taught her in the past that the obvious suspect was very often the right suspect—she accepted the logic of the position, unexciting as it might be to the more tortuous mind. Kevin John had arrived at Adelaide Square that very morning with the avowed intention of doing Chloe some violence and had then proceeded to beat up Jemima. He had later quite gratuitously admitted to shinning up the scaffolding and entering the penthouse itself; depositing a geranium right next to the room where the murder had been committed. He thus had motive—by his own lights—and opportunity. What was more, Kevin John Athlone was certainly strong enough to wield that brutal knife, with the efficient hands of one whose profession was to live by them. Had he not begun life as a sculptor? Jemima had a dim memory of some unwieldy sculptures in Chloe's Fulham house, attributed to Kevin John in youth.

It was true that there were certain inconsistencies in the idea of Kevin John as the murderer. First of all, it had to be faced that the revelation of Chloe's pregnancy did complicate the issue. The obvious theory of Kevin John as the spur-of-the-moment killer need not be abandoned; but it needed expansion. If Kevin John had indeed struck her down, his motive was likely to have been jealous rage at this—to him—highly inflammatory piece of news. The repeated stabbing when Chloe was already dead, or at least visibly dying, did indicate some storm of passion. But if one accepted this as Kevin John's motive, that led to further questions. For example, why had Chloe elected to break the news to Kevin John in the first place? When did she tell him? When, and above all why, had Chloe re-entered the penthouse in her white broderie anglaise petticoat?

The alternative was to accept that Kevin John had murdered

Chloe in a fit of rage quite unconnected with her condition. It did not do, as Jemima knew, to insist on neat solutions where murder was concerned. It might just possibly be that the two facts—the murder and the pregnancy—bore absolutely no relation to each other.

At the same time, Jemima was aware that her curious presumption of Kevin John's innocence antedated Pompey's confirmation of Chloe's pregnancy. For the second inconsistency in the theory of Kevin John as murderer centred round his known behaviour during the late afternoon. There was something implausible in the notion of a man who had cruelly slaughtered his ex-mistress settling down for a nap in the hall of the same house where the deed had taken place; having first advertised his forcible entry to her flat, not only by the presence of a glaring pot plant, but also in conversation thereafter with Jemima Shore.

According to Pompey, the bedroom—and the knife handle—had been wiped clean of fingerprints. That showed a deliberation, an instinct for self-preservation, at variance with Kevin John's general behaviour in the last twenty-four hours. Jemima could, unfortunately, believe that Kevin John had flung himself on Chloe like a mad bull, and as it were gored her to death rather as he had uncontrollably beaten up Jemima. But after that, what would have happened? Was it not far more in character for Kevin John to collapse weeping?

"I love her, I love her." His distraught words in the flat that morning, as he blubbered, virtually round Jemima's neck, now rang in her ears. She would have expected Kevin John, the fell deed done, to have cried out like Othello: "O Desdemona, Desdemona O!"

But Chloe's murderer had coolly wiped the kitchen knife handle; had wiped prints from the bedroom; and had donned gloves to clean up his own traces. Jemima told Pompey that Chloe's kitchen gloves were missing; and she could not envisage Kevin John pausing in his path of mayhem to don a pair of kitchen gloves. Rather, like Othello, he would have slaughtered Chloe in a fit of passion; killed first, wept afterwards. Either way, it was difficult to imagine that Kevin John would choose to slump down in the hall of 73 Adelaide Square and fall stertorously asleep.

There was yet another inconsistency—that anonymous and Irish voice issuing threats in the late-night and early-morning telephone calls. Kevin John, despite his name and lineage, had no trace of an Irish accent, but rather an unexpectedly cultured English voice. Jemima had been tempted even at the time to acquit Kevin John of responsibility for these calls, impressed by his denial. If not Kevin John, then who?

The obvious suspect, leaving out of account Kevin John Athlone, was Sir Richard Lionnel . . . yet, if the police doctor was right and Jemima's dating of the crucial TV programme was accurate—a reasonable assumption in both cases—there was another inconsistency here. Sir Richard Lionnel could hardly be the father of Chloe's child. The old question arose: if not Lionnel, then who?

Chloe's own attitude to her pregnancy had been, to put it mildly, ambivalent. She had certainly not entrusted Jemima with the secret—but then Jemima, the latter reflected bitterly, had been destined for quite another role in Chloe's scheme of things than that of confidante. Yet Chloe had deliberately arranged to visit her elderly parents—unvisited for many months—in order to break the astonishing and perhaps shocking news. Failing to make the expedition on her way to France, because of Lionnel's date at number ten, she had then proceeded to summon her aged stepfather to London, having broken the news of her condition in advance on the telephone.

What sort of meeting had Chloe envisaged between Mr. Stover, in his seventies, bowed but dignified and still capable of fierceness, and her new lover, the Lion of Bloomsbury? Was old Mr. Stover intended to arrive with some form of metaphorical shotgun and force on the union? In short, was Chloe, in one of her intricate seemingly artless schemes, intending to palm off the baby on her new lover, using it as a weapon to persuade him to marry her?

Certainly the summons of Mr. Stover to the same building as Lionnel, indicated that some kind of confrontation had been planned. At the same time, these thoughts reminded Jemima how very much Lionnel had to lose from this revelation of Chloe's pregnancy—if he believed himself to be the father. According to Valentine, Lionnel feared any type of scandal at any time before the announcement of his new CARI appointment; the brooding Lady Lionnel, Valentine's Medea, could hardly be expected to take such news calmly. To say the least of it, Chloe's death had come at a convenient moment for her latest lover. Lionnel, like

Kevin John himself, would do well to produce a cast-iron alibi for the lunchtime hour when the murder was committed.

Jemima yawned. She felt it was very late, although it was in fact only ten o'clock according to her little gold watch. The ormolu clock on the mantelpiece told some fantasy time of midnight which belonged to another world where the Lion of Bloomsbury had lain down with his pretty lamb of a mistress. Tiger who, once Pompey had departed, had decided to crouch on Jemima's lap, had gone to sleep. Jemima used his inertia as an excuse to let her own curiosity roam once more back over the known facts. She knew from experience that this curiosity, once aroused, would not let her sleep until everything, at least within the confines of her own mind, was ordered.

Fallen Child, Fallen Angel . . . but Chloe if she had remained a child, had been no angel . . . Angel—yes—angel, that was the word which was important, "My former angel" . . . Chloe's soft breathless voice, so penetrating despite its capacity to sound as if it were borne on the wind, came back to haunt her. "My former angel who was . . ." Yes, that was the clue which was teasing her. What *was* the identity of Chloe's former lover? Who was also, presumably, the true father of her child . . .

Restlessly Jemima fingered the telephone, more because it was within her reach without disturbing Tiger than with any clear idea of who to telephone. Who on earth at this hour would provide her with the background information she sadly needed about the last months of Chloe's life? Valentine Brighton she ruled out; she had had his story already. But it was the thought of Valentine which drew her on to the subject of the ill-fated novel, and so, inexorably as it seemed to her afterwards, to the subject of Isabelle Mancini.

At the time she felt it was pure inquisitive impulse which led her to dial Isabelle's home number for further interrogation of that transatlantic acolyte, Miss Laura Barrymore. That and the fact that Jemima, who had a good head for telephone numbers, remembered it from the morning. She was nevertheless startled when the telephone was answered immediately and by Isabelle Mancini herself.

"Isabelle, I thought you were in Paris . . ."

"Jemima, oh my God!" cried Isabelle, as though Jemima had not spoken. "I've just heard the news. Oh my God!" she repeated. "Oh my God!" Possibly she was crying or had been crying very recently.

The richness of her French tones was unmistakable. It called to mind instantly not only her warm personality, but the full rich French figure which matched it, wide-hipped, generous-bosomed; even Isabelle's thick black bun, with its elegant silvery streaks, had a special wealth, a heaviness about it. For Jemima, the habitual floating grey of Isabelle's clothes—she wore no other colour—conveyed more warmth than other women's pinks and reds.

But there was nothing warm about what she was now saying, only despair, a mixture of passion and despair.

"I wanted to ke-e-el 'er," Isabelle was saying. "I came back from Paris to ke-e-el 'er. And now she's dead." The rest of her words were swallowed up in prolonged and convulsive weeping.

Chapter Ten

A Carnal Encounter

Isabelle's hysterical sobs suddenly stopped. It sounded as if the receiver had been taken away quite sharply from her. Another voice came over the wire—that of Laura Barrymore. In contrast to Isabelle, she sounded smoothly calm; it was as if she were spreading her own remarks like butter over Isabelle's previous utterances.

"Isabelle is naturally very upset at hearing the news of Miss Fontaine's death. She's also not quite herself since she's been working so very hard in Paris. She had to come back early to get some rest. And she was of course quite unprepared to take your call at this late hour." Through the politeness came a slight implication of reproach. "I've been trying to get her to take a sedative—"

"Who told her the news? I'd like to speak to her again." Jemima knew how to inject a certain authority into her own voice.

"I'm not sure—"

Isabelle grabbed the telephone, her French accent more pronounced than usual. "Valentine 'as told me. And 'e was told by the police. 'E's in 'is flat in Bloomsbury—" It was a word to which Isabelle brought her own special pronunciation. "And so 'e telephones me. Just like zat. My 'eart, I think it stop. Because I 'ave come back from Paris exprès, no Laura, cherie, don't stop me, eeet's true—to ke-e-el 'er—"

"I thought you weren't coming back till Sunday—I spoke to Laura this morning."

In the background Jemima could hear the sound of some angry expostulations from the formerly cool Miss Barrymore. Isabelle resumed in a slightly less emotional tone: "Silly child. No, not you, dulling, *la petite Laure*, e-e-diot child. She thinks I am telling you things which are dangerous. So swe-e-et. So loyal. No, no, dulling, what I am telling you is this. I came back at lunchtime specially to ke-e-el Chloe, she was a monster that one, wait till you 'ear, I wanted to choke her, strangle her for what she's done to me." Dramatic pause and change of tone. "And another thing, Jemima, Laura tells me an absurd story about Chloe going to the Camargue for us. For us? With Binnie? Who, by the way, is in Capri, with some terrr-r-rible pr-r-r-ince. More terr-r-r-ible even than her usual pr-r-r-inces. Chloe in the Camargue for us?" Isabelle wheezed with rich indignation. "Had the child gone mad?" she repeated.

"I suppose that would be quite out of the question." Jemima sounded tentative. She was anxious not to cut off this helpful but sensitive source of information by an unfortunate word. But Isabelle by now was in full flood.

"That book," she was exclaiming. "It was so 'or-r-r-ible, so disloyal, something precious laid out like that for all the world to see. I shall never, never agree, I said. Over my dead body. I pleaded with her. I wanted to ke-e-el her." Isabelle's vehemence became strangled. "Oh God, dulling, and now she's dead," she concluded in the calmer of her two voices. It was impossible to know whether she had realized the significance of what she had said.

Jemima decided to come out into the open. She assured Isabelle that she had not read the offensive book, knew of its existence only from Valentine, and furthermore no one would ever read it now. "But, Isabelle, tell me one thing, Chloe's style was generally so cool, so carefully ironic, hardly full-blooded, you know what the critics say about her, used to say. I'm rather puzzled you were quite so upset."

"Upset, what are you saying?" Isabelle's voice rose perilously. "She used my letters, my own letters to her; foolish, foolish letters; there they were, written down for all the world to see, the letters of a foolish old woman." Jemima tried to interrupt, but Isabelle was in full Gallic flood.

"And Valentine, too, what did he do, the ter-r-r-aitor, he asked her to edit a whole book of letters, and so she laughed, that pretty laugh, she too a terr-r-raitor, and said she would put them, some of my letters in her anthology. Letters of an Unknown Woman—"
At this point Laura evidently intervened again. Isabelle's voice,

still audible despite the fact that either she or Laura was now masking the telephone, was fierce.

"E-e-ediot child!" Jemima heard her say. It was the opposite to Isabelle's other famous cry: "Swe-e-et boy (or girl)." *"Non, non Laure* no, of course not, why should I be such a fool, I? Not *murder* her, kee-e-el her, you understand me." Isabelle was now speaking directly to Jemima. "And when I come back I 'ear she is dead." A pause. "And then of course I am sorry." Isabelle was sobbing again. "Little Chloe dead. What fiend could have done that?"

Jemima listened as Laura Barrymore recovered the telephone and in her politest manner attempted to enlist Jemima's help in securing the return of the aforesaid letters—a task she thought Jemima would be able to perform with some ease since they must, surely, remain in Adelaide Square. Miss Barrymore's tone implied that this small favour was something in the nature of passing on the name of a good hairdresser.

Jemima decided to press home her advantage. Laura Barrymore was assuming that Jemima was still in Chloe's flat; Jemima did not disabuse her of the notion. She had brushed aside an earlier warm invitation from Isabelle to join them in their own cosy apartment without comment on her present whereabouts. She realized that she had something at least to trade in return for further information from Isabelle. Personally she saw no reason why Isabelle should not have her pathetic letters back—"the letters of a foolish old woman"—as soon as possible, although Pompey might take another view as he conscientiously unravelled the webs spun by Chloe, the fallen child. Still, even if the police read them and analysed them (Pompey had probably removed them by now in any case) she, Jemima, might be instrumental in securing their discreet return at the appropriate moment.

She assured Laura Barrymore to this effect, and in return was able to put one last question to Isabelle without having the Barrymore vigilance interrupt her.

"I suppose poor Valentine is very upset about Chloe," she ventured.

"Oh, Chloe was so terr-r-rible to him. She behaved so badly to him," Isabelle expostulated.

"I'm beginning to think Chloe was terrible to all her lovers."

A Gallic exclamation. "Lover, dulling, Valentine, no. A peck on the cheek, perhaps, no more. Too well br-r-red, too much of an ar-r-r-ristocrat."

"It doesn't necessarily follow," murmured Jemima, with memories of certain encounters of her own in the past. Isabelle gave an unexpectedly bawdy chuckle. Jemima had forgotten her propensity for gossip; Isabelle had taken the allusion.

"Ah, wicked Jemima. No, this was different. Valentine adored Chloe, he loved her in his own sad way, the way of a moth perhaps, fluttering towards the——" Isabelle paused before the cliché and rushed on—"star. Yes, that was it. Kisses like a moth, don't you think, there is something so swee-e-eet about Valentine. But he was much too ar-r-r-ristocratic to think of marrying her, to frightened of *la Maman*, perhaps, and so he would torture himself hearing of her *affaires*. I tell you, she was ter-r-rible to him."

Privately Jemima considered that Valentine had sought his own fate; she had no great sympathy with emotional masochism herself. Still, it all made sense. Whoever Lover Unknown was, he was not Valentine Brighton; thus Valentine as the father of Chloe's child could be eliminated. All the same, Valentine's movements on this particular Saturday still needed further examination—had he for example an alibi for the crucial hour between one and two o'clock when the murder had taken place? It had been just after two o'clock when she found him slumped in the Reading Room, and the police were inclined to favour an earlier rather than a later time.

Reassuring Isabelle that she would work on the problem of the letters, Jemima put down the telephone.

Isabelle? Was it possible? Should she be added to her list of potential suspects? A lot depended on the time when Isabelle Mancini had actually returned to London from Paris. "Lunchtime" was sufficiently vague to make anything possible and in this case covered a very important area of time. Isabelle's alibi if any—that was one for Pompey and his boys to iron out. The investigation of movements was easy for them, their speciality. But all these hysterical threats—how were they to be regarded? The character and probably the behaviour of Isabelle Mancini—that was in Jemima Shore's line of business. Jemima reflected wryly that the distinction between ke-e-elling and murder was not one that the man in the street or for that matter her friend Pompey would readily accept: but it was also true that the word "ke-e-el" was frequently on Isabelle's lips in the most unlikely conjunctions, as all her friends would testify. The word testify brought Jemima up short. She hoped, most sincerely, that it would not come to that. There had been enough havoc already, wreaked by Chloe—or Chloe's death, whichever way you liked to look at it.

Time to sleep. Jemima supposed that she must soon retire to the so-called office bedroom suite, where Sir Richard had displayed, without comment, an Empire bed, imperial eagles on the bedhead, upholstered in rich dark green; the walls were hung with the same material. The room seemed to show yet another decorative hand at work—a far more successful one. Its atmosphere was deliberately grand as well as masculine; Jemima felt her own intrusion into this room to be exotic enough as to be exciting—Chloe, had she too felt that?

Jemima yawned again and wondered which of the three rooms if any represented Sir Richard's own taste; she hoped it was not the modern horror on the third floor.

Here the balcony onto the square had a high concrete edge, making the front area of it dark and cavernous. It was time to push Tiger off her lap—he had endured the long telephone conversation without movement—and retire. The balcony windows were wide open, and for Tiger's sake, Jemima decided to leave them that way. She knew that a policeman was posted at the entrance to the building; Pompey had taken away the keys to Chloe's flat in his pocket.

Tiger stretched, that long lazy movement which completely altered the shape of his cosy domestic body into that of a hunting animal, and then vanished into the shadows of the scaffolding, lit up from place to place by the street lights. Jemima heard the cat scurrying about making little sounds, scratching.

For a moment she stood looking at the square, listening to the faint rustle of the wind in the trees. Then she leant over the concrete parapet. It was a comparatively short drop into the square itself; she could not actually see the police sentinel, perhaps he was under the eave of the porch. It was typical of the meaningless modernity of this building that whereas the parapet of the penthouse was too low for absolute security, here on the first floor it was too high for comfort.

Jemima looked idly into the shadows. The proximity of the scaffolding would have made a lesser woman nervous, but she herself had never been frightened of the dark, or indeed of solitude. She thought of her more highly strung friends—poor Chloe, for instance, had always been intolerably nervous when alone: perhaps that was the true explanation of her amazing promiscuity . . . Chloe would have made anxious patterns out of these shadows and backed hastily away from the balcony for the safety of the lighted flat. In particular the shadows threw into relief one patch of greyness amid the scaffolding, very close to Jemima, which an over-imaginative person could well have fashioned into some lurking face.

Jemima's own eye travelled casually downwards. On the floor of the balcony was a pair of shoes. They looked like white gym shoes. So convinced was she still that this was purely a trick of the light, that it took her several seconds to take in that she was actually gazing at a pair of white shoes, shoes with real feet inside them, with bare ankles rising from them into the darkness above. And it was several seconds more before she finally realized that someone was actually standing in those shadows, motionless, staring at her, face almost touching hers, and had been standing there all the time, face a grey moon, face level with her own.

Jemima stood absolutely still in her turn. It was as though their two figures were engaged in playing a game of statues with each other. The hidden figure was the first to move.

"How amusing it is meeting like this," said Adam Adamson, stepping out into the light. "You've seen me at last. I was wondering how long I could hold my breath. My heart was beating like a mad gong, I'm amazed you didn't hear it. I seem destined to give you delicious shocks, don't I? Now, goddess, we can have a good talk, without interruptions."

He bent down and patted Tiger.

"You, me, and of course, Puss. Goddess as you may be, you have a great deal of explaining to do to a mere mortal like myself. Never mind, the night is young."

Putting a courteous but firm hand across Jemima's shoulder, Adam Adamson wheeled her into the lighted drawing room of the first-floor flat.

"You fool!" Jemima's momentary panic made her sound both crosser and more intimate than she intended. "Don't you know that the police are here?"

"Raffles the Gentleman Cracksman at your service." Adam Adamson drew off an imaginary hat with a flourish. "I did see a stalwart bobby standing at the front door of the concrete prison;

nevertheless it proved the work of a moment for your humble servant to elude his stern but straightforward gaze and shin up the ever-convenient scaffolding. Courtesy of the Lion of Bloomsbury. Then, lo and behold, what do I see, illuminated in the first-floor window, like the goddess you are, fit for worship, but Pallas Athena herself. Ho ho, thinks I, has our fair goddess set the sleuths upon me? And for that matter what might she be doing in the Lion's official den? So I decided to pay a call—"

His grip on her shoulder remained firm.

"Let me go." But Adam Adamson didn't let her go. Instead he guided her further into the room and sat her down on the deep comfortable tawny sofa. Then he sat down beside her, quite close. She could have touched the golden down on his freckled cheeks and stroked the curly chestnut-coloured beard had she so wished.

"First question, why did you shop me to the police? I had quite an unpleasant moment seeing yon arm of the law standing there."

"You fool," Jemima repeated. "I didn't shop you. Don't you *know* why the police are here?" Jemima felt herself breathing heavily, even panting; Adam Adamson's physical presence, which once she had found oddly attractive, now seemed to threaten her. Perhaps it was the late hour, the tantalizing and rather sinister circumstances of his arrival.

"I rather imagined that they had rumbled the salubrious presence of the Friends of the House, as symbolized by your humble servant and were e'en now making sure that he did not effect any further revivifying entrances." He put his hand on hers; she noted the golden hairs on the back of it. It was a strong hand with a spatulate thumb.

"My dear Adam—" Jemima stopped. Both their intimacy and the situation itself were developing too rapidly for caution. Jemima Shore, Investigator, was in danger of losing a key opportunity of making a few pertinent enquiries of her own, before Pompey reached Adamson.

"Where have you been, then?" She tried to stop her voice sounding too brisk. "I saw you leave the house about half-past five just as I was coming back."

"I like to walk round London at night. Like Puss here I see the sights and smell the smells. Especially this part when it's empty. A little spying perhaps for the organization. Some beautiful empty houses doomed for demolition, no lights on, no security. We reconnoitre them at night."

"A long walk. But then I suppose you'd been cooped up in that terrible flat all day. You must have enjoyed the change of scene."

Adam did not answer the implied question. His expression was hard to read. Jemima feared that hers must be more open. She remembered Adam's apparent ability to read thoughts.

"So what are the police doing here?" He spoke more abruptly.

Jemima balanced the advantages of telling him—and thus proceeding further in her enquiries in a straightforward way—against the advantage she still possessed of surprise. While she still hesitated, Adam moved even closer to her:

"No, don't tell me, you're going to lie to me, goddess, I can see it in your green eyes. And your archaic smile. Let me do this instead." Adam Adamson, putting one hand on her breast, pinched the nipple quite hard. Before Jemima could cry out, she felt her lips impressed by his and he half kissed, half bit her.

"No," she panted when at last she had freed herself.

"Why not? I rather thought you might like that kind of thing," replied Adam coolly. "More fun for us both than your telling me lying stories about the police. I hate being lied to, don't you? In fact I take very great exception to it. It's the one area where I generally take my revenge."

"I've no intention of lying to you." Jemima carefully checked the collar of her dress as though it was that not her breast which had suffered the assault of his hand. "Someone was killed here today, killed, murdered. In the upstairs flat. The police are guarding the building."

"No chance of its being Sir Richard Lionnel, I suppose?" Adamson sounded extraordinarily composed; of the two of them, she was the agitated one.

"It was Chloe Fontaine, as a matter of fact. The owner of the top-floor flat. My friend."

He stared at her in silence.

"Ah. I'm sorry. I'm sorry your friend died."

After a long pause, Adamson sounded conventionally sad, no more than that. "Chloe the Tragic Nymph. There's probably a curse on this building you know, since I tried to put one on it myself. I'm sorry it was a nymph that died and not a villain. She should never have come here."

"You didn't know her?"

"I didn't say that. I didn't know her real name until you told me yourself this morning. Dollie, she called herself to me, Dollie

Stover. Then I saw her photograph on the back of a book you were carrying and recognized it. Dollie—Chloe—you see, was a nymph by nature, a Nymph Errant, and I—sometimes—am a Knight Errant. We met, as such characters are prone to do, somewhere in the mazy land of the Errant where the most wayward one is king."

Memories of Chloe's breathless words came back to Jemima—"A little, a very little, adventure . . . a casual encounter you might say, a carnal encounter perhaps." Was this little adventure then shared with Adam Adamson? If so, Jemima had filled in two names out of the three she had listed as the most recent admirers of Chloe Fontaine.

"A casual encounter?" she asked. She tried to make her tones sound equally offhand.

"I like them, don't you?" Adamson had in the meantime placed his arm along her shoulders; it was a more overtly friendly gesture than the fierce advance he had just made. Nevertheless Jemima still felt threatened; she could not deny that she also felt increasingly excited by his presence, his proximity.

Jemima Shore returned to business.

"So you had a carnal encounter with Chloe?" She stopped, slightly embarrassed by the Freudian mistake. It was all very well for Chloe. Jemima proceeded more firmly. "Did you meet in the gardens, by any chance? She was locked out, she told me. Forgot her key. Climbed into the gardens and had what she called a *casual* encounter."

Adam smiled. "Ah. An indiscreet girl, my Dollie, or at any rate it appears that your Chloe was indiscreet. I didn't know that she was in the habit of confiding her errantry. Yes, if you want me to say so, I'll say I met her in the gardens. I'll tell you something else about my Dollie which may or may not apply to your Chloe. It was she who told me about the empty flats here. Slipped me the key. Said she got it from a friend who was a decorator. Said she was living here as a kind of superior squatter. So it was you, Jemima Shore, goddess of wisdom, who informed me not only of the rather surprising news that my Dollie was your Chloe—literature's Chloe so far as I can make out—but also even less pleasingly that she was a lawful tenant in this concrete prison."

"Did you see her after that?" Jemima persisted. "Your Dollie?"

"A goddess of wisdom should know everything without needing to ask." His hand was placed on her thigh, where it rested;

with his other hand, he touched her cheek. "No, I never saw her again. I don't think I would have been interested to do so. It wasn't, you know, a great romance. Only what you so aptly called it just now, a carnal encounter. A pleasant phrase that, by the way."

"It's hers, Chloe's. It *was* hers."

"Ah. Pleasant phrase all the same, pleasant phrase and pleasant activity. No, I didn't see her again. But I can see that your sleuth-like instincts are aroused and as I'd rather like to arouse a different set of instincts in you, I'll begin by setting your curiosity at rest. Here goes. I stayed in the upstairs flat all day, I slept, I read Dante—it seemed appropriate to the inferno in which I found myself—also some Petrarch, but that was for a different reason, and went out about five-thirty to get something to eat. When you, I gather, saw me. No, I heard nothing. Enough?"

"You'll have to tell this to the police," began Jemima. A terrible feeling—or was it so terrible? Merely exciting or, in dead Chloe's own phrase, carnal?—was stealing over her that the conclusion of the evening was going to be exactly as Adam Adamson planned, and not as Jemima Shore intended.

A little later she made no protest when Adam took her by the hand and led her into the dark green Empire bedroom. He stripped off the heavy rustling bedspread, and the soft white bedclothes tumbled out.

His slight body—the hips round which she could have put both hands—looked quite different naked; not vulnerable as so many naked bodies did, especially those of the young, but powerful and triumphant.

"Goddess," he said facing her, "it's your turn to worship me."

Chapter Eleven

Curiouser and Curiouser

When Jemima finally awoke the next morning, it was with an instant sense of happiness, content. That sensation quickly vanished when she first felt, then saw, the figure of Adam Adamson, lying across the Empire bed. He was fast asleep. He looked everything he had not seemed the night before; innocent, uncorrupted.

"Oh Christ," said Jemima Shore aloud. He did not move.

She longed absolutely and passionately for him to be gone, magicked away from the flat; as much as she had longed for him to make love to her for ever the night before. Why could not such a mythologically minded man bear in mind the story of Cupid and Psyche? Cupid had insisted on leaving the mortal maiden Psyche before the light came. Very sensible of him. After all, dreadful consequences had ensued when Psyche had attempted to defy the ban by lifting her lamp of oil to view her unknown lover.

In this case, Cupid had overslept.

"Oh Christ." Unbidden the visage of Detective Chief Inspector John Portsmouth came into her mind; unlike the Cheshire Cat he was not smiling, but deprecatingly shaking his head. It had to be admitted that there was something to shake his head about . . . shades of Chloe Fontaine (although that too was an unfortunate phrase).

She became more resolute. After all *in its own way* it was an investigation. Jemima was fond of using the phrase *in its own way* on television when attempting to justify the unjustifiable. The Press sometimes mocked her for it. The memory of such—

affectionate—attacks compelled her to admit, fair-minded person that she was, that given the opportunity she would undoubtedly behave in exactly the same way all over again.

Given the opportunity: but not however on Sunday morning. This particular Sunday morning at any rate. No one was going to be given any opportunity this morning. Adam Adamson, great causal encounter as he might be, was going to the police. She, Jemima Shore, was going to—well, first of all—have a cup of coffee.

She stepped gingerly from the white bed on which there were now no bedclothes at all and pulled her navy blue silk kimono from her suitcase. Adam did not stir as she left the room.

Some minutes were occupied in searching out first the coffee and then the method of making it in the immaculate but curiously ill-appointed kitchenette. In the end Jemima discovered a tin of Nescafé stuck behind the rows of clean cocktail glasses and made do with that, there being no apparent method of filling or making work the elaborate gleaming Italian coffee machine.

She sat meditatively on the single kitchen stool—uncomfortable and the wrong height. Was this kitchen intended for anything except getting ice cubes from the fridge? The coffee was too weak and tasted disgusting. As she sipped it, she heard the noise of the front door opening. Someone was coming in.

"Oh Christ," she said for the third time.

The intruder had to be Sir Richard Lionnel. The police, so far as she knew, did not have a key to the flat and would in any case have rung first. Awkward and embarrassing as it might prove for him to use his own key without ringing the bell first, she supposed she could hardly object. The kitchen did possess a small digital clock. It was 11:30.

Jemima tied the sash of her kimono still more tightly round her and stepped out into the little hall with its Georgian mirror and table—the prettiest and simplest room in the flat. There was no one there. The drawing room was empty and the door to the office remained locked. It took her a few moments to realize that what she had heard was the sound of someone leaving the flat rather than entering it.

It was true. The green bedroom, now lit in a theatrical manner by one shaft of intense sunlight coming through the gaps in the heavy swagged curtains, was empty.

The light fell upon a note, written on a piece of paper headed "From the office of Sir Richard Lionnel."

"Dear Psyche," it read, "I'm afraid Cupid overslept but at least you didn't pour boiling oil over him. Thanks for everything. A. P.S. I've taken all the rest of this headed paper. Rather useful in the cause of revivification, don't you think? P.P.S. Don't worry, goddess, I'm going to the police."

The rest of Sunday was much less exciting. Jemima forced herself to read an Edwardian diary taken out from the London Library; the small print acted as a special kind of discipline.

The call she awaited was from Pompey. It came about four o'clock that afternoon.

"Well, my dear," he began, "we've talked to your squatter friend."

"*My* friend?"

"The one you met in the third-floor flat. Adam Adamson he calls himself. That's not his real name by the way. He's Adam all right but the rest of it is not quite so plain English. He tells me you advised him to go to the police. And very proper, too." Pompey chuckled.

"Naturally. You know me, Pompey, Honest Jemima Shore. The good citizen." All the same Jemima was not totally happy about all this jocularity. She could picture Pompey shaking his head.

"One thing did surprise me a little. He said *you'd* asked him no questions about his movements. Simply told him what had happened and said it was his duty to go to the police. And so, being a squatter—he calls it some funny name, doesn't he—but not a slaughterer, those were his words, along he came to the station. Now, I wondered, where was the natural human curiosity of Jemima Shore, Investigator? *No* questions about his movements, alibi if any, connection with the deceased?"

Pompey might be wondering about her incuriosity but Jemima herself was speculating how Adam Adamson had eluded the policeman at the door; not so much last night but this morning in broad daylight.

Pompey answered that question for her.

"Mind you, our chap on the door, PC Bland, is still rather baffled as to how *your* friend got into the building last night. *Your* boy—" Jemima wished Pompey would stop the emphasis— "swears he just walked in, and has indeed made a statement to that effect. He noticed no policeman and, in so far as a squatter can be said to do so, minded his own business. Spent the night upstairs, emerged this morning, met you, you told him—but then you know the rest of it, don't you, my dear?"

"And the murder period?"

"His statement says that he spent the day in the third-floor flat. He even had an alibi for the first period, though we haven't checked that out yet. Says he heard nothing, neither the deceased woman entering the flat with her companion whom we assume to be her murderer, nor any sounds of a struggle or cries. You wouldn't expect the latter, not with that slash across her windpipe, she would have died more or less instantly. Says the door is exceptionally thick and the flats—he called them some very rude name and tried to incorporate it in his sworn statement—are soundproof, at least above and below. Left the flat at about five-thirty to get something to eat, confirmed by one Jemima Shore. Did know the deceased woman but as Dollie Stover, not Chloe Fontaine. No prints of his in the bedroom but the murderer wiped that clean in any case."

Pompey did not pause before adding in a completely different almost official voice: "Ah, well, all this is of no great moment, because you see, we've picked up the artist." Immediately Jemima's professional curiosity drove out all other considerations. "Beyond that, we've checked out two alibis. Sir Richard Lionnel—he does prove after all to have an alibi, quite a good one as a matter of fact. The restaurant was called 'The Little Athens,' and he did have lunch there, no question of that, with a lady—now that's amusing—not your friend, naturally, seeing as her throat had been cut at the time, but a lady, A Nonny Mouse." Pompey chuckled. "Second alibi, Mrs. Mantovani, Mancini, whatever, the female editor. You mentioned her. Perfect alibi. Plane lands at Heathrow at one-fifty. Bus reached the airport proper—due to delays—at two-ten. She can't be in Central London before two-fifty and that's stretching it. She's out—as we see it.

"And I've another piece of news for you," he continued remorselessly, "my boys have spoken to the maid, Rosina Whatnot or whatever her name is. Visited her this morning. Another funny piece of deception there. No sick child. Very healthy child bawling away out of sheer bloody-minded healthiness according to my boys. They don't know how to bring up kids without spoiling them to death, Italians, do they? Be that as it may, *your* friend Miss Fontaine gave her a few weeks' holiday. Out of the blue. Said you didn't want anyone disturbing you."

"I probably didn't," Jemima felt bewildered. "But I certainly didn't say so. I never had a chance. No, wait, Pompey, don't you see? She, Chloe, didn't want Rosina Whatnot hoofing about, talking to me perhaps about Lionnel, or about anything. Much safer not. She's a great talker, I gather. Is that true?"

"One of the greats. Screamed, cried, screamed again, told my boys everything, absolutely everything they wanted to know. All about Lionnel. The Sir she called him. The Big Sir—isn't that a hippy place in California? And one or two other details which may be useful. However, she's no good for the actual murder, of course, because she'd been on holiday all the previous week. Still she is valuable background material."

"I might visit her. I should perhaps sort out financial arrangements with her, cleaning up the flat and so on. I hardly imagine old Mrs. Stover will want to do that."

"Why not visit her, my dear?" Joviality was the order of the day.

"And Athlone?"

"That's a very different story. Picked him up in a pub this morning. Twelve o'clock. Opening time. Very much the worse for wear. Slept rough I should imagine, or as near to it as you can get. You could smell the drink a yard off. No alibi for the vital time, beyond a confused story about drinking with someone called Dixie. Then we picked up Dixie in the next-door pub and he was the worse for wear too, but not so much that he was prepared to vouch for his mate. Very shifty character, Dixie, and knew which side his bread was buttered where the police were concerned; no alibi there, oh no. Won't swear beyond the fact that he met Athlone some time before lunch, but rather fancies it was between eleven and twelve. Very damning, Dixie. Particularly the last part of his statement."

"Which was?"

"Athlone asked him for a razor."

"Ah, the razor." Jemima let out a long sigh. The whole question of the razor on the floor by Chloe's bed could not be pushed to the back of her mind for ever.

"Dixie couldn't help. Did the silly bugger think he carried a razor about with him to every pub he visited? Those were Dixie's exact words. Not the words of the sworn statement, however.

109

Besides, Dixie has an enormous beard which shows no sign of having had a razor near it in years. Athlone swigs down two double Scotches, departs, swearing that he'll first find a razor to make himself beautiful for her Royal Highness the Lady Jezebel, and then tear her to pieces like the cur he is. And he won't even need the assistance of all the others curs in her life."

"The latter being a Biblical reference, as I don't need to remind you," was Jemima's tart comment.

"As well as hearsay evidence, as I don't need to remind *you*. Dixie—I repeat, a nasty piece of work—only tells us that Athlone made those remarks."

"Go on. Kevin John certainly never made any secret of his violent intentions towards Chloe and even had a dress rehearsal with me. What's his story about the razor?"

"Athlone takes the line that he doesn't need a story about the razor because he obviously hasn't shaved for several days. That at least is true. Athlone fervently denies returning to the building until about four o'clock. According to his own statement, he spent the intervening hours wandering about Soho looking for flowers. Wanted red roses. Red roses not available. Finally found a pot plant, to wit Exhibit J.H.P. 10, one red pelargonium found on the floor of the lounge of the deceased, climbed up the scaffolding, found the balcony window unlocked, deposited the aforesaid plant and let himself out of the door. Felt a little weary after the climb and maybe the drink, as he used to be an athlete but described himself as none too fit these days—accurate that. Slept in the hall. Never went into the bedroom."

"And of course he *didn't* need the key to get out of the flat. Because it wasn't double locked. You've suddenly reminded me that when I returned from the Library I didn't need to use the second Chubb key. Yet I'm almost certain I double locked it when I went out."

"We found the deceased's own set of keys in the bedroom. Two keys to the flat, one to the front door of the building, and two more which we have identified as fitting the office suite."

But Jemima pursued the subject of Kevin John. "And *never* looked in the bedroom? When he was searching for Chloe?" This time Jemima was incredulous and Pompey was calming.

"Ah, my dear, but according to his statement he wasn't looking for Chloe Fontaine. He'd already cased the flat in the morning, hadn't he? No, he thought you might be resting in the bedroom.

Being a gentleman he didn't like to disturb you. Deposited the plant and quit. As you have pointed out, the second lock was not in operation. It was easy to let himself out."

"In its own way I suppose it does make sense. If true," said Jemima slowly. "Tell me, how did he take the news, the news of her death?"

"I can only say that he howled. Gary Harwood, one of my lads, good-looking young fellow, you'll remember him—was with me. He can confirm that. A howl like a dog. And then blubbered like a baby. Still, that means nothing. You'd be surprised at the ways of some murderers. Cry like babies on being shown a corpse they themselves have battered to death. No my dear, it must be said that things do look rather black for him. First of all, lack of alibi. Then attempt to get a false one out of his friend. Between ourselves, we picture it this way. He returns to Adelaide Square. Meets Chloe Fontaine, perhaps on the stairs, perhaps in your—her own—flat fetching something. More likely the latter. She has let herself in with her spare set of keys. She gets him the razor, takes it into the bedroom, they have a quarrel—perhaps she breaks him the news of her pregnancy—and he grabs a knife from the kitchen and stabs her to death."

"Why is she in her *petticoat*?"

"Very hot day. Everyone is out of the building. More like a dress than a petticoat, wasn't it?"

"For obvious reasons, I don't remember it too well. Perhaps you're right. It's still unlike Chloe to wander round any building in her petticoat. She is—was—always very neatly dressed."

"Maybe he and she were going to"—cough—"you know. She *was* an adventurous lady, after all." Pompey broke off discreetly.

"Anyway, continue—"

"He leaves the flat. The second half of his statement about bringing the plant and so forth is true. We've found his prints all over the scaffolding by the way."

"I find it psychologically unconvincing, the return of a murderer—and why linger in the hall?"

"Murderers are funny people." Pompey's voice sounded solemn down the line. Jemima could picture the shake of the head. "Besides, he was drunk. Drunks are funny people too. And drink leads to murder. The demon drink. None of this would have happened, would it, if your friend Kevin John hadn't had a great deal more Scotch than was good for him?"

"You still have to prove it."

"Certainly we do. Proof not psychology or feminine instinct—with due respect to you *and* Mrs. Portsmouth—has always been my motto. Beyond all reasonable doubt, what's more. And we shall, we shall. He may well confess. I know the type."

"Is he still at the station?"

"No, we let him go for the time being. We have to tie up the loose ends first. You know the form. He's staying in Chelsea now; we have the address—rather a good one: he's got rich friends as well as rough types like Dixie. No, he won't go far. I know the type." Pompey coughed and then gave a particularly rich chuckle.

"By the way, my dear, there's something else which might interest you about your late friend's flat. Quite a way-out piece of information. We don't think the artist is involved in this. But my boys have found a spy hole through the bedroom wall. Small but perfectly formed. Behind a loose brick and right through that indecent red picture. There's modern building for you. Anyone applying their eye to it would have a good view of what went on in that bedroom." He chuckled again. "Easy for an outsider to come up the fire escape onto the small kitchen balcony, remove the loose brick and—er—apply the eye. The reason we don't think Athlone is involved, is nothing to do with its being his own picture, he might even enjoy damaging that in a good cause—you know artists. No, it's because there are a lot of fingerprints. We're just checking them out, but we already know two things. They all belong to the same person and that person is not Athlone."

"What?" This time Jemima was genuinely shocked. "My God, the caller—the anonymous caller. My secret view, he called it, something like that. It's in my statement." She said in a controlled voice, "curiouser and curiouser."

"Exactly," said Pompey with great satisfaction. "Curious is exactly what it is."

"To think that I slept there!"

A cough. "I take it you *were* alone on that occasion?" Jemima reminded herself that this was to be taken as one of Pompey's little jokes, and not as a dig.

"Not only that, but you can take it that I never did like that picture," was her fervent reply.

Pompey had had his fun. "Now, my dear," he continued in a graver voice, "I'm afraid you're going to have the Press round you any minute if you haven't already. The death will be announced on the early evening news. But you'll handle that with your usual charm. They can't get into the building itself. No point in that."

After Pompey had rung off, Jemima went to the balcony and peered discreetly over. It was true. A little knot of photographers was grouped on the pavement; there were also a few anonymous women, like extras in a crowd scene. PC Bland was staring straight ahead.

There was of course nothing to be seen except an ugly modern concrete building. The lure of murder had brought these people together; if the demonstrators returned on Monday would they mingle with this tourist crowd, still bearing their placards which vowed destruction to the Lion of Bloomsbury? In principle Jemima preferred the applied spirit of the demonstrators to the prurient curiosity of the women outside; but she wondered whether the demonstrators were as idealistic and the spectators as ghoulish as she conventionally imagined. Perhaps some of these spectators would shed real tears for the lurid death of Chloe Fontaine, beautiful, defenceless, fragile, slain by a brutal murderer, even as they goggled at the site of her death. While probably not one of the demonstrators—engaged in saving bricks and mortar—would feel much of a pang for the death of a human being, given that she had been the mistress of the Lion of Bloomsbury.

The presentation on the news programmes of both television channels was comparatively restrained. The BBC showed that still picture of Chloe under her parasol which had attracted Adam Adamson's attention. It looked highly incongruous alongside the announcement that the police were treating her death as murder. ITN rather more dashingly showed a short clip of Chloe chatting soulfully about literature, her face framed by a stiff white lace collar like a ruff; the clip must have been taken from that same programme where she met Sir Richard Lionnel. But he was not included so most likely the connection was unknown; even if there were rumours, ITN would not have risked making such a libellous inference. ITN did refer to the title of Chloe's last novel as *Fallen Woman*—a mistake corrected later in the programme—but that was probably carelessness. The BBC referred to the same novel as *Fallen Children* and did not correct their mistake later.

Nothing else happened that evening till about ten o'clock. Jemima deserted the slightly frivolous narrative and small print of the Edwardian diary for the more rewarding discipline of Nadine Gordimer's novel.

When the telephone rang, she found that with concentration on such a spare and stern book had come peace. She therefore received Valentine Brighton's late-night call with equanimity. It had been, all things considered, a bloodless Sunday. Not that Valentine himself sounded bloodless. He was breathing heavily; his voice was agitated and quite jerky compared to his usual airy tones. He did not sound at all himself.

He began at once: "I've got something I've really got to heave off my chest about all this. I need advice, your calm approach, Jemima darling. You know about the police, don't you? That man Portsmouth, I seem to remember you worked with him in the past. You see, I've always given them a wide berth—in London that is. Our local man at home is quite a decent fellow. Mummy does the Right Thing and asks him to lunch at Helmet from time to time. But up here I've always tended to agree with Mrs. Madigan in *Juno and the Paycock* that 'the Polis as Polis in this city is Null and Void.' "

His badly rendered accent represented a ghastly attempt at his usual light-heartedness: there was nothing properly light about Valentine's approach.

He proposed a meeting the next day. "Now how would you like to do it? I hardly want to come to Adelaide Square. Poor divine Chloe. Surrounded by Press, I daresay. The building I mean. I don't expect you want to come to the Brighthelmet Press. How would you like the Reading Room of the British Library? I imagine you'll be trying to get back to work on the Golden Goodies." He gave the impression of having planned it all out in a way she could hardly refuse.

It was while listening to Valentine's unaccustomedly emotional accents, and above all his rendering of O'Casey, that Jemima made a discovery. In not sounding like himself, Valentine Brighton had not exactly sounded like a total stranger. Curiouser and curiouser. Taking into account Pompey's final rich revelation of the peep-hole through the picture, it was not too difficult to make the connection.

The Irish accent clinched it; this was the intense voice of the anonymous telephone caller on the night before and the morning of Chloe's death. One phrase in particular was almost identical: "Now how would you like to do it . . ." "Now how would you like it . . ." had breathed the unknown caller. "In that bed . . ." Yes, she would certainly meet Valentine Brighton in the Reading Room the next day. She had become very curious indeed about the role of Valentine Brighton in the life of Chloe Fontaine.

Chapter Twelve

Shattered

Jemima, heading straight for Row B at the end of the Reading Room by pre-arrangement, spotted Valentine's fair head from a long way off. He was engaged in reading something which looked like a typescript. On this occasion he was not slumped down upon the dark polished desk. Nor, for that matter, was Jemima herself disturbed by premonitions of violence. The habitual mental litany, as she ticked off the rows of seats, manifested itself in words of comfort: A for Adorable, B for Better and Better . . . This time no secret shapes of dread intervened to kidnap her private alphabet.

On Monday morning, early, the Reading Room was already filling up rapidly. But as readers strode about purposefully looking for a seat, interweaving amongst assistants carrying piles of books marked by white slips, the confusion and slight noise created a favourable impression upon Jemima. The Reading Room, on this occasion, offered a haven even for Jemima Shore.

The noiseless surface of Adelaide Square had been shattered for ever by the murder of Chloe. Whatever the interior turbulence of the building before her death, it was as nothing compared to the maelstrom which now held it in its sway. It was as though the doll's-house front of the building had been stripped away, leaving Jemima, the last inhabitant—except for Tiger—exposed to the prying gaze of the outside world.

Thanks to the jolly camaraderie which existed between Fleet Street and the police, Jemima's own role in the discovery of the corpse had become known. Her present location, even the private telephone number of Sir Richard Lionnel's office suite, had also not proved beyond Fleet Street's powers of discovery.

Since she had a great many friends in Fleet Street, Jemima

regarded the approaches of the journalists as quite inevitable. As a professional herself, she certainly wasted no time in resenting them (although her own kind of journalism was very different). She was after all quite capable of looking after herself, giving pleasant noncommittal answers where necessary, as well as confirming facts. She refused for example to be drawn on the question of Chloe's colourful private life beyond what was known already.

"I only know what I read in the papers," Jemima would say charmingly. Having time and space at their disposal—unlike the television channels the previous evening—the morning papers had indeed provided their readers with some titillating details of *la vie bohémienne* as it had been apparently lived by the late Chloe Fontaine. Chloe's taste for having herself so frequently and so dramatically pictured, made love to as it were by the camera, brought unexpected financial benefits to the photographers concerned, who found their studied romantic portraits, veterans of Chloe's book jackets, pressed into service once more in the coarser medium of newsprint.

"Isabelle's pet, young Binnie Rapallo, must have made a killing," thought Jemima. "Evidently she was still able to sell her pictures even from darkest Capri surrounded by wild princes."

The word Bohemian was employed quite lavishly to describe Chloe's life style. Her two marriages provided some of the material. Lance Strutt, an actor who had been at Cambridge with Chloe and Jemima, was on tour in Canada. He described himself as "utterly shattered" in the *Mail* and "very shocked" in the *Express*. Both statements were probably true. The further statement that he and Chloe had remained good friends after their break-up was to Jemima's certain knowledge not true.

Lance, at any rate until he became wise to Chloe's errant conduct, had been a nice but rather dim character. Igor, on the other hand, although his travel books and articles never quite raised him out of the medium-dim class as a writer had not been nice at all. About the only thing to be said for him was that he had at least been more satisfactory than Kevin John Athlone for whom Chloe had left him. Igor speaking from Venice was however nice enough to be "shocked" in the *Mail* and "shattered" in the *Express*. And he was honest enough to admit to having been on bad terms with his ex-wife.

The "live-in" relationship with Kevin John Athlone (no comment available) also received a great deal of publicity. A photograph of him in a white polo-necked jersey, wonderfully handsome and somewhat thinner than of late, received almost as much prominence as photographs of Chloe. Kevin John in his turn was described—but not by himself—as being "shattered" at the break-up of their relationship and "emotionally distraught." Hints of his drinking, also employing the word "emotional," were fairly heavy. The very detailed but soberly phrased account in the *Telegraph*, ended: "Mr. Athlone, whose present whereabouts are unknown, is believed to have volunteered a statement to the police on Sunday."

The inference, to those used to such things, was obvious. Jemima fancied she detected the hovering hand of the police in these mentions of Kevin John. A word in time, of a discreet nature, from the police, helped the Press to direct their eager noses in the right direction; and the Press in their turn helped on the police by their own enquiries. It was after all only an amplified version of Jemima's own relationship with Pompey.

Unlike the television channels, the Press gave no significant mention to Chloe's literary works. The measured warmth of Jamie Grand in the *Guardian* was the honourable exception (J.S. Grand, editor of *Literature,* writes: "A talent to observe . . ."). Otherwise the person was considered so much more newsworthy than the *oeuvre*. Jemima thought that Chloe would have found in that personal concentration matter for regret, despite the vast publicity given to her death—but could she be sure of anything to do with Chloe any longer? Perhaps her friend would have relished the street fame, the passionate popular interest . . . No, surely not, a writer must always hope for the elevation of the work over the personality. And Chloe, whatever her other qualities, had been at heart a writer. In that at least Jemima had not been deceived.

There was not even the merest hint in the Press of Sir Richard Lionnel's connection with Chloe. Even the fact that she had lived—and died—in that controversial modern building, creation of the Lion of Bloomsbury, 73 Adelaide Square, received little emphasis. Only the *Telegraph* seemed remotely interested in the subject, and this interest was limited to the phrase: "recently in the news due to student protest at the demolition of Adam's work."

Did she also detect the hovering hand of the police here? More likely the hovering hands of Fleet Street's eagle-eyed libel lawyers. No point in going for the (almost certainly) innocent Sir

Richard Lionnel, armed with his own equally watchful lawyers, when the (almost certainly) guilty Kevin John Athlone, a picturesque enough killer for any editor, was there for their delectation.

Jemima's favourite editor, Jake Fredericks—brother of her own boss the ebullient Cy—did ring her up from the *London Evening Post* and suggest a piece about Chloe.

"I gather that handsome brute of a painter finally went over the top and did it," he observed cheerfully. "I never could stand him myself. Irresistible to women, I am assured, blows and all. Maybe I should deliver a blow or two myself. I must check with Eveline sometime. Anything to please. I used to meet Athlone at Cy's parties when he was with Sophie and he used to beat her up something terrible then. She went to hospital, needed stitches, all that kind of thing. And I think Oonagh Leggatt had something of the same experience. Ugh." Jemima repressed a smile at the thought of the charming rather motherly Eveline Fredericks entering into some kind of sado-masochistic relationship with Jake. Unlike Cy, Jake had been happily married as long as Jemima could remember. "Good painter, though," he added. "Still it's not quite enough, is it? We can't have our lady novelists dying like flies, can we?"

Jake Fredericks' notion was, as he expressed it, that Jemima should set the record straight about Chloe. "After all she was a very good writer, as well as a grand horizontal, wasn't she? My colleagues have concentrated so far on the latter angle. Here at the *London Evening Post* we have always believed in a woman's right to be both."

Jemima was not to be drawn. Thanking Jake politely, she declined and headed for the British Library. She felt depressed. Things were getting blacker for Kevin John. A known record of violence towards the women in his life was not going to help his case forward with Pompey—or, if it came to that, with a jury. It remained to be seen whether Valentine Brighton, in heaving something off his own chest, would also relieve Kevin John Athlone in some way of the burden of guilt.

But Valentine Brighton, pale but composed, speaking in a low voice in view of the regulations of the Reading Room, did no such thing.

"I saw him." It was as bald as that. "I was shattered. No, no, not doing the murder—" His voice rose slightly. "Just afterwards. It must have been just afterwards."

"Sssh" came very angrily from the middle-aged woman of foreign appearance at the desk next to Jemima's. "Here iss not a place for talking." Jemima, in her own state of shock at what Valentine had just said, vaguely resented the interruption but made no effort to curtail Valentine's stream of words.

"And further I must tell you, you are sitting in the place of Professor Leinsdorf," hissed the woman, after a moment, plucking at Jemima's sleeve. It was true. Jemima had been waved to B10 by Valentine, but Professor Leinsdorf's books, as they presumably were, were neatly stacked in the corner. The theory of economics, mainly in German. As Jake Fredericks would say, ugh.

Valentine Brighton was at this moment saying: "Jemima, I've got to use you as my mother confessor. Do I go back to the police and tell them? How on earth do I explain what I was doing there? My God, do I have to explain about—well—I mean will it all come out, be in the papers? It will kill Mummy, I tell you it will kill her—"

His voice, never particularly deep, rose to an accompanying angry "Sssssh" from the friend of Professor Leinsdorf.

"It *did* kill Chloe Fontaine," Jemima hissed back furiously. "Or rather someone did. And of course you must tell the police what you saw. Besides, they already know a good deal of it—look, Valentine, I may as well tell you now. They found the peep-hole." Pompey had confirmed the prints as being Valentine's that morning.

For a moment Jemima thought Valentine was actually going to faint. His slightly sweaty pallor increased dramatically and his eyelids closed and flickered. He swayed in his seat.

"Oh God, poor poor Mummy," he groaned. Professor Leinsdorf's friend stood up and regarded the pair of them with extreme disfavour; she arranged her own books and belongings all over her desk as though to prevent the possibility of any further territorial infringement by Jemima. Jemima noted the label on her briefcase, a surprisingly smart object of black leather, considering its owner's own careless appearance: Dr. Irina Harman, it read, and the address was somewhere in Cambridge.

"I go to have a coffee," Dr. Irina Harman announced. Then: "Those are the books of Professor Leinsdorf. It iss not in the rules to sit at that desk." As Jemima did not react, she said in a louder voice: "It is occupied." Then Dr. Harman stumped away.

"If it gets into the Press, I can't bear it. I simply cannot bear it," Valentine was saying. "I'll go and live abroad."

"Oh for Christ's sake, Valentine. This is not the nineteenth century and you are not the wicked Lord Byron. *Do stop thinking about yourself.* What's a little harmless voyeurism among friends?" She forebore to remind him that she herself had received two of his calls.

Valentine groaned again. Jemima's furious flippancy only seemed to make him feel worse. For her part, she wanted to shake him.

"I take it you saw Kevin John Athlone—in Chloe's bedroom."

"I don't know why I do such things. It started when I was a child. Perhaps because I was lonely. Anyway, where Chloe was concerned it all began one day by accident. I found the way up the fire escape when her buzzer didn't answer. There was a loose brick—I was looking for a key. She was somehow so provocative, Chloe, wasn't she? I mean I almost felt she *wanted* me to watch her. But how can I tell the police that? As for Mummy—"

"Valentine," Jemima whispered as calmly as she could. "What did you actually see? The police aren't interested in your private tastes, they're only interested in you as a witness to murder."

"I went up the fire escape and I looked through the peep-hole," he said. "Chloe hadn't turned up here. I had some vague idea of warning her about Francesca Lionnel. I'm not quite sure what I expected, I never am when I do these things. I suppose I also thought I might see you. I called you, you know, the night before and in the morning." He spoke quite flatly. He seemed to have no shame where Jemima herself was concerned. Perhaps he imagined that life in television had inured her to such things.

"Leinsdorf? Your books." An Asian carrying two large grey volumes was standing over Jemima. He deposited them without waiting for a confirmation. He was handsome and quite young; and was wearing a red T-shirt with the face of Marilyn Monroe on it. Jemima recognized him. He had tried to deliver some books to her desk—commissioned by someone called Hamilton—on Saturday. This time she accepted the Leinsdorf books without comment.

"Go on."

"I saw him, Kevin John Athlone. In her bedroom. He was alone. At least I think he was. He was holding a razor in his hand. You can't see the top of the bed you know. The hole is too high.

Only the bottom of the bed, the rest of the bedroom and the door. He was just standing there. Looking right at the picture. At me. I was terrified he'd see right through it and see me. And she'd promised me it was all over. I felt quite sick. I went away. Then I saw you walking towards the British Museum and I followed you. I followed you right into the Reading Room. I watched you looking for a place. I moved someone else's books just ahead of you and sat down. I made a place for you. You see—I wanted you to find me. I pretended to be asleep so you wouldn't suspect. I was still feeling sick."

"Ah. The wrong books which were delivered—" Jemima began.

"Oh, Jemima, couldn't *you* tell the police? Explain I'm not feeling at all well, and I'm not, absolutely not up to it. Poor Mummy, how will she bear it—"

"You *must* make your own statement; it's vital, don't you see that? I can't give *your* evidence."

"Pardon me, but I believe those are my books," said a polite soft female voice above Jemima; this time the accent was not mid-European but American. "Since I had not purposed to vacate this seat, you should provide yourself with another one. And adjust your seat number accordingly on any request slips you may have already filed." Professor Leinsdorf spoke in the terminology of a firm but courteous public notice.

But contrary to Jemima's mental image, the Professor besides being female was comparatively young. She wore a neat white blouse and pale grey skirt, with a soft grey chiffon scarf at her neck. She might have been a member of some modern nun's order, which wore contemporary dress. She was also rather pinkly pretty with full lips and a high natural colour: although she wore no visible makeup, she hardly needed it to enhance her wholesome and attractive appearance.

"I'm so sorry," said Jemima hastily, leaping up. "Valentine, we have to talk. Let's go outside. Right?"

Valentine made a movement she interpreted as a nod. Professor Leinsdorf also nodded with the confident air of one who was used to restoring things to their rightful order wherever she went, and sat down.

She heard Valentine's voice calling rather faintly after her and returned. This time his message was only whispered: "Give me five minutes to recover, old girl." The sobriquet was somehow pathetically sportive. "I won't rat on you," he added, in the same Kiplingesque idiom.

"Sure. Meet you by the head of Rameses in, say, ten minutes' time? I'll fill in a book slip or two for when I return." Valentine gave a rather more vigorous nod in which she discerned relief.

Jemima took herself off to find a new seat, succeeding finally among the Ls; a rather noisy position due to the presence of a row of machines behind her being cranked by readers to show microfilm. Still L for Love had good connotations; she speculated whether Valentine's dogging her footsteps on the fatal Saturday had not been responsible for the strange aberration of her mental alphabet on that occasion.

On her way Jemima passed Dr. Harman who shot her a look of malevolent triumph. The doctor's heavy figure, ill suited by her brightly flowered skirt and green blouse, stockingless white legs in flat sandals, together with her mouse-coloured hair scraped back into a tight bun, made her the prototypical figure of the earnest female scholar of the old style, just as the fresh and soignée Professor Leinsdorf (who could have been photographed for *Taffeta* in one of its serious moods, just as she stood) epitomized the new. Yet it was possible that the two women were in fact about the same age.

"It is not good to take the seat of another person," said Dr. Harman in a loud voice. "You will learn." Jemima ignored her.

Finding the press mark in the catalogue—a list of numbers— and filling in a white slip to order a book was a famously aggravating task. In another area of her mind Jemima, as she coped with the heavy catalogues, was also turning over what Valentine had told her. She too was shattered. A few minutes' respite for them both was perhaps not a bad thing.

Moreover the catalogue appeared to have taken on a life of its own; it was a creature of mood, and in this case a peculiarly perverse mood. It sent her scurrying from one quarter of the alphabet to the other—a shift of numerous volumes—as a book written by one Marion Miller frustratingly turned out to be listed under her maiden name of Evans. As Mill*er* had also proved to be Mill*ar*—a shift of another volume—and the literary Evanses were innumerable—more than one heavy volume of entries—the whole operation took a great deal of time.

Jemima concentrated on filling in the order slip accurately; a mistake in the catalogue number would send her back to the start of the whole ponderous process. Slip finally filled and deposited in the box provided, Jemima made for the exit. On her way she glanced towards Row B. Valentine had gone on ahead. The typescript he had been perusing in his capacity as a working publisher was however still there, sheets spread about the desk. Clearly he intended to return and collect it.

Jemima hoped that Valentine's pause for recovery would only have crystallized his intention to make a clean breast of his story to Pompey as soon as possible. Valentine's own first-hand evidence—rather than her second-hand report of it—was both crucial and devastating where Kevin John was concerned. So far as Jemima knew, this was the first positive proof that Kevin John had been at the scene of the murder during the lunch hour. Under the circumstances her own irrational belief in Kevin John's innocence was fast fading. To say the least of it, Kevin John had lied about his movements to the police in his sworn statement (and to Jemima herself on the afternoon of the murder, for that matter).

Jemima was amused to see that Professor Leinsdorf and Dr. Harman had also abandoned Row B. Perhaps some economic conference of their fine minds was being held elsewhere in the building? Their respective papers and books however were spread about ostentatiously; no chances were being taken of another alien invasion.

She wended her way to the end of the Reading Room and proceeded to the checkpoint where a couple of uniformed officials, one woman and one man, maintained a search of bags and belongings to ensure that the valuable rare books of the British Library did not stray.

Jemima's prettily patterned notebook was always subjected to a peculiarly rigorous search as though some exciting rarity was being smuggled out, although half the pages were blank and the other half filled with her own hand-written notes. Jemima was just giving her automatic speech—"That's my own hand-writing; no, it's not the property of the British Library; look, no press marks; yes, it's my *own* notebook" when she was interrupted by a familiar guttural voice—speaking even louder than before.

"*Ja, ja*, it iss her! It iss she who took the seat of Professor Leinsdorf." Panting heavily as though she had been running, Dr. Irina Harman was standing at the exit and pointing in the direction of Jemima. "Stop her!" A middle-aged man in a jacket and tie stood at her side.

It was really too much. Jemima, already tense about her rendezvous with Valentine—she suddenly feared she might have allowed him enough time to change his mind—felt her patience beginning to snap. The whole incident was so absurd.

"For God's sake," she began angrily as the official stepped forward. He looked acutely embarrassed, particularly when he recognized Jemima; Jemima for her part rather thought she recognized him; he was the superintendent, or held some other fairly responsible position, and they had met in a discussion group about the future of the Reading Room.

"Excuse me, could I have a private word with you?" he asked in a low but firm voice. "It's Jemima Shore, isn't it? We've met." His embarrassment deepened still further. "And you were sitting in Row B just now, and holding a conversation—"

"For God's sake," Jemima repeated in a furious voice which she did not bother to moderate. "It was only a tiny episode and I've already apologized. This lady seems to be quite obsessed—"

"No, no, you don't understand, Miss Shore. I'm afraid the gentleman you were talking to just now collapsed very suddenly at his desk. We're trying to track anyone who knows him—"

"Collapsed! But I only just left him—"

"I know. It was very sudden, according to this lady here. Some form of heart attack, I fear. We've summoned an ambulance. But I ought to prepare you—"

"He iss dead," interrupted Jemima's quondam accuser in a heavily lugubrious voice. "He spoke to uss, said some words which are odd, then he iss dead. There iss nothing even Professor Leinsdorf could do for him. She had tried respiration immediately. Your friend iss quite dead."

Chapter Thirteen

Strong Women

"Fatal heart attack. Could have happened any time. Heart in a terrible dickey state. Mother—strong woman that, by the way, remarkable fortitude—confirmed it." Chief Inspector Portsmouth gave a shake of the head which under the circumstances was positively blithe. "Mind if I do?" He poured himself another pale whisky and water, courtesy of Sir Richard Lionnel. "What about you?"

Jemima in turn shook her head.

"But why did it have to happen *then*?" she asked despondently. "When he'd told me so much—but not everything. Not every detail. And he hadn't told you—second time round—anything at all. No sworn statement."

"My old mother, another woman of remarkable fortitude, always used to say, 'Into each life a little rain must fall.'" Pompey was maddeningly cheerful. You would not think, to look at his spare relaxed figure, once more installed in the gracious *Country Life*-style drawing room of Sir Richard Lionnel's flat, that he had just lost a prime witness in a murder case.

It was Tuesday evening and Pompey had invited himself over for an "after-work chat" as he put it. Jemima envied his aplomb. She herself was suffering from a feeling of irrational guilt that she had prematurely frightened Valentine to death by dragging his story from him, instead of letting him tell it all to Pompey. She knew that it was ridiculous: Valentine needed, indeed had deliberately sought out, her encouragement. Yet she was haunted by the memory of his pallid face, his groans as he contemplated the exposure of his private tastes to a mocking world.

"And you won't even pay attention to his last message," she

concluded in a gloomy voice. " 'He came back'—maybe someone came back to the flat, someone we don't know about."

"Certainly he came back. Athlone came back. Your voice from the grave is most convincing," Pompey responded happily.

Jemima's depression over the death of Valentine—and after all they had been friends long before Valentine proposed a professional relationship—was increased by the grotesque circumstances which had accompanied it. The detached kindness and carefully worded statement of Professor Leinsdorf hardly compensated for the irritation engendered by further contact with Dr. Harman. What was more, the two women were not only staying in the same hotel, close to Adelaide Square, but as Dr. Harman made absolutely clear, actually sharing a room.

"It iss, you understand, a very large room," she stated in her usual ponderous manner which seemed to convey some threat even when the words were palpably innocuous. "Professor Leinsdorf iss most generous. Each year we meet like this. We see only each other. And off course we do our work." She shot a look of ferocious devotion in the direction of her companion. "Each year it is Professor Leinsdorf who pays."

All the same the two women proposed to give Jemima tea in the hotel lounge, an arrangement for which Jemima was duly thankful. Intimate contact with their domestic arrangements would only bring further embarrassment. Already Dr. Harman could hardly allow the Professor to pour the tea without patting her hand; at one point she even pushed back one of the Professor's soft brown curls which had strayed onto her cheek.

"Yeah, it needs a good cut. I know it," was all the younger woman said; she gazed speculatively at Jemima's corn-coloured bell of hair.

"John of Thurloe Place—" said Jemima hastily, hoping to fend off further intimacies from Dr. Harman (whose own hair could have done with some attention).

The passions of others being notoriously unfathomable, Jemima reflected that she would probably never understand what drew the Professor, a charming woman by any standards, towards her uncouth watchdog; it was much easier to sympathize with the latter's evident infatuation. The attraction had to be in Dr. Harman's mind, since in Jemima's humble opinion it could hardly lie in her personality or her appearance; no doubt the appeal of Dr. Harman's thoughts on German economics, or whatever the

Professor's special subject might be, was overpowering . . . although an annual idyll with the good Doctor would hardly be Jemima's idea of amusement, it had to be admitted that this intellectual approach was also to the Professor's credit. She was interrupted in these frivolous thoughts by a loud and almost girlish laugh from the Professor.

"I guess Irina has just never got over her younger sister earning more than she does!" she exclaimed. "Why if she came to the States, she could put us both up at the Savoy . . . As it is I have to leave Henry once a year to look after himself. I'm always on at her to make the switch. It was just my good fortune I went to the States when I did."

"Ach, no, Poupa—" Jemima could not help being extremely relieved that the adoration in Dr. Harman's eyes had now been revealed as sisterly in origin. It was still slavish.

At Jemima's request Poupa Leinsdorf—as she must now learn to call her—ran through Valentine's last actions and stumbled words yet again.

"He looked very sick. He gave some kind of cry, more like a cry than a groan, would you say, Irina?" The doctor nodded, her enchanted gaze held to her sister's face. "He half put out his hand, I guess he wanted water or something. I jumped up. You got up too, Irina, at that point." The doctor nodded again. "I asked him if he needed some assistance. He didn't answer right away, just said nothing at all for approximately twenty seconds. Then he said, and this is my precise recollection, and I believe Irina will confirm it: 'He came back.' Those three words. Then: 'I've got to tell her.' Quite distinct, wasn't it, Irina? Then he slumped forward. The rest you know. He didn't speak again, nothing that could be understood as more than a groan. Irina thinks he muttered something like 'Mother' or 'Mummy' but I would not want to be too positive about that."

Back with Pompey, who had already perpetuated the Professor's information in the form of a statement, Jemima tried rather hopelessly to think of any way in which Valentine's words were not peculiarly damning to Kevin John. Her heart was no longer in it. Even without the help of Valentine's last words—to which Pompey refused to pay attention—it was going to be very difficult to persuade Pompey that Kevin John had not committed the murder: the prime suspect now known (if not proved) to have been present at the scene of the crime.

"We'll get him," said Pompey of Kevin John. "Other witnesses will come forward. He'll confess. You see if he doesn't. You, my dear, have been most helpful in what you have remembered. Good memory inside that pretty head."

"I hope so, Pompey," said Jemima in a pious voice. "It's a question of the trained mind rather than the pretty head, by the way. Like Dr. Harman."

"Oh myself, I like women to have both beauty and brains; no objection to that at all. I've made that quite clear to Mrs. Portsmouth from the very start of Women's Lib. Any time she wants to go to the Open University, Adult Education, evening classes—you name it. No holds barred. Instead of which she prefers to direct *my* gardening out of articles she's read in the evening paper with her feet up. I ask you! Women simply won't grab their opportunities."

Pompey then abandoned the elaborate teasing which appeared to give him much pleasure and reverted to his brisk manner.

"The Coroner's inquest opens tomorrow, by the way. Purely formal—you won't be needed. In view of our current enquiries, we'll suggest an adjournment. You see, now we know exactly what questions to ask Athlone. We know, for example—without being able to prove it, naturally—that he lied about his lunchtime visit to the flat. The net is closing, my dear. The net is closing. We're bringing him in for questioning again, right away. The only fly in our ointment at this stage is Punch Fredericks. He's been brought in on the act."

Jemima whistled. "Punch Fredericks! Very impressive. How did that come about?" The youngest of the three Fredericks brothers was a well-known radical solicitor interested in a number of social causes, including law reform; he was notorious, at least to the police, for believing in bail-for-everyone-including-murderers (as Pompey sardonically put it) and armed with the traditional will and energy of the Fredericks family, very often secured it.

"Friend of the gallery owner who looks after Athlone, I believe. Very rich, very left-wing, lives happily in Chelsea, you know the type. Creep? No, that's wishful thinking. Creed. At all events Creed is putting up Athlone, so he's probably hired Fredericks at the same time. Bail-for-everyone, indeed!" Pompey shook quite fiercely.

For the rest of the week Jemima abandoned her research in the

British Library. This was not only the result of an aversion towards the scene of Valentine's death—Jemima would have thought it her duty to conquer that kind of feeling. No, the fact was that Jemima was in some doubt as to whether the Brighthelmet Press itself would survive with the sudden demise of its energetic proprietor-cum-chairman-cum-managing director. In its future the survival of her own contract was only one petty problem. Jemima herself was constitutionally incapable of working without, as it were, a deadline. She had once been prepared to toil unsociably for the whole of August, disappearing into a noiseless borrowed flat. The flat was no longer noiseless, thanks to the furore engendered by Chloe's murder. Now her actual motive for research had been removed by the death of her publisher. And what was more, she had lost two friends in a week.

Work being Jemima's cure, she badly needed a substitute if this disastrous summer holiday was to be rescued. Fortunately there was work of a sort to hand: good useful work which might at least avenge Chloe's death and unravel the mystery of her last hours.

And if work was Jemima's cure, curiosity was her stimulus. The first-floor flat at Adelaide Square was still at her disposal, Lionnel Estates having not yet proffered an alternative although Jemima received twice-daily calls from a Miss Katy Aaronson, describing herself as Sir Richard Lionnel's private assistant—"No, not his secretary, Miss Shore, his private assistant." She was reminded of Laura Barrymore, Isabelle Mancini's cool "personal assistant."

In fact Miss Katy Aaronson turned out to have a secretary of her own, who put through her frequent calls to Jemima in an important voice; that again reminded Jemima of Laura Barrymore.

The call which Miss Katy Aaronson made on Thursday morning, apart from being made at 8:20 A.M.—half an hour earlier than Miss Aaronson's wonted hour which was early enough—brought with it an additional surprise in the shape of an invitation to lunch from Sir Richard Lionnel.

Miss Aaronson did indeed apologize with her usual suavity—another Barrymore touch—both for the earliness of the hour and the shortness of notice. Her use of titles as opposed to Laura Barrymore's transatlantic employment of Christian names possibly indicated the difference between a personal and a private assistant.

"Unexpectedly Sir Richard finds himself free for a late lunch in

London, since he is taking an ordinary commercial flight from Glasgow to Heathrow . . . before going down to Sussex by helicopter later in the afternoon to join Lady Lionnel at Glyndebourne. And the Minister, that is to say Lord Manfred, accompanied by Lady Manfred, hopes to join them by car from Hastings, where the Minister will have inaugurated . . . So if we sent the car for you at one-forty-five . . . There's a Greek restaurant in Percy Street just off the Tottenham Court Road where Sir Richard likes to lunch late . . . He finds the ambience . . ."

What on earth made tycoons' assistants imagine that the complicated social arrangements over which they themselves were destined to toil were of equal interest to the rest of the world, Jemima wondered irritably. The stately movements of Sir Richard Lionnel across the British Isles both dispensing and pursuing culture were no concern of hers; but Miss Katy Aaronson took care to inform her that Sir Richard had been lecturing at some Festival of Scottish Industrial Architecture in the presence of the youthful arts-minded Prince Frederick of Cumberland as well as other notables.

The apology, for all its suavity, was purely ritual. Jemima was not expected to refuse; if she had any other arrangements she was expected to put them off—in fact she had invited Isabelle Mancini to lunch to talk about Valentine and she did put her off; nor was Jemima expected to cavil at the late hour or the choice of Greek "ambience."

What would have happened, she wondered, if she had firmly opted for the Savoy, stating (untruthfully) that she hated Greek food? But Jemima always preferred other people to make the choices, not so much out of indecision as out of an observer's interest in the tastes revealed.

She contented herself with one flash of independence: "No car, thank you, I'll walk to 'The Little Athens.' It's only a few minutes away. I know its ambience well."

Imagining she would have quite a wait for Sir Richard, whose Scottish plane would inevitably be delayed, Jemima brought her Nadine Gordimer novel with her. The prospect of a concentrated read in the pleasant little restaurant, with its wide plant-filled window embracing Percy Street, was not displeasing. But when she arrived, she recognized the unmistakable figure of her host—well-cut fawn tweed suit, white shirt, black knitted silk tie—seen through the window as though in a frame. He was reading a magazine and laughing.

From its format, Jemima recognized *Jolly Joke*. Its pages were perpetually filled with rather crude satirical attacks on Lionnel and his ilk—this week's issue was no exception. For a man supposedly sensitive to Press criticism, Sir Richard was certainly showing remarkable sang-froid in laughing quite so freely. However at her approach Sir Richard covered *Jolly Joke* with a copy of Christie's catalogue illustrating a sale of antique clocks. Still the impression remained of a man in one way at least indifferent to public hostility.

Was Lionnel sufficiently indifferent to it to go further, divorce his wife and marry Chloe? And at the same time aim at respectability and the chairmanship of CARI? Perhaps Lionnel would not recognize the conflict: he would simply see it as a problem to be managed.

Chloe had been so specific about the marriage to Valentine, it was difficult to believe there was nothing in it. Just as this thought had formed in her mind—against a background of urbane conversation, quick efficient ordering of whatever she cared for in the line of food and drink, almost as though Miss Katy Aaronson had previously reconnoitred her tastes—Sir Richard surprised her still further by openly contradicting it.

Jemima had anticipated—obviously—that they would discuss Chloe; she did not flatter herself that Sir Richard had taken a sudden irresistible fancy to her on the strength of one brief meeting under traumatic circumstances. Nevertheless the directness of his approach confused her.

"The most attractive woman in the world. I was absolutely mad about her, don't you see?" he was saying, leaning forward and fixing his mesmeric black eyes upon her. The black ring of curls lifted in the faint breeze of the window, but Jemima had the impression that they were also flickering with his own personal electricity.

"But of course I would never have left Francesca. No question of that." He was not only direct but, as on the night of the murder, strangely lacking in embarrassment. "She's wonderful, Francesca. Wonderful hostess—you've never seen Parrot, I suppose? You never stayed there with the Hampshires? Retta Hampshire is beautiful in somewhat your style—cat's eyes—she's much older, of course."

"I've never even met the Duchess of Hampshire."

"You must come down, you positively must. What Francesca has done there is quite amazing; everyone says so. Even our match-boxes are eighteenth-century adaptations, I believe. The Hampshires had let it go terribly down hill." The thought of match-boxes reminded Sir Richard to strike up yet another black cigarette; he used a lighter very similar, if not identical, to the one Kevin John Athlone had discovered in Chloe's bedroom. Jemima wondered if the police had returned it to him—or did he perhaps have quantities of such elegant *objects*? Had they also returned the razor which had been found by Chloe's bed?

"Did you read the article in *Taffeta*?" he was saying. " 'Francesca goes Lionnel-Hunting'?—they meant all the original furniture she dug out of antique shops. Marvellous photograph of Francesca by that jolly little girl photographer, do you know her? Short black hair. Dresses in knickerbockers for some extraordinary reason, but very fetching."

"I know Binnie Rapallo." Jemima had definitely not come to lunch, chucking Isabelle for the occasion, to discuss the lissome but curiously irritating Binnie Rapallo. She was therefore somewhat startled to hear Sir Richard declaring himself "mad about" Binnie Rapallo, in much the same language as he had used to express his admiration for Chloe. Even the tone in which he expressed enthusiasm for his own wife's taste—hardly a fault that, it had to be admitted—was remarkably similar. These repeated enthusiasms, couched in terms which were almost schoolboyish, gave an overall impression of lack of passion rather than the reverse.

Surely there was some difference of degree—between Binnie and Chloe at least, even if Chloe and Lady Lionnel were mentioned in the same breath. He was astonishingly open about it all. Throughout the conversation Sir Richard chain-smoked his black Sobranies, but otherwise showed no sign of embarrassment.

When he had finished the packet he requested the proprietor of the restaurant, a handsome but sad-eyed man with the heavy fleshy build of a successful opera singer, to request another from his chauffeur.

"Sir Richard is feeling better today?" said the man conversationally when he returned.

"Thank you, Stavros. I certainly am. But it was my wife who was ill not me," replied Lionnel with a flash of the satyr's grin.

133

"Now I bet you're never ill," he said looking at Jemima as the proprietor turned deftly away, too experienced to look embarrassed at the mention of a wife, but somehow conveying apology for having instigated a conversation about one lady in front of another. "Francesca has rotten health. London for example simply doesn't suit her. She feels right as rain at Parrot—sea air and all that kind of thing."

"But I take it she comes up sometimes? Here, for example?" Jemima's curiosity about Sir Richard's domestic arrangements was aroused in spite of herself.

"Oh absolutely. In fact we had lunch together here on Saturday." It took Jemima a second or two to realize that he was referring to the day of the murder.

"I thought you were alone—" she exclaimed, startled.

He grinned.

"Alone except for my wife. What can I say? Lunch with my own wife. Embarrassing, wasn't it? Originally I told the police I was alone in order to keep Francesca out of it. And I kept vague about the restaurant. Chloe never knew; I only rang her beforehand, to be frank, to check she was safely stowed inside the flat. Not to invite her out. As you know, she never answered. The police know now, of course, and our friend Stavros here has vouched for me. For some reason Francesca insisted on coming up to see me before I went on holiday and I got the lunch hour off from number ten."

But Jemima knew the reason which had brought Francesca Lionnel pell-mell to London: the information about Chloe Fontaine's trip to the Camargue, carelessly or maliciously passed on by Valentine's mother at tea the previous day. Exactly what had transpired that fatal lunchtime? If Francesca had become "ill" in the restaurant there must have been some kind of scene. Had she taxed Lionnel about the affair with Chloe and had he confessed? But Jemima realized she was unlikely to be told the truth of that now and it was—probably—no longer important. Sir Richard had clearly mended his fences with his own wife since Chloe's death, if not before.

She understood however what Pompey had meant when he told her that Lionnel had proved "after all" to have an alibi—"Quite a good one as a matter of fact. A lady. A Nonny Mouse." Then Pompey had chuckled. He was right. There was a kind of grim humour about Sir Richard deceiving his mistress with his own wife.

Jemima decided to wrench the conversation back to the subject of Chloe Fontaine. She was still uncertain whether Lionnel was carefully rewriting history. With Chloe no longer around to contradict him, he was busy making it clear that their affair had never amounted to more than "one of my little flings" as he put it. "I fall head over heels in love, don't you?"

Jemima in response gave her famously enchanting smile, made famous that is to say by television, curling the corners of her wide mouth, and revealing the perfect white teeth with which Nature had thoughtfully endowed her for the purposes of her chosen profession. It was also a mechanism for concealed emotion. The real answer is—yes, I do fall, and head over heels, from time to time, she thought, her mind on Adam. But not in love. Love is another matter.

The mention of Lady Lionnel and her talents for decoration suddenly concentrated Jemima's mind. The flats, the various styles of decoration, how were they to be explained if they were not the creation of that paragon of virtuous good taste, Francesca Lionnel? In response to Jemima's careful probing questions, Sir Richard was even more startlingly frank.

"Katy Aaronson did the office suite, I think," he said rather carelessly. "You know Katy, don't you? She keeps me straight, rules me with a rod of iron all day then home to mother and father in Highgate in the evening—well, most evenings, anyway. No personal life at all, well, nothing outside work, awfully pretty too, first-class brain and legs like Betty Grable. Pity in a way they didn't let her go to Cambridge like her brother. Still it's been my good luck. What more could a man ask in his private assistant? I think she decorated the office suite—she's always wanted to do something like that, it seemed. Something more feminine than her usual work. I chose the mirror and table in the hall—picked them up for a song when I was quite a young man and had time for those things. Then who did the bedroom? Was it that smashing Czech Countess I met at Jane Manfred's? Or did Katy do the bedroom and the smashing Czech do the drawing room? Do you know that Czech girl? I'm absolutely mad about her. Quite beautiful and she does it all herself with a spray-gun and scissors; amazing. Come to think of it, she certainly pinned up all that green stuff on the bedroom walls."

"And the third-floor flat?" Jemima hoped Lionnel would not ask her how she had penetrated it. He did not.

"Oh that. The photographer. You know, we were just talking about her. The one who wears knickerbockers."

"Binnie Rapallo," suggested Jemima in her coldest voice.

"Ghastly, isn't it?" Sir Richard gave one of his happy grins; his black eyes flashed and bulged, like the eyes of a wrestler in a Japanese print. "That never did work out." Did he mean the relationship or the décor? While Jemima was still trying to puzzle this out, Sir Richard Lionnel leant forward and picked up her hand where it lay on the tablecloth, sharing it now only with a large ash-tray and some untouched turkish delight on sticks, thoughtfully provided by Stavros.

He turned it over and gazed at the palm. What he saw there either reassured or inspired him. The next thing he said, black eyes fixed hypnotically upon her, was:

"Miss Shore, Jemima—may I? My friends call me Dick by the way—why don't you redecorate it for me? Any way you like. Just let Katy know about the bills. Don't worry about the expense, just talk to Katy as and when it's necessary. She looks after all the empty flats."

The role of decorator of Adelaide Square in the life of Sir Richard Lionnel had suddenly become alarmingly clear to Jemima. Hastily she extricated herself from what might have been an embarrassing situation,—although for one moment, was she perhaps tempted? . . . *No*, definitely not, she reminded herself sternly, definitely not to clear up the area of decorative disaster created by Binnie Rapallo. And she would not call him Dick either. Which meant she could hardly revert to Sir Richard without being rude; she would have to call him nothing at all for the time being.

"What will become of Chloe's flat?" she asked at the end of lunch in a suddenly sad voice. She had the answer to her original question now: Chloe, the great deceiver, in her last relationship had been deceived. Or at least had deceived herself. This man had never intended to marry Chloe Fontaine.

"The lease belonged to her. Not the freehold of course. Katy tells me there's probably no will. No husband, no children. That means it goes to her parents, and they will presumably want to sell it. We'll buy it back—we have first refusal. I'm trying to persuade Katy herself . . . time for even the nicest Jewish girl to leave home . . . Highgate can be quite awkward sometimes . . . Stifling environment, no wonder the brilliant brother dropped out."

Sir Richard Lionnel was shown the bill by Stavros but was evidently too grand even to sign it; he waved it away with a smile, merely adding to it a large note.

"It would never have done," he said, leaning back easily in his chair. "Not because of me, but because of her. She was so wayward, wasn't she? That's what attracted me in the first place. You see, I'm surrounded by strong women. Francesca—very strong in her own way; Katy, a Tartar; my mother—still as strong as a horse at eighty-three. You're a strong woman, we should get on very well together—"

Jemima smiled at the flattery. But the compliment proved to be double-edged.

"Love is another matter. I've always been fatally drawn to the other type. A dash of adventure in my life—I need it. There was nothing strong about Chloe, was there? She was like an eel. And a liar! She lied as she breathed. She was pregnant, did you know that?"

Jemima nodded. A splash of red. Kevin John to Chloe, Adam to her, Chloe to Richard Lionnel. Apparently they all needed it.

"Not my child. Then who was the father?"

"You're sure? I know the dates make it improbable—"

"Quite sure. We have no children, Francesca and I. It's not her fault, it's mine. Boyhood illness. It's never bothered me; and Francesca has come to terms with it—as I told you, she is a strong person." He paused. "Then who was the father? I would like to know that before I close the books."

"I haven't the slightest idea," replied Jemima quite truthfully. She really did have no idea who might have been Chloe's lover, or even her partner in a casual encounter, about three months ago. At least Adam Adamson was out of the question since their relationship had developed only within the last few weeks.

"I suppose the bastard killed her."

Afterwards Jemima refused the offer of a lift; it was after all only a step from "The Little Athens" to Adelaide Square. She watched Sir Richard's Rolls-Royce purr away in the direction of Whitehall. Sir Richard himself, bent over some papers, was accompanied by an exceptionally attractive young woman with auburn hair who apparently had been waiting for him in the back of the car. Katy Aaronson? Or any one of the other innumerable women Lionnel surrounded himself with. As far as he was concerned, the incident of Chloe Fontaine was clearly closed. His attempts to pump Jemima about Chloe's lover having failed, he would probably spare the dead woman no further thoughts.

When Jemima let herself into the office suite, the telephone was ringing. Detective Chief Inspector Portsmouth was in a jovial mood.

"The artist fellow, Athlone," he said merrily. "We're charging him with murder tomorrow. Witness saw him leaving the building between one-thirty and two. Besides, he's admitted it. He was there all right."

Chapter Fourteen

Back to Athens

Lunch with Isabelle Mancini the next day, Friday, was dominated by the news of the arrest and charging with murder of Kevin John Athlone. After a brief early-morning appearance at Bow Street Magistrates' Court, he was remanded and taken to Brixton.

As Jemima walked once again in the direction of "The Little Athens"—for her own reasons she was minded to pursue her acquaintance with that restaurant—she speculated on Kevin John's present whereabouts. She hated the thought of that great handsome bull's head butting against fate; horns now tangled officially with the police. It was curious how sympathetic to Kevin John she had become, now that he was in a sense Chloe's victim as well as her alleged assassin. It was particularly odd, since she had never felt even covert sympathy for him before, and regarded the memory of their two encounters in Adelaide Square with distaste. The fact was that as Chloe's webs-after-death began to pull him down, she saw his involvement with her late friend in clearer colours.

Whatever a jury would find—and they were hardly likely to view his undeniably violent proclivities with favour—she would always believe that Kevin John had struck down Chloe in the face of some kind of intolerable provocation.

Oddly enough, Isabelle Mancini shared Jemima's view: another woman who had never been a fan of Kevin John's in the past and had, for example, never dreamt of featuring the artist in her cherished *Taffeta*.

" 'E was forced to ke-e-el 'er" she declared passionately after their first contretemps over the menu at "The Little Athens" had been resolved. "Chloe made everyone who loved 'er want to ke-e-el 'er. Danger—it turned 'er on . . . Ah, Chloe, ee-ee-diot child.''

Isabelle's eating was temporarily afflicted by two quite different considerations. In the first place the ethnic nature of any given restaurant had to conform to her somewhat confusing but strongly held political views. Laura Barrymore having made the new appointment and dropped her employer at "The Little Athens" in her chic smoky-glassed black Mini, Isabelle was apparently unaware of the nature of the venue. There were some moments of difficulty while Isabelle sorted out her political attitude to that particular geographical area represented by this particular restaurant. And where might that be?

"You know, Athens, darling," murmured Jemima sardonically, "Athens, Greece." Her voice was not heard as Isabelle eagerly questioned the proprietor. Stavros, handsomer, heavier and gloomier than ever under this treatment, was transparently in a mood to agree with whatever opinion it was that Isabelle so strongly held. The exact nature of this was however rather more difficult to elicit. At last Isabelle relaxed.

"*Bien.* 'E agrees with me about l'Arménie, 'e says, and 'e's never 'eard of l'Albanie," she declared. "Agh, eet's probably not true—" She stopped. Jemima did not dare ask what agreeing with Isabelle about Armenia involved—was that really a topic of the day? But by now Isabelle's attention was distracted by her second consideration, that of food.

Isabelle was on a diet, a diet almost as particular as her political views. Furthermore, as a former cookery writer and restaurant guide, Isabelle was not to be fooled by bland discussions of ingredients. Stavros' courtesy remained impeccable throughout their long-drawn-out negotiations, while Jemima covertly drank a great deal of retsina, a wine that Isabelle, it seemed, despised both for its content and its political implications.

Finally, with a rather good French wine to reassure her—how fortunate it was for Isabelle that France, her native country, through all its vicissitudes remained mysteriously politically and gastronomically O.K.—Isabelle settled herself back in her chair and turned back to conversation. In her flowing grey draperies she made a dignified if substantial figure; the pretty pearl-handled fan with which she cooled herself ("Perfect for zose boiling collections, darling") was perhaps a little too delicate for her looks, which were, like those of Kevin John, on a large scale. The heavy silver bracelets which clanked in time to the airy motions of the fan were more suitably massive. But as the talk flowed, Jemima derived all over again that pleasure from Isabelle's company in which her ample physical presence was merely the outward manifestation of her generous spirit. The loyalty Isabelle demanded, she certainly also dispensed.

"Paris—a nightmare. Where was I, darling? Yes, Kevin John—'ee was forced to ke-e-el 'er. For 'e loved 'er. Valentine too, 'e loved 'er; she wanted that, you know, violence, she loved it; that's what poor Valentine could never give 'er. Swee-e-et boy. Even I—" Isabelle paused only for a moment. "Even from me she wanted something, some 'atred perhaps, when all I 'ad for 'er was love. Why be so cruel to me? *Why*? I ask myself now, with zat book, zose letters—steell, we don't want to talk about that now, do we?" Isabelle rushed on, "Poor Valentine. If only 'e 'ad been able to give her something like that. If only . . . But then 'e would not have been so sw-e-et, would 'e? And life—ah life—" Isabelle paused again and then plunged on, "Life would 'ave taken a different turn for Chloe."

At the end of lunch, Laura Barrymore arrived to fetch Isabelle. She was wonderful and long-legged in grass-green trousers and matching T-shirt, down which irregular green glass beads set in gold cascaded, revealing every tense sinew of her muscular but graceful body: she must have been every inch of six feet and barely weighed more than eight stone. Jemima watched Laura coiling herself back into the black Mini like an elegant green snake.

Through the smoked glass Jemima could not even discern the heads of the two women, as she had been able to watch Sir Richard and his female companion being borne away on Thursday. Nevertheless it occurred to her that both Isabelle and Lionnel, highly successful in their respective spheres, understood the necessity of binding their acolytes to them. A loyal acolyte was something Chloe Fontaine had not even desired unless one counted poor Valentine and even he, rightly or wrongly, had detected in her a provocation: "She made me watch her. I had a feeling she wanted it."

Jemima was due to visit Chloe's domestic acolyte, Rosina, later that afternoon: perhaps there would be a loyalty there. In the meantime she had some unfinished business at "The Little Athens."

"Mr. Stavros—" she began, flashing her television smile. But it was hardly necessary. Stavros was quite enchanted at the presence—two days running—of Jemima Shore, Investigator. The exact significance of her title did not bother him as he brought some more wine—"a present for a lovely lady," given with a smile as wide and ravishing as Jemima's own. He also banished the restaurant's traditional sweetmeats on sticks at Jemima's request—what would Isabelle have made of these glutinous lumps, politically and gastronomically? With the departure of Isabelle, and in the absence of Sir Richard Lionnel, Stavros' melancholy had quite vanished. He became a mine of information on the restaurant trade, on which he was delighted to think that Miss Shore might be planning an autumn programme.

The transition to the subject of Sir Richard Lionnel was made without too much difficulty and somehow even Lady Lionnel was introduced . . . Stavros rolled his eyes. After all he had had to answer similar questions from the police; a television enquiry was not so different after all, just rather more comforting to its subject. Jemima made it clear that in her case lunch with Lionnel had been in the line of business . . . since she was not concerned to pump Stavros about Lionnel's ladies, but only his movements on that particular Saturday, the task proved relatively easy.

Yes, poor Lady Lionnel had become ill. "She was a little upset, yes, upset, definitely." Yes, Sir Richard had summoned the chauffeur to take her to the station but it was too early, the chauffeur had not yet come back. In fact he had only just gone for his own lunch.

"About half-past one?"

"Something like that. It was a one o'clock booking. But Sir Richard was early. He always is."

"I noticed."

"And Lady Lionnel arrived soon after that. She just had time to taste some taramasalata—then, pouf—" Stavros' face was expressive. "Tears."

"And—how did she leave then?"

"Ah, then no car. He looks angry. He does not say so. I know it. He thinks, the car should be there all the time. He goes out, himself, I cannot stop him. He moves very quickly that man, and looks for a taxi. He comes back and puts her in it. Face of thunder. Both Sir Richard and the lady. He comes back, sits here. 'No reason to waste an excellent meal, Stavros,' he says. But he eats and drinks nothing. Later he says: 'I'm afraid I'm not feeling very well, Stavros.' He reads a magazine, a book maybe. Very calm. When the car comes back he is no longer angry. He waits reading until about two-thirty, and then his car takes him away."

"To number ten Downing Street," concluded Jemima thoughtfully. "And you told all this to the police, just as you told me."

Stavros smiled and flung his hands open.

"I told it, yes, most of it. But I am a businessman. I do not tell them about the tears of Lady Lionnel. That is private to Sir Richard. Besides they are not interested in her, only in him. And the fact that he is here from twelve-forty-five to two-thirty. To that I swear and so do Nicky and Spyros." He indicated two further melancholy men, younger and thinner, but in somewhat the same mould as Stavros. "Sir Richard Lionnel, he too is a businessman. It is a pleasure to see him here. He knows what he wants—we give it to him. The other lady—please forgive me, Miss Shore—your guest. What does *she* want?" Jemima left hastily, before she should be drawn into discussing the political-gastronomic ideals of Isabelle Mancini. She also paid the bill in cash: despite Stavros' evident desire to make that another present "for a lovely lady."

Jemima remained thoughtful on her journey to see Chloe's daily woman. She was haunted by a feeling that she had received an odd and valuable piece of information in the course of her visit to "The Little Athens." It was as though an insignificant chip in a jig-saw had been handed to her; if she could only place it correctly, the whole pattern might become clearer.

Jemima enlivened the walk to Tottenham Court Road tube station by re-running her conversations with both Isabelle and Stavros through her mind like a tape.

As she came to Stavros' revelations, she realized that the striking piece of information she had received concerned the precipitate departure of Lady Lionnel—the Medea of Parrot Park—from "The Little Athens" at about 1:30—back to the station. An item of information as yet unknown to the police, who had contented themselves with establishing Sir Richard Lionnel's alibi—lunch with his wife—with the aid of Stavros and his waiters.

That needed further quiet thought. Lady Lionnel? It was odd to think that this Medea who unquestionably had a motive for wishing Chloe removed from her husband's path, had also been vouchsafed an opportunity to effect this removal.

Something else—less obvious perhaps—some remark of Isabelle or Stavros—continued to haunt her.

She was still re-running the scene in her mind when she reached Tottenham Court Road station and bought a copy of the *London Evening Post*. A recent photograph showed Kevin John's face, anguished, pop-eyed, slightly reproachful, staring at her from the front page. His huge eyes with their improbably starry eyelashes, seemed to be imploring her help.

Jemima shivered and turned down the steps to the moving staircase. The text accompanying the report was short: there was after all very little to be said. There was, however, a short interview with one Miss Kim Lee Ho, who described herself as the "steady girlfriend" of the accused, and was also temporarily lodging with Kevin John's artistic patron, Crispin Creed, the owner of the Aiglon Gallery.

A joint photograph was provided. Inspecting it with interest, Jemima could see a dark pretty Oriental-looking girl; her small figure was almost masked by the robust presence of Creed, a man whose affectionate nickname of Creeping Croesus had been earned by a combination of inherited wealth and commercial perception. This then was the submissive girl of Eastern origin to whom Chloe had so casually referred. Jemima was vaguely pleased that Kevin John had some feminine support. It made her feel less guilty in the face of those reproachful eyes. Kim Lee Ho, who, give or take her Oriental ancestry, had a certain disquieting resemblance to Chloe herself, was described in the evening paper as a model—whether artist's model or fashion model was unspecified. Chloe, despite her photogenic looks, had always rejected the fashion offers which had come her way, even when poor and out of work after Cambridge. "I'm a model nothing," she used to say.

She had not, it seemed, been a model employer. Mrs. Rosina Cavalieri received a rather hot and fussed Jemima in a small depressing street north of Tottenham Court Road, a neighbourhood with little else to commend it except the convenience of the tube for working in Bloomsbury. Rosina was indeed, as Chloe had pointed out and Pompey confirmed, a compulsive talker; her son, Enrico, no more charming than Chloe had predicted, clung to his mother's skirts and regarded Jemima with enormous baleful eyes set in a full white face.

Enrico's distinctly plump figure, however, was immaculately

dressed notwithstanding the heat in a white silk shirt which buttoned on to grey silk trousers, white socks and black patent shoes. Despite his tender years, Enrico had an excellent sense of when the conversation was taking an interesting turn, and at this juncture infallibly grabbed his mother, demanding a biscuit, some other comestible, or orange juice. Thanks to these interruptions, it took Jemima longer than she had anticipated to elicit Rosina's impressions of life with Chloe Fontaine.

First, as Pompey had indicated, Rosina was most impressed by "the grand Sir"—Sir Richard Lionnel. Second, she was not impressed, rather the reverse, by the fact that Chloe had apparently shared her favours with others during the same period. This kind of disloyalty, Rosina made it clear, was unthinkable in the particular society in which Rosina moved. At one point she even clutched the sulkily acquiescent Enrico to her breast, sticky chocolate biscuit and all, to emphasize the point.

With flashing eyes and heaving bosom—indeed, in more ways than her emphasis on loyalty, Rosina bore a general Mediterranean resemblance to Isabelle Mancini—she enquired how such matters as *"bambine"* could be managed with ladies of such wayward tendencies. If her language was not quite so high flown as that of Isabelle, her English accent was an improvement. It was clear what Rosina meant especially as she appealed from time to time to the example of little Enrico, the son indubitably of his father, big Enrico, who would kill anyone, and she, Rosina, would also kill anyone if they suggested . . . This dramatic monologue on the subject of marital fidelity was broken only by the protests of Enrico, who, biscuit finished, struggled free from his mother's arms and demanded "Orange! Orange!"

But Rosina had not expounded in vain. Jemima derived the very definite impression that Rosina, by some means or other—a doctor's letter left carelessly about, a telephone call overheard—had suspected Chloe was pregnant. It was true that Rosina had denied all knowledge of such a distasteful subject to the police—but then Miss Jemima Shore was so very different, wasn't she, to the young male detective who had interviewed Rosina. Handsome as Pompey's protegé—the dashing Gary Harwood—might be, he was no substitute for a real-life television star. Miss Shore was so very friendly, so very famous . . . There was an enormous television set in pride of place in the tiny sitting room which presently Enrico insisted on having switched on for his own delectation. Miss Shore, Rosina declared, was like someone she had known all her life, her own sister, for example.

More than prepared to accept this helpful hypotheses, Jemima narrowed her questions to Chloe's other callers, especially those prominent in the period when Chloe had first moved into Adelaide Square, which had coincided with Rosina's arrival to work for her. Since Chloe had been roughly three months pregnant when she died in the first week of August, the father of her child must have been someone she knew long before the move to Adelaide Square towards the end of June; conception had to have taken place at the beginning of May.

Rosina, predictably, was gracious about the "poor lord," meaning Valentine Brighton, whose sudden death had been brilliantly brought to her attention by Enrico when he recognized Valentine's face on the television news with a shriek. The "poor lord" had helped Chloe with her move into Adelaide Square, putting his Rolls at her disposal.

No, Rosina was full of approval for the poor dead Lord Brighton: *"Che gentile! Che simpatico!"* and so on. At any point Jemima expected her to join Isabelle in her cry of "Swee-e-et boy." It was an approval which did not, however, extend to someone she termed the "*studente*." Jemima, despite herself, felt her heart give a little jolt.

"*Studente*, there was a *studente*?" she probed, hoping that Enrico would not choose this moment—there was a commercial break—to demand another orange. She need not have worried: advertisements as well as programmes held Enrico entranced.

"Ahdum," Rosina pronounced the name with scorn. "Ahdum Ahdum: he was a *studente*. A foolish name." She implied that his youthful status was no excuse.

"Not *then*, Rosina, surely." Jemima knew that she sounded agitated. "Not in June. Not when she first came to Adelaide Square. It was later, wasn't it, a week or so before she died that she met the student?"

"But no! It was the end of June like I tell you." Rosina's indignation rose. "It was the day after the birthday of Big Enrico, June twenty-six. It was then I tell you. The *studente*. In the empty flat with her, that first day, no furniture, no bed even. They were in the bedroom, all the same. I knew. She just called out: 'I'm resting. Come back in an hour!' And later when I do come back, all those stairs again, I pass him. The *studente*, with his little red beard, his *barba*, you understand? She was running down the stairs and calling: 'Ahdum! Ahdum!' Then she saw me and stopped. She said: 'Mrs. Cavalieri, this is Ahdum, a friend of mine from Fulham. He's been helping me with the move.' But the room, it was still empty."

"What did he say?"

"Ah, he spoke in a funny voice, funny words. He was young, too young for her. He said he liked it here, better than in Fulham, and he might come and live here himself if she asked him. He laughed. They both laughed."

At this point Enrico, maybe in a jealous rage at the thought of the laughter of others, let out a prolonged and angry bawl. "Ma-aama!"

"He is tired with our talking," said Rosina apologetically. "And the television is tiring—when they are young," she added hastily in case she seemed to denigrate Jemima's profession. "Perhaps you will come another day, Miss Shore. I would like to ask my neighbour to tea, Mrs. Pollonari, she likes television *very* much."

Jemima was left to wend her way home by tube in the Friday rush-hour, missing for the first time in a week the easy passage her Citroen gave her through weary London.

She pondered a world in which not only Kevin John Athlone had lied to the police about his lunchtime movements but Adam Adamson had also lied—if not to the police at least by implication to Jemima Shore. He had definitely allowed her to believe that he had met Chloe for the first time a few days prior to her death. Now it emerged that they had been friends—no, more than that, lovers, long before Chloe moved to Adelaide Square. They had been lovers in Fulham, Fulham where Chloe's child had been conceived.

"I suppose the bastard killed her," Sir Richard had said of the unknown father of Chloe's child. With a heavy heart, Jemima acknowledged that it was a possibility at least worth exploring: and Kevin John's large imploring eyes gazing out at her from the folded front page of the evening paper, called on her mutely to proceed.

Chapter Fifteen

A White Petticoat

Jemima planned to move out of Adelaide Square over the weekend. On Friday evening Miss Katy Aaronson telephoned with the offer of a furnished flat—another penthouse—in Montagu Square. Under the circumstances Jemima decided to take it. She felt she had had enough of Bloomsbury; nor did she particularly wish to approach her own American tenant with a view to shortening the let by a couple of weeks. That way lay the possibility of an unwelcome intimacy with the need to ask a favour. Anonymity in Montagu Square, near Marble Arch, an area without associations, away from friends and strangers alike, if not quite the holiday she had planned, was at least the most dignified way of ending it.

Shortly afterwards a Lionnel chauffeur came round with the keys of the Montagu Square apartment. Miss Katy Aaronson had very politely excused herself from a Saturday rendezvous. She liked to spend the day with her parents in Highgate, starting with a Friday eve-of-the-Sabbath supper.

"And since Sir Richard is generally at Parrot Park on Friday nights—although house guests are invited in time for Saturday lunch, but in any case the housekeeper is at the disposal of Lady Lionnel for those arrangements—and Sir Richard's personal assistant, Mr. Judah Turpin, has the flat in the old stables, should business matters arise—"

Jemima was happy to cut short this catalogue of undoubtedly admirable arrangements and arrange to arrive at Montagu Square at leisure, at a time of her own choosing, and under her own terms. She rejected the offer of a Lionnel car to convey her. The anonymity of a taxi was another personal choice. Making it clear that at Montagu Square, for the next week, her privacy was to be regarded as sacrosanct, Jemima arranged to leave behind her own keys to the Adelaide Square office suite. The efficient Miss Aaronson possessing several spare sets, would arrange their collection.

It was a pity that Tiger would have to make two moves in rapid succession—for Tiger would be coming back with Jemima to Holland Park Mansions. It was as though he had been pre-ordained to replace Colette. No one else showed the slightest interest in the fierce golden cat. Mr. Stover, on being consulted on the telephone, had revealed the existence of a rival Stover pet, Nipper, a terrier of great age and uncertain health—"although where cats are concerned, he's still pretty much on the ball, I can tell you that." Mr. Stover obviously regarded the possible incursion of Tiger into his dog's declining years—"mind you, he's not called Nipper for nothing"—as symbolic of the whole cata-strophic confusion wrought in his own existence by the death of Chloe. Jemima was left to reflect that Mr. Stover and Nipper were no exception to the oft-quoted rule that over the years pets and their masters grew to resemble each other.

Jemima did not flatter herself that she had in any sense won Tiger's affections—Colette had been from the first a far more domesticated animal—but she recognized their alliance as inevi-table. And that kind of recognition was often more binding than a sentimental attachment.

Fortunately Tiger had already shown himself to be a survivor where moves were concerned. He had adapted himself to Blooms-bury after Fulham; carefully treated he would survive the short-term stay in Montagu Square, the final move to Holland Park.

Fulham and Tiger: Jemima caught her breath suddenly at the memory of Adam Adamson and Tiger on that day of their first acquaintance. Had she not sensed something strange even then about Tiger's eager disappearance into the third-floor flat? It was obviously explained by the fact that to Tiger, Adam was a familiar figure. Adam had not exactly lied to Jemima in this respect: indeed, throughout their conversations he had shown a remark-able, jesuitical regard for avoiding the direct lie, while not telling the whole truth.

He had not actually denied knowing Tiger, only: "Nice cat . . . it wanted to come in"—followed by compliments about her own appearance. No wonder Tiger, accidentally excluded from the upper flat, had peregrinated towards the least hostile terrain.

Jemima however still believed that Adam had been genuinely puzzled over Chloe's true identity. Was it possible that he could have been fooled by the pose of Dollie Stover? On consideration it was: Chloe, the mistress of deceit, had presumably conducted her carnal encounters with Adam elsewhere than in her Fulham house—in his own former dwelling, whatever kind of revivified pad that might have been. Adam's menacing comment about Chloe and her deception—"I hate being lied to"—was, she would swear, genuine.

Perhaps their carnal encounters within Adelaide Square itself had taken place on the third floor? And literally so, in view of its lack of furniture, Jemima reflected wryly; her slight sense of crossness was almost proprietary, but since all proprietary feelings about Adam Adamson were so clearly a mistake, she dismissed the whole train of thought as unworthy of her. Back to the question of Adam and the penthouse: by keeping him ignorant of her lease of the top floor, Chloe would have run no danger of him ferreting out the incriminating copies of her own works, those exquisite tell-tale photographs on the back.

Besides, now that Jemima—far too late—was coming to some new understanding of Chloe's character, she had an intuition that the encounters in the empty flat, with her own immaculate penthouse above, and Sir Richard's secure opulence below, would have given Chloe exactly that rich spice of danger she sought.

As Jemima waited for Pompey to bring her back the keys to Chloe's flat, in order that she might pack up her remaining belongings over the weekend, she continued to ponder on the subject of Adam. Adam—"my former angel"—Adam, presumably the father of the unsought child, Adam with his fertile youth and impetuosity giving Chloe the child which she had either avoided receiving or refused to accept from two husbands and at least one steady—ridiculous word in the context—lover in the shape of Kevin John. There had been at least one abortion, possibly two, in Chloe's past, hadn't there?

Jemima was a little hazy about the details: Chloe's marriage to Lance breaking up, impossible to bring a child into the world under such circumstances, Chloe desperately writing her second novel, trying to support herself financially as a meagre-selling novelist, impossible to take on the burden of single parenthood.

Jemima, not closely involved herself, knew that Chloe had always had plenty of excuses to offer—and goodness knows Jemima herself did not believe dogmatically in unwanted children coming into the world, having investigated too many of the resultant miseries. At the same time Jemima had always suspected that Chloe's deep-seated reason for avoiding motherhood was her unwillingness to tolerate the arrival of a child in her life while she herself remained in so many respects wilfully childish and irresponsible.

That left open the question of the carelessness . . . the lethal carelessness which had led to at least two, possibly three pregnancies. What precautions had Chloe taken? One had to assume that she had not been on the Pill, or at least not regularly. It was certainly true that there were plenty of medical reasons to be quoted against the continuous long-term use of the Pill for any woman. Jemima herself had quoted them—as ever giving both sides of the question—in that programme about the Pill, to which Pompey had alluded. Yet Jemima wondered once again at the surprising contrasts evinced by Chloe's character; the neatness and domesticity of her surroundings, the meticulous care of her writing, versus the dangerous abandon of her private life, carried surely to excess in her reckless attitudes to the question of her own fertility.

It did not affect matters that on this occasion Chloe had tried to turn her pregnancy to good account as part of her intrigue to get Sir Richard Lionnel—hitherto childless—to marry her. Chloe had gone to her death without knowing how that particular plot was always doomed to fail. She died, with her stepfather on his way to London as a kind of angry witness to the confrontation. Jemima was glad that at least all three parties had been spared that dreadful moment when Chloe would have been denounced as a liar, and furthermore a promiscuous one. Lionnel had to live with the knowledge now; he clearly did not find it easy. Yes, dangerous abandon had certainly been what Chloe had displayed.

Dangerous abandon—the thought suddenly struck Jemima that if Adam was Chloe's former angel, that left the identity of her casual—carnal?—acquaintance from the square gardens still unknown. Was there some mystery to be unravelled there? Or was the whole episode of that nocturnal spree as unimportant to the world now as it had been to Chloe at the time?

That certainly was the point of view taken by Pompey. He was in a joyous mood. He had rounded off a hardworking Friday, which began with the formal charging of Kevin John with murder at the police station, by having "a jar with the lads," as he put it, of a mildly celebratory nature. And he seemed to regard his visit to Jemima as a further postponement of his return to Mrs. Portsmouth and the intellectual principles of gardening.

"The lover in the gardens!" he exclaimed, shaking his head repeatedly like a mechanical toy—a fox perhaps, in a man's suit—which had just been wound up. "Sounds like a Sunday newspaper headline to me. No my dear, Athlone did it. No question about that now. His second statement was a great deal more to the point, as well it might be. You see, your squatter friend made a statement saying he had seen him leaving the building between one-thirty and two; looked out from the third-floor balcony where he happened to be, *not* minding his own business, still it's convenient for us that he was. Described him exactly. Not only does he have his own little alibi for that period, as I told you, but *his* story was confirmed by a very different kind of witness.

"One Flora Elizabeth Powell, fifty-eight, spinster, who came into the station in response to our enquiries and made a voluntary statement. No, my dear, not a hysterical spinster, just a hard-working citizen, employed in a local cafe on the early shift who was on her way home, some time after one-fifteen when she knocked off work in Great Russell Street and two-five pm when she noticed a local clock in Hammersmith, where she lives, and reaches by tube, when she saw him coming out of a house in Adelaide Square. Can pinpoint the house of course: 'It's the lovely modern block, isn't it? Which the Queen Mother declared open the other day. I saw the crowds. I couldn't quite get to see her, but my friend said she looked lovely.' Never mind the fact that the crowds she saw were demonstrators *against* the building." Pompey chuckled. "And the Queen Mother was at University College round the corner. Flora Elizabeth is our witness all right. Very particular about the blue T-shirt. Better still, she remembers seeing someone in a white shirt—that's the squatter of course—on the upper balcony. Came out with it on her own accord; couldn't have made that up; didn't know we were interested, you see. Remarked that she was happy to think the building declared open by the Queen Mother was already occupied, not like that Centre

Point, since it might have worried the Queen Mother to know—but I'll spare you the rest."

Pompey chuckled again. "What does feminine instinct say to all that?"

"My feminine instinct has nothing to *say*. It never does. It just nags at me in the watches of the night. I don't doubt you. I don't doubt either of them for that matter—my squatter and your spinster can hardly be in league to fool us," said Jemima rather wearily. "It's just that I like the loose ends being tied up. The identity of the lover in the gardens—I love the headline, by the way—continues to intrigue me, although I dare say you're right and it's not important. Tell me at any rate, before I read it in the newspapers of the trial, about Athlone's second statement."

"He admitted it. To being there, that is. Still utterly denied killing her. But that's par for the course." Pompey shook gently, as if confirmed once again in his low—but not necessarily contemptuous—view of human nature. "He came back at lunchtime—to apologize to you. Felt he'd behaved like a cad—well he had, hadn't he? All that violence towards a woman," said Pompey in stern parenthesis. "He was surprised to find the penthouse door open *with* the keys in the lock."

"*Open?*"

"Exactly. Listen, this is his statement, not mine. In he goes. No one there—not you, and not at this point, his ex-mistress, Chloe Fontaine. He decides, believe it or not, to have another go at finding a razor."

"I do believe that!" exclaimed Jemima. "That razor was obsessing him. He left Dixie in the pub saying he was going to find a razor."

"Believe that if you like. It's immaterial to our case. But a rational woman like you, Jemima—in the daylight hours"—a gallant shake—"may find the rest of it a little more difficult to accept. Athlone finds a razor—right?"

"The same razor, we assume, which is later found beside Chloe's bed—"

"Exactly. In some drawer or other. His prints were all over the bathroom and bedroom anyway—except in those areas wiped clean by the murderer—as a result of the morning's search for that same razor. He decides to shave. And not before time—" This was clearly the reproving voice of Pompey speaking. "But he's still pretty angry, he's drunk a good deal of whisky, feeling not

153

only angry but violent as he himself tells us. At this point his eye lights on the picture—'The Red Paintpot,' whatever it's called. He decides suddenly that she, the deceased that is, is not worthy of 'my effing work of genius.' His exact words." Pompey paused. "Except he didn't say effing."

"So, listen to this." Pompey's tone was now more portentous. "He takes a kitchen knife, yes, the same knife we assume to be the murder weapon—for he remembers deliberately choosing the biggest of the knives available. He goes back into the bedroom. He proposes to massacre the aforesaid work of art. Again his own words. He is going to slash it to effing pieces and throw them over the balcony to feed the lions of Bloomsbury."

Pompey leaned back. He gave the impression of being rather pleased with his imitation of Kevin John, which did not however in Jemima's opinion contain any of the sheer craziness of the original; there was too much devilry, too little dash in Pompey's delivery.

"But before he can carry out this felonious plan—it's not his property"—Pompey shook—"although it's not exactly like desecrating the Mona Lisa, is it, not exactly—he's disturbed."

"Disturbed? By whom?"

"By her, of course. The recently deceased Miss Chloe Fontaine. I'm anticipating her state somewhat, it's fair to say. So there he is, razor in one hand and effing great kitchen knife, to borrow his phrase, in the other."

"And there she is," cried Jemima, "in a white petticoat, I suppose. It reminds me of that nursery riddle:

> Ninny nanny petticoat
> In a white petticoat
> The longer she goes
> The shorter she grows.

The answer's a candle by the way. Appropriate to Chloe, a flame, snuffed out. But why, Pompey, why?"

"Now that's very sharp of you, Jemima," said Pompey approvingly. "Because that's the first thing he said to us about her. 'The C-blank' "—cough—" 'wasn't even dressed.' He objected particularly, you know, to her parading round the building in her petticoat. Thought it unseemly, or as he put it, effing disgusting."

"And then?"

"*He* says they had a flaming row. I can't recall the precise colourful phrase he used to describe it. She, the deceased, absolutely refused to explain her presence in the penthouse beyond telling him, Athlone that is, that she had borrowed the first-floor flat from 'a friend'—identity not revealed—in order to have some working peace for this anthology she's supposed to be editing. She had returned to the top floor to fetch some forgotten necessity for her work like a notebook; cat slips out; she goes to rescue cat, leaving keys in the door. They're her own keys, having given you, Jemima, the second set."

"Pretty thin story," commented Jemima gloomily. "Except for the bit about the cat. That's probably true. Tiger did that to me. A restless type, I fear, like his former owner. If the cat went down to the basement, that would give Kevin John time to get up the staircase without passing Chloe on the way."

"Athlone thought the story was pretty thin, too." Pompey sounded equally gloomy. "He wasn't too interested in the subject of the cat, one way or the other; but he was interested in the identity of the helpful 'friend' who had lent her the first-floor flat. Thought it was certain to be male, and a lover.

"Hence the row," he went on. "She tells him to get out of the flat. Taxes him with following her about, harassing her, when everything is over between them. He accuses her of having a rendezvous upstairs and wants to know when and with whom. Then she really insults him, goes for him, past present and to come. Never loved him in the first place, you know what ladies can be like"—cough. "Anyway at those words, it all changes. He drops the knife. He just leaves. Leaves her there."

Jemima let out her breath. Pompey went implacably on: "After that he sticks to his original statement. Had a few more drinks. Decided much later to drop in the flowers. For you or her, that's not quite clear. Probably for you: he'd promised you flowers. Admits to being pretty drunk by now. Climbs the scaffolding, deposits the pot plant. Opens the door from inside—it's shut but not doubled locked. Bangs on the first-floor door. No answer. Goes on down to the hall. There he collapses. Has some vague idea of waiting for her to come back, or emerge from the first-floor flat. He may trap her new lover. That's not quite clear. Collapses anyway. The next thing he knows, you're standing over him."

"And he never looks in the bedroom? On that second visit?"

"So he says. We, of course," said Pompey gently, "think he killed her on the first."

On Saturday evening, Jemima found it took more determination than she had expected to mount the stairs to the penthouse flat again. Yet it had to be done, before she could shake the dust of No. 73 from her feet. She opened the door of the office suite. The stairs stretched upwards as though pointing to her duty; seeing how they curved out of sight towards the top floor gave her an odd presentiment that the end of the Chloe story was likewise still hidden. Yet the clues which pointed to any killer other than Kevin John were so extremely slender that only instinct—and natural obstinacy—prevented Jemima from abandoning her consideration of the case altogether, in favour of Pompey's rational certainties. Pompey for example was convinced that Kevin John had returned via the scaffolding only in order to clear away all incriminating traces of his earlier presence—which was certainly more logical than his own explanation.

Jemima let herself into the penthouse flat, using both keys. She was not a nervous person; nevertheless the atmosphere seemed to her not so much silent as sepulchral. That was the right word: the penthouse was now like a tomb for all Chloe's hopes and works and plans and lies and plots.

The murder charge arising from Chloe's death meant that no burial order had yet been given for her poor little body, once the giver and receiver of many strange pleasures, lacerated first by her murderer, then by the pathologists. Frozen in death, it remained waiting for the possible trial of her murderer. In the meantime would there be some kind of memorial service?

The obvious arranger of all such matters would have been Chloe's publisher, Valentine, especially since Chloe had no literary agent, preferring to trust herself entirely to what she had termed Valentine's "aristocratic but mercenary mercies—still, in his own way, he can be an angel you know—I hardly need *more* mercenary mercies from an agent." But Valentine was dead.

In the meantime this flat, until it was dismantled by the combined offices of Miss Katy Aaronson and the Stovers— certainly more the former than the latter—remained Chloe's true sepulchre.

The images of Chloe were everywhere. Lying flat on their backs, faces of Chloe, under her parasol, on her swing, the provocative *Fallen Child* pictures, stared up at the white ceiling from the jackets of her books. They were ranged round the pale carpet. Had the police stacked them so? Presumably. Other belongings were neatly piled and sorted. Everything was immaculate. The comparison to the hideous dust and mayhem which had possessed the flat a week ago was inevitable; Jemima did not find it particularly comforting. But she had to admit that the police had cleaned up after themselves most professionally.

The flat, if clean, was airless. Putting off the moment when she must open the white louvred double doors to the bedroom—for that gesture reminded her too clearly of the past horror—Jemima concentrated on pushing back the balcony windows. They were not locked; but the lock itself was not conspicuous and whoever shut them—the police? Katy Aaronson?—might have thought they were self-locking.

Something soft and furry caressed her legs. Tiger, on his noiseless pads, had followed her up the stairs. He put his golden paws up on the scaffolding to the left of the balcony, and sniffed delicately. Jemima rejoiced constantly in the inquisitive tendencies of cats; it reminded her that her own curiosity was in the natural order of things.

Then she observed that the earth in the pots containing the grey-leaved plants and white-flowering geraniums which had pleased Chloe's bleached sense of decoration, was quite hard and dry. What happened to plants when people died? These had been sufficiently loved by Chloe for her to bring them from Fulham to Bloomsbury. Jemima could not imagine the Stovers conveying such plants back to Folkestone, any more than they had welcomed the intrusion of Tiger. She pictured Mr. Stover's large crimson roses—Ena Harkness perhaps—bristling at the arrival of these sophisticated urban cousins.

As for Jemima's own taste in such things, she recognized it to be prettier but somewhat less tasteful—pale pink roses in her case, New Dawn and Albertine, ran riot in huge dark green tubs on her own balcony, with purple pansies and gypsophila, daffodils and blue hyacinths in the spring. She certainly felt no impulse to adopt Chloe's primly matched plants, but the Rousseau-like savage Tiger was a different matter. In the end, it was the abandoned side of Chloe's nature which magnetized her.

As if to emphasize his freedom from constraint, Tiger was now bounding about the balcony and tossing a leaf, a pretended mouse, in his paws; it was a game at once playful and sinister.

The plants in comparison, if not exactly wilted, looked depressingly arid. Jemima sighed. Whatever their ultimate fate it was not her nature to leave them unwatered. One way of getting herself through those bedroom doors was to fling them open, march through and fetch a watering-can from the bathroom—she had a memory of something rather charming and painted, a kind of Marie Antoinette of a watering-can, in the corner there.

Then she would organize her own belongings into a suitcase. It was now about nine o'clock. The air over Adelaide Square was sultry. Scarcely a rustle disturbed the mighty trees. It had been about that hour of the evening that she had looked in vain across the square for Chloe's departing figure. Oppressed by the memory, Jemima turned away and, striding firmly across the thick sitting-room carpet, flung open the bedroom doors.

Then she heard herself scream, and that scream was succeeded by another, and another, and another. The sound seemed to come from outside, so that she was still listening for further screams, even while she stood panting, and now silent.

On Chloe's white bed, motionless beneath his own violent red picture, vast bulging blue eyes staring fixedly towards her, lay Kevin John Athlone.

Chapter Sixteen

Straw into Gold

An instant later, the vast blue eyes shut. Relieved of their intense stare, Jemima lost her panic and moved gingerly forward. A rumbling noise—yes, it was really a snore—greeted her astonished ears. Kevin John Athlone, whom she had imagined for one feverish moment to be dead, was actually sleeping. The fixed stare which had greeted her corresponded to nothing so much as a coma, an unseeing coma.

It was an appalling thought, but had he actually escaped from Brixton?

He was wearing a white shirt, two or three buttons undone; a black tie, carelessly half unknotted, still slung round his neck; light grey trousers which belonged to a suit because a matching grey jacket was roughly slung over the back of a nearby cane peacock chair. In the top pocket of the jacket, incongruously neatly folded, was a white handkerchief. Black shoes, demonstrably polished, were disposed near the bed. Kevin John's feet, sticking out across the bed like those of the corpse he somewhat resembled, were still covered in dark socks.

The formality of the sleeping man's attire struck Jemima forcibly since she had not seen him previously in anything save jeans, T-shirts, and the most rugged polo-necked jerseys. She presumed they were the same clothes in which he had been remanded at the Magistrates' Court: Crispin Creed was probably responsible for them. In the photograph printed in the evening paper Kevin John had looked heavily handsome, like some debauched film star leaving the divorce court for the third time. In the flesh he looked younger.

Jemima looked at the sleeping figure with more irritation than horror. Her vague intellectual feelings of the necessity of justice towards an innocent man had quite melted away in his physical presence. And even the first feeling of dread at her predicament if he *had* escaped from prison, was less strong than her sheer annoyance at the sight of this great snoring bull, lying so inconveniently prone before her.

It was essential to cope with the problem he presented—and at once. Jemima took another delicate step forward.

The next thing she knew there was a noise, an eruption rather like a mountain in blast, and Kevin John had uncurled himself off the bed, bounded forward, and was clasping her in both shirt-clad arms.

Slightly corpulent as he might be, he was astonishingly muscular. There was no escape. Jemima stood there mutely while Kevin John gave her two quick succulent kisses on the cheek with his rubbery lips.

Then he panted: "You'll save me, sweetheart, won't you? You'll save me?"

He did not let go of her hands. He continued to stare at her. The blue of his eyes was even more amazing than she had remembered; the numerous red veins in the eyeballs were bright and clear as though running through white marble. His long, ridiculously long black eye-lashes fluttered slightly; but his gaze itself did not falter. Coquetry was absent; on this occasion Kevin John Athlone was in deadly earnest.

Alcohol, the pungent disgusting smell of stale alcohol, a great quantity of it, came reeking towards her on his breath as on that fatal Saturday morning a week ago. Only the new formality of his clothing was a present reminder of all that was tragic which had happened in between.

"And if you won't save me, Jemima Shore, Investigator," said Kevin John, puffing slightly as he spoke, but in no way slackening his grasp, "I'll keep you here till you do." From the severity of his tone, the new sound of purpose, Jemima had to assume that the flutter of his lashes which accompanied his words was purely automatic. She also wondered exactly how drunk Kevin John really was, despite the odour of alcohol palpitating from him with every breath exhaled.

"A hostage," he added, "in case there's any doubt about my intentions. A hostage to misfortune—mine." He smiled in what was obviously intended to be a winning manner; this time the flutter of his lashes was deliberate; nevertheless it was all a cold parody of the flirtatiousness which he normally exhibited to the female sex. "I've an idea, sweetheart, that nothing too bad can happen to me while I've got you here."

A surge of fury filled Jemima. The memory of her previous sympathies for Kevin John merely enraged her further. She wrenched her hands free from his. She particularly disliked the notion of physical imprisonment, both in theory and practice, when it was allied to injustice.

"How the hell did you get in here?" were the first words she managed to say.

"I knew you were living here. I thought you would help me. You're famous for helping people." The threatening note beneath the wheedling was still more marked. "So back up the scaffolding I came. Window not locked again."

"I'm not living here—" Jemima broke off. She did not propose to give him any more information than he had already. "Anyway I thought you were in Brixton. For God's sake, don't tell me you've been fool enough to escape."

Kevin John gave a dreadful leer, into which he appeared determined to inject as much boyish innocence as he could muster.

"Now would I do a thing like that?" he cried. "Not your Kevin John. No, sweetheart, for me it was the jolly old Judge-in-Chambers." He pronounced the words proudly and with enormous care. "The jolly old High Court judge his very self. Saturday afternoon and all, when you would have thought all decent judges were at the races or denouncing vandalism at football matches . . . but not my judge. The merry old soul sat up all night, I mean sat up all the afternoon to receive the application of my solicitor, the well-known Red, Punch Fredericks, God bless him and all other Reds,—and what did he say? He said: Yes. Kevin John Athlone shall go free. On bail, of course, but Creeping Croesus was very handsome about that, as well he might. Anyway, out I popped from Brixton. It was just like the prisoners' chorus in *Fidelio*. And I was singing a pretty merry song myself, I can tell you. Now *that* is no place for a gentleman and an artist . . ."

Reluctantly, Jemima came to the conclusion that Kevin John, in his circumlocutory fashion, must be speaking the truth. His temporary release seemed to have been secured by the energetic action of Punch Fredericks, rightly classed by Pompey as belonging to the bail-for-everyone school. A receptive High Court judge had done the rest. As far as Jemima could make out, Kevin John had merely been requested to surrender his passport: Crispin Creed had been required to go surety for some vast sum, and also put up with Kevin John as his official house guest in Chelsea.

Jemima suspected rather cynically that Creed was animated by more than philanthropy in coming to the aid of an artist in which his Gallery had such a large stake. She only hoped that he would find the bargain worth while.

These thoughts were rudely interrupted as Kevin John suddenly pounced upon her. He shoved Jemima down hard upon the white bed, and felt deftly in the skirts of her thin silk jersey dress. From the hidden pocket he took first the keys of the first-floor flat which he rejected, then the keys of the penthouse.

He held them up.

"So! I recognize these. The keys of the kingdom! Our kingdom. No departure for either of us until you've solved the problem of the day. In short, who killed Chloe Fontaine?"

So saying, with that light athletic walk which his figure belied, Kevin John headed for the front door of the flat. He shut and double-locked it. Then he held up the keys once more.

"Shall I make you beg for them? On second thought not. There is no need, is there, for that kind of game between us? With your brains and my assistance, you should easily find the answer to the conundrum. Don't discount my assistance, will you? My charms are a snare; I'm not nearly as witless as I look. I shall lend you plenty of help, my celebrated hostage."

Jemima put out a hand. Afterwards she was not quite sure what she had intended. Was it to grab—or perhaps simply possess—the keys from this unwelcome invader?

Kevin John stepped back one pace. "One last thing to encourage you." The broad sitting-room window was open. Without looking behind him, he tossed the keys upwards and outwards in a great arc. They swung heavily through the air, tinkled against the edge of the scaffolding, and touched something else, probably the low concrete parapet. Then, before Jemima's eyes, they vanished from sight downwards.

"Now we're all locked in for the night, as the old lady said in the ghost story," observed Kevin John conversationally. "No, no, you don't—" As Jemima lunged in the direction of the balcony, Kevin John neatly fielded her with his broad strong grasp. "No maidenly cries for help, if you please. When you've solved the problem, Jemima Shore, Investigator, we'll telephone the police together. Till then—silence." He put his finger to his stretched smiling lips.

The first few hours of Jemima's imprisonment at the hands of Kevin John passed very slowly. The manifest absurdity of her situation, kept like some latterday Rapunzel in the concrete tower, did nothing to reconcile her to it.

Rapunzel was the wrong fairy story to bear in mind. Jemima Shore was not being asked to let down her rippling corn-coloured hair for any likely prince to climb up it. The appropriate fairy story was that of the unfortunate peasant girl married off by her father to the king on the boastful (and erroneous) grounds that she could spin common straw into gold. Once wed, so far as Jemima could remember, the wretched girl had been shut up by her royal husband into a tower room well stocked with straw and told: "Spin!"

In much the same way Kevin John seemed utterly convinced that if only he kept Jemima incarcerated long enough, she too would spin the few straws of evidence at her disposal into the gold of liberation.

The time also passed slowly because for the first few hours of her imprisonment, Jemima refused to listen to Kevin John's harangues and protestations. Nor would she discuss the case.

Kevin John let her sit down on the sofa. He shut the balcony window but—Jemima noted—did not lock it. Perhaps he too imagined the catch was, as it appeared to be, self-locking.

"I don't want anyone else coming up the route I took," he remarked casually. Jemima did not deign to answer.

Kevin John took one of the large white armchairs and placed it opposite her, with his back to the balcony. He gazed at her with his curiously unwinking blue stare.

"He'll fall asleep," thought Jemima scoffingly, "and then I'll grab the telephone. The police will break the lock." She was not carrying Pompey's private number with her since all her personal possessions, including—how foolish!— her handbag, were still in the first-floor flat. However under the circumstances, 999 would do just as well.

But Kevin John did not go to sleep. For some time he kept up a long self-pitying monologue on the subject of his relations with Chloe. He referred entirely to the past. The events of the last week were ignored as though they had not taken place: or perhaps he was hoping to tease Jemima into posing some pertinent questions. As it was, she did not respond. And not only was there self-pity; there was a perpetual air of self-justification in all he said.

"Beat her up!" he said at one point. "Of course I beat her up. For one thing she was a"—obscenity—"a Jezebel, a ruiner of good men's lives. And for another, mark you, she liked it."

Jemima, thinking that in some twisted way that was probably true—Chloe had both hated and been fascinated by the violence she produced in Kevin John—still would not answer.

But in the end it was Jemima who fell asleep, not Kevin John.

When she woke up, the sitting room was lit by candlelight— one short thick white candle in an opaque holder was standing on the glass table. It was dark outside except for the glow of the street lights. Kevin John was bending over her, or as it turned out, he was bending over the table itself, depositing a tray. It contained a bottle of wine, opened, two glasses, some digestive biscuits, and a large plate of sardines.

"Nothing for me to cook for our candlelight supper. Pity: I'm a wonderful cook. Almost as good as Chloe—was. But I've done my best. Not many provisions you've allowed yourself, by the way, something less than perfect as a housekeeper, aren't you? Do your television fans know? Fridge turned off as well. Warm wine—"

While he was talking, Jemima made a quickly planned dive and succeeded in grabbing the little white telephone. She was frantically dialling the second digit as Kevin John disentangled himself from the tray by dropping it and sprang towards her. In the mêlée the bottle of wine rolled over and liquid started flowing fast along the glass table, then splashing off it onto the carpet. Biscuits and sardines were mashed together into the thick pile.

Neither gesture—neither her lunge nor his counter-spring had any point. Kevin John wrenched the receiver out of her hand and listened to it; then it dawned on him that there was no dialling tone.

It was Jemima who said bitterly: "Cut off. This flat is empty, you know." Momentarily she became reckless as to what information she gave Kevin John.

"Then you—what are you doing here?" It was his first visible moment of uncertainty.

"Packing up. I moved downstairs after—after she was killed."

"It was luck, then, me finding you up here."

Jemima favoured him with her ironic smile, not the lovely open smile which made the public adore her on television, but the other smile, the one which made government spokesmen, for example, with weak cases to defend slightly uncomfortable in retrospect. "That Shore woman, not all sugar and spice, is she?" they would murmur questioningly in the direction of their wives once the interview had been shown.

"Luck, indeed."

"So who *does* know you are up here?" He was quick to pick up the point.

"The police," replied Jemima smoothly. "They gave me the keys. A police officer will be along to collect them shortly." Even to her own ears, the lie did not sound convincing. She did not dare consult her little gold bracelet watch, but she was aware it must be nearly midnight.

Kevin John snorted. His disbelief was clear.

For the first time Jemima found herself wondering rather desperately exactly when and by whom she would be missed. Not by Pompey, alas, nor by any member of the police force, or at any rate not for a very long while, longer than she cared to contemplate. The keys to Chloe's flat, destined for Miss Katy Aaronson, were to be left downstairs in the office suite.

Pompey had not taken the Montagu Square number although he could easily ascertain it if he so wished. The trouble was that Pompey and Jemima had made no precise plans for a future meeting, their relationship in general depending on *ad hoc* consultations on either side. Besides Jemima had a shrewd suspicion that with the arrest of Kevin John, Pompey would be free and thus obliged to spend the weekend taking cuttings for the autumn in his greenhouse under Mrs. Portsmouth's direction—for such he had predicted to be his fate.

"The gardening columns really get going at this time of year," he had confided to her with gloomy resignation. "And Mrs. Portsmouth gets going with them."

Miss Katy Aaronson was happily immured in the bosom of her family in Highgate enjoying the ritual of the Sabbath. Sir Richard Lionnel had picked up the broken threads of his life with astonishing ease and was at his home in the country—how quickly that abortive holiday with Chloe had been forgotten: the waters of fresh official engagements, such as entertaining that peregrinating minister, Lord Manfred, had already closed over his diary.

Frankly Jemima could not envisage anyone else likely to enquire about her whereabouts with any urgency. It was not that she did not have friends, lovers, admirers in plethora; just that she had taken the fatal decision to disappear in London . . . What an absurd ring the words now had in their original meaning!

Neither she nor Chloe had succeeded in bringing about any kind of effective disappearance. Something—no, someone—had caught up with Chloe in the flat she had pretended to abandon and pinned her down to it for ever like a butterfly in a case. Only in this case the pin had been a long sharp kitchen knife. .

As for Jemima, her disappearance out of her own background, away from Holland Park Mansions and Megalith Television, had only succeeded in plunging her into the far murkier waters of her friend's life. Now Jemima was human enough to wish profoundly that some zany impulse would cause her assistant at Megalith Television, Guthrie Carlyle, to question exactly where she might be, and pursue that thought with his usual executive efficiency. For that matter, when was her secretary, the ebullient Cherry, Flowering Cherry as she was sometimes admiringly known within Megalithic House, due back from Corfu? Jemima, who had so often suffered from Cherry's over-zealous arrangements, was depressed to remember that she was not in fact due back until the end of August, shortly before Jemima would be repossessed of Holland Park Mansions.

Jemima Shore had finally succeeded, quite inadvertently, in disappearing in London. It would be many days before anyone missed her in earnest and, so far as she knew, many days before anyone came to unlock the penthouse flat. Not that she really expected many days to pass in this ludicrous form of captivity. But Jemima was honest enough to admit that the unpleasant prospect was not absolutely out of the question.

It seemed even less out of the question the next morning when Jemima awoke into the dawn. An exhausted grey light filled the sitting room, more reminiscent of a long night past than redolent of the promise of day. She squinted at her watch. Close on five o'clock. The candle had guttered to a standstill. Congested wax had spilled onto the glass table. It joined the debris of the crashed tray which Kevin John had not allowed her to clear up the night before.

She was aware that some noise had caused her awakening. Kevin John was still sitting opposite her—for they had finally fallen asleep as they sat, she rejecting with unrepressed horror the offer of Chloe's bedroom. His eyes were closed; he was emitting gentle half sighs, half snoring sounds which reminded her of how many bottles of wine he had consumed the night before—unaided but also undisturbed by her abstinence. The penthouse was at least well stocked with wine. His sighs, however, were not responsible for her waking.

It was Tiger, a dark golden blur outside the balcony window, who had roused her with his delicate infant's wail. He looked and sounded reproachful. Jemima guessed he was hungry. Knowing that she could open the balcony window, her first impulse was to let him in and feed him with the remnants of the sardines from Kevin John's tinned supper. Then she realized that here was a possible opportunity to summon help—supposing there was anyone around to summon at 5 A.M. in Bloomsbury on a Sunday morning.

A note dropped, perhaps? One thing she did not propose to attempt was a descent via the scaffolding; and she had a gloomy feeling that the kitchen door to the fire escape at the back—poor Valentine Brighton's voyeur's route—would have been well and truly locked by the police.

"Don't do it, darling," said Kevin John with only a flicker of his eyelashes to indicate wakefulness. "*If* I'm the bully boy the police say I am, I wouldn't hesitate to cast you off the balcony after the keys would I, rather than let you yodel for help? Wait till you've solved our little problem. Then we'll both celebrate together."

He put out his arm, brown, hairy, and very strong-looking, exposed from the sleeve of his white shirt, which was now like his grey trousers in a very crumpled condition.

"I was going to feed the cat."

"Let him starve. I loathe cats: selfish little buggers. When do they ever put down a saucer of milk for you and me? Even worse than women."

"He might appreciate the sardines more than I did."

"Not a fishy sniff shall he have till you come up with your solution."

But it was not until nearly eight o'clock, when the slight Bloomsbury bustle indicated the beginning of modest Sunday traffic, that Jemima finally agreed to listen.

Under the promise of coffee—thank God the remaining stores

in the flat did not consist solely of white Muscadet—she bent her weary mind yet again to the problem of Chloe's murder. It had after all obsessed her all the week, until Kevin John's bullying had brought about a counter-reaction.

Besides, she had in mind asking for a bath once he was sufficiently mollified. The hot water system was still working. Tiger by this time had vanished, and she hoped that he had managed to scavenge a meal elsewhere.

"If not you, then who?" It was the old question: Who, Who? "I'll accept your premise that you're innocent for the time being. Hostages can't be choosers. So long as you let me have another cup of coffee."

"The bitch—I refer to your late friend—was meeting someone up here. I never believed that crap about looking for her notebook. Passed it on to the police, mind you. I could see it only made things worse for me if they thought I'd surprised her with someone else. Then I really might have done her in."

"And him, too, I suppose."

Kevin John favoured her with a boyish smile. "Not necessarily, darling. We men stick together. We'd probably have a lot in common if she treated him as badly as she treated me. You know, the sweetness, the sex—she was very keen on that by the way, breathless, begging for it—then the torture of it, the infidelity, never knowing where she was. Oh Christ—"

He put his great black head in his hands.

"She's dead now," said Jemima in a softer voice. "And we're going to find out who did it. Look, I'll buy that," she went on more rapidly, "the fact she was meeting someone else. I've had my suspicions all along. Little things—the petticoat she wore, for example. Chloe was so particular, wasn't she? When she was working," she added hastily. "Then there's the question of her other lovers. Three of them. Bear with me—" She raised her hand as he gave a half groan. "You want the truth. You promised to help me."

Kevin John poured himself yet another glass of white wine. "Shoot, sweetheart," he said. Jemima herself swigged her coffee in great gulps from the oatmeal-coloured mug.

"After you split up, Chloe had three lovers. I'll call them, with great originality, A, B and C. A was a young man, a kind of drop-out, squatter, whatever you like, she knew him in Fulham.

He also came here with her, to this building, probably not to this flat, squatted on another floor—"

To her surprise, Kevin John interrupted her: "A is for Adam," he said heavily. "I know that. She told me about him. She boasted about him—the young body, like a Greek god, all that kind of shit. She could be very cruel, you know. That was the last time we met. In Fulham. So he was here, was he? Well, why the hell don't the police think *he* killed her?" His indignation was gathering momentum. "Why pick on me?"

Jemima hesitated. Kevin John obviously did not know that Adam had sworn to seeing him leaving the building, evidence corroborated by an outside witness.

"Lack of motive chiefly. And lack of proof. I believe he has some kind of alibi. The police also don't think he did it because they think you did, I suppose. He *could* have killed her. He could have come up the fire escape from the third-floor flat." Jemima briefly described Adam's hideout.

"And what do you think?"

"I suppose I think he's not the killing type."

"And I am? Poor Kevin John, a lambkin among mankind, to be labelled a killing type just because he lays about him with his fists when the drink is in him—"

"Did you know Chloe was pregnant?" Jemima interrupted the tirade.

Sudden tears came into his eyes. "The police told me. Asked me if I was responsible. Of course I wasn't. The only child we had, we could have had, *she* killed. That was a killing—a real killing—she said we weren't getting on, I was drinking—true enough, but it was *her* fault—she drove me to it."

"I believe this Adam was the father."

"There's your motive then!" The change of mood was mercurial. "The young fellow doesn't want to be a father, kills her to avoid the responsibility. You know what the young are." He gave a ghastly parody of a Harrods' matron's accent.

"A bit far-fetched, isn't it? In an age of abortion on demand. Besides, you haven't heard about B and C yet."

"Get on with it then!"

"B was a man of substance, a famous man, whom Chloe hoped would marry her. We think she intended to palm off this baby on him; she certainly intended to use it to lure him away from his wife. B certainly had a motive to murder Chloe, scandal, a lot to lose. But unlike A who had opportunity but not motive, B had no opportunity. B, you see, was having lunch in Soho with his wife. It is also unlikely that B would arrange a rendezvous in the penthouse—but that's another matter."

"I suppose you won't tell me who B was?"

"Correct. You haven't heard about C yet. I think I ought to call him X rather than C because X is the man of mystery in all this. Someone unknown whom she met in the square gardens. One night when she was locked out of here, forgot her key. A casual encounter she called it. Supposing she was meeting that person, X, up here."

"And he goes and does her in? Why?"

"I don't know yet. Maybe he sees her with you, gets the wrong impression."

"And that might be anyone!" exclaimed Kevin John. "That bitch was capable of having it off in the bushes with anyone, man, woman, in between—"

"You've no clues? Nothing she said?"

"My God!" he stopped. "No, that's impossible."

"Nothing's impossible. It's not even impossible that *you* killed her. Anyone leaving the building? Anyone she talked about?"

"What I was going to say, that's what I meant is impossible. But, wait, another train of thought. A famous man you said, a man of substance. Another impossible thing. That man, the tycoon, Lionnel—"

"You *knew* then—"

"Wait, Lionnel, the monster who put up this appalling building, but not such a monster after all, a man of taste and judgement, since he bought one of my pictures. Binnie Rapallo fixed it and since she has no taste whatsoever, he must have some himself. That Saturday, morning, lunchtime, whenever it was—I was so pissed, *and* pissed off—I saw him. I ran away from him. Didn't want to talk about any damn modern art under the circumstances, as you may imagine. You know what tycoons are, buy your work, and think they own you, including your merest conversation."

"Where was he?"

"Outside this building. Coming from the Tottenham Court Road. Walking very fast. I thought he was coming towards me. I had the impression he ducked. Perhaps he saw me, or someone else he knew. I veered off. I was pissed as a newt, as I told you."

"The time?"

"How the hell do I know? As I left the building. Whatever the police say. It was odd that he was walking so fast. I remember thinking that. I thought tycoons were unhurried. Or else had chauffeurs. Or both."

Silence fell between them. Kevin John poured yet another glass of wine. Through Jemima's orderly mind were proceeding the following thoughts: not Lady Lionnel leaving the restaurant early in a taxi, but Sir Richard fetching that taxi for her; Sir Richard running out into the street in the absence of his chauffeur; evidence not given by Stavros to the police because it touched on a family row and Sir Richard was a good customer. Valentine's dying words—"He came back"; Lionnel walking fast to Adelaide Square from "The Little Athens," only a few minutes away across the Tottenham Court Road, and back again . . . About 1:30, the time Kevin John left the building . . . About the time Chloe Fontaine was killed. Above all, Valentine's "He came back."

Sir Richard Lionnel with motive *and* opportunity . . . Had the queen, shut up in her tower, succeeded in spinning straw into gold?

Chapter Seventeen

Lovers in Disguise

"Now let me go," said Jemima. "I've kept my word."

"You think he did it—that art-loving tycoon. Why is it, incidentally, that all the worst of them are art-loving?" Kevin John still sounded lugubrious. But he did not stop her when she walked to the balcony and pressed the catch to open it. "Puss—Tiger—" she called into the morning air. Its freshness was a relief. But Tiger, once scorned, did not reappear.

"I need to prove it. The police too will want proof. I need to talk to Stavros, the owner of the restaurant."

"A Greek colonel, eh? All those bastards are in league together."

"No, an honest man. But a businessman."

"If I let you go, what happens if you shop me to the police?"

"Shop you! You're on a murder charge already. Have you forgotten?" Dazed with wine and lack of sleep, perhaps Kevin John had forgotten. "Next problem," Jemima continued briskly, "is how we get out. Do you recommend hollering blue murder—sorry, red innocence—flying a white flag, or dropping a brick on the head of the nearest passer-by in Adelaide Square—"

A mumble sounding like: "You've promised, Jemima Shore, Investigator," was his only reply. And then: "You'll see me all right." Jemima had an awful fear that the drink was overtaking him. True to her dread, Kevin John slipped further down the chair and finally onto the floor. He had fallen asleep or at least into that coma-like state which with him passed for sleep.

Oh my God, she thought, now how do I escape? Hollering was the least attractive of the alternatives. She did not wish for public attention at this moment: she needed to get to "The Little Athens," re-examine Stavros, work out a few times precisely, and then perhaps call Pompey with new evidence.

It might be easier to break a lock. Jemima inspected the kitchen door to the fire escape. The bolt she could draw back, but the police had also locked the door, and the key was missing. The glass was reinforced with wire. The front door was out of the question.

There was nothing for it but the balcony. Kevin John did not move as she stepped onto it. She was grateful for that. If she had to cry for help—with all the possible public consequences—she would prefer not to be accompanied by a drunken artist out on bail for murder.

Inspection of the scaffolding provided a happy surprise. Jemima had imagined that Kevin John's successive scalings of it had been an example of exaggerated intrepidity possibly due to inebriation. Now she saw that anyone even moderately athletic, with a head for heights (or the self-discipline not to look downwards), could have achieved this feat. The scaffolding was stoutly built, a credit to the Lionnel Estates. Even Kevin John's ability to elude public notice during his climbs was now more explicable. The scaffolding was quite deep as well as securely slung together. A man could well have worked there, in the shadow of the building, and not been spotted by a random passer-by.

Right. Where a drunken Kevin John Athlone could ascend, a sober Jemima Shore could descend. Slipping off her golden thonged sandals, which laced up her legs, Jemima tested her toes against the metal. Her dress remained a problem. Was a Jean Muir silk jersey dress, with all its virtues, really the right apparel in which to shin down scaffolding? It was tempting to strip to her bra and pants—but the arguments against reaching the ground in her underclothes, like those of crying for help accompanied by a man on a murder charge, were conclusive. Jean Muir it would have to be.

With brilliant improvisation, or so it struck her at the time, Jemima belted the flowing dress twice round her narrow waist with the gold thongs from her sandals. Barefoot, she embarked.

The journey was not so much long as, in spite of the solidity of the scaffolding, nerve-wracking. With relief, Jemima flopped down onto the staging-post of the concrete third-floor balcony. It was fortunate that she did not suffer from vertigo; she felt she might do so in future.

She was immediately aware—with another spasm of relief—of the presence of Tiger. Sleekly, he rolled onto his back at her feet, revealing the pale yellow fur of his tummy, and began to purr. This unprecedented friendliness was no doubt to be explained by the presence of a large bowl of milk in the corner of the balcony, and another bowl of something chopped, white enough to be chicken. There was a smaller saucer of water.

All in all, Jemima was not totally surprised—but once more relieved—to find the balcony window slightly ajar. At least she would be saved further perilous descent.

She peered through the smoked glass without being able to discern anything very clear except the confused swirl of that subterranean blue and something which looked like low modern furniture on the floor, cushions perhaps, which had not been there before. She inched the window open.

Then and only then the confused shapes of the cushions separated themselves and became white or rather pale; they also became two shapes. A Laocoon-like figure, writhing legs and arms, on the floor, resolved itself into Adam Adamson, naked; some unknown figure, equally naked except for a string of gold chains, rose hastily but gracefully from the floor, like some greyhound starting, gave a much less elegant squawk of dismay, and vanished in the direction of the subterranean bathroom.

Adam Adamson, undismayed, lolled back on his elbow.

"Pallas Athena," he said. "What strange moments goddesses choose to call. I was just tangling with the goddess Artemis, as you may have noticed." He gazed at her.

His body had that confidence of nakedness associated with statues of the gods.

He went on: "Yes, in that strange tunic effect and bare feet you really do look like a goddess. Why don't I imitate you and slip into something similar?" He rose, strolled into the bathroom in his turn and re-emerged with a towel knotted round his waist. Only the ugly geometric design, in keeping with the rest of the flat's aggressively modern décor, disturbed the picture.

Behind him, at least an inch taller, and clad in a bright green cat-suit, lurked a young woman with a highly sulky expression. From her small head, disdainfully carried on the long neck, and excessively long legs and narrow flanks, she might have been a model.

"The goddess Athena, the goddess Artemis," Adam waved his hand.

"Miss Shore and I have met," said the goddess Artemis; her accent was more gracious than her expression. Extending her hand, whose long fingers were serrated in gold rings, in a parody of a bountiful greeting, the girl in the green cat-suit said: "I'm Laura Barrymore, Isabelle Mancini's assistant."

Had they ever met? Jemima really did not remember. There were many Laura Barrymores in the world. Nor did she particularly care, for that matter, why and wherefore Laura Barrymore was passing the time of day with Adam Adamson. Her concern was to find her way out of this flat and to a telephone. Then she could raise Stavros, Pompey, even Sir Richard Lionnel himself. The keys to the first-floor, which now seemed like a paradise of a refuge, were still in her pocket.

Baldly, she addressed herself to Adam: "Get me out of here. I don't care what you're doing here, by the way, just let me out. No questions to you, none to me."

Adam raised an eyebrow but it was the measure of his unhurried self-confidence that he seemed prepared to do as she asked without further ado. It was Laura Barrymore who disturbed this amity.

"Miss Shore, I am truly aware that you must be wondering," she began in a rush, "but on my honour, I swear to you that I first came here with the absolute firm intention of rescuing Isabelle's letters, letters from that dreadful woman, well, of course one doesn't want to speak ill of the dead—" she paused, having evidently lost track of her explanation, then continued more firmly. "That Saturday morning, you remember, when you telephoned. I thought that if *you* were in Miss Fontaine's flat, we could search together, you're famous for being so warm and understanding about human problems, I could explain to you—"

Jemima shot Laura Barrymore a look which was anything but symptomatic of those warm qualities recently ascribed to her.

Adam, who continued to regard Jemima with a slight smile, threw in: "It's true you know," he said. "Our friend was fairly on the prowl. The trouble was she came to the wrong flat, and then, as they say, one thing led to another. I read her some Petrarch when I discovered what her name was and that seemed to turn her on. I never could resist goddesses you know. That coldness, that aloof air—"

"She was here—a week ago—" exclaimed Jemima incredulously.

"Oh yes, for a couple of happy hours. She went back and found her friend—shall we call her the goddess Hera, another jealous type—had arrived back unexpectedly from Paris, was there waiting for her."

Jemima addressed herself directly to the girl.

"Is that true?"

But by this time Laura Barrymore, who had been knotting her long streaky blonde hair the while and pinning it on top of her head, had fully recovered her poise.

"And if it is," she enquired coldly, "what the fuck is it to do with you?" The refinement of her voice, from which all the mid-atlantic was now missing, made the obscenity sound far worse than it might have done, for example, on the vigorous lips of Kevin John Athlone.

"The police knew. I told them," contributed Adam in a tone of mock helpfulness. "You particularly instructed me to tell them everything."

Yes, thought Jemima, not the killing type indeed; although there might be something to be said about Adam Adamson along the lines of not loving wisely but too often. And too precipitately. Still, as Miss Barrymore had so aptly observed, it was nothing to do with her. Adam's alibi, in its full irony, was now revealed; and the future of Isabelle Mancini and Laura Barrymore was even less her concern than that of Adam and Laura.

For her, another chase was on. The fox was Sir Richard Lionnel.

Adam Adamson went to the door, and towel-clad as he was, swept it open with style.

At this point Jemima observed with some surprise that the third-floor flat, the dark-blue subterranean cave, bore more rather than fewer signs of occupation than when she was last inside it. The image of the writhing white furniture had not been totally illusory. There were two new white plastic shapes on the dark floor; pushed together they might serve as some form of armchair or even sofa. Recently, however, they had been pushed widely apart; Jemima had a mental image that this had been effected by the athletic coupling of Adam and Laura.

There were other new traces of domesticity including a small table and some lamps. Yet by any reasonable calculations Adam should have given the place a wide berth once he had made his statement to the police. That had taken place on Sunday morning. A week ago. Even the most ardent revivifier might have twitched his cloak and passed on to fresh squares and buildings new after an experience like that.

Disregarding Laura Barrymore, who was now coldly buffing a long and glittering pearlized nail, Jemima said abruptly to Adam: "You come and go as you please. Revivifying—squatting— whatever you call it. That's not quite the picture I get. You *live* here. That furniture wasn't here before. Explain if only to satisfy my curiosity. Then we'll both go out of each other's lives."

"Why shouldn't he be here?" Laura Barrymore had glided to the position she seemed to prefer, which was just behind Adam's shoulder, her small snake's head clearly visible above it. "It's his flat, isn't it?"

"Oh come now," Jemima spoke coldly—the interjections of this grass-green Lamia were beginning to irritate her. "To call it actually *his*—isn't that carrying revivification rather too far? Does Isabelle plan an article on the subject in *Taffeta*? 'Back to Adam—modern style' with photographs?" These remarks, Jemima realized the moment she had uttered them, were not exactly those of the all-wise goddess she wished at this moment to personify. Adam clearly shared her opinion.

"I realize now to the full the difficulties presented by life upon Olympus," he remarked plaintively.

Jemima smiled, her own sense of the absurd restored. "How do you cast yourself then?" she could not resist asking. "Please don't suggest Dionysus. No one I assure you is going to tear *you* into pieces . . ."

"Something in disguise," he said gently. "A minor god in a minor disguise. Perhaps I should reintroduce myself. We are all sons of Adam, as I told you, but I am also the son of Aaron. Adam Adamson by choice, preferring the old Adam to the old Aaron, but Adam Aronson by birth."

"Ah!" A short pause. "Adam, brother of Katy. The brilliant one who dropped out from Cambridge."

"Where he was studying architecture. The same."

"How much of the rest of it was lies?"

"It depends on one's attitude to the truth. I first had the idea of revivifying this building from listening to my sister. She's an admirable girl, but no lover of the arts, to be frank. Listening to her endless disquisitions on the subject of Sir Richard Lionnel—she's madly in love with him of course—she and Francesca Lionnel have an unspoken alliance to fend off the rest—and thinking him only slightly less monstrous than his own building, I started to demonstrate. Katy didn't like it: she never really likes anything I do, ever since I got a scholarship to Cambridge and then dropped out, the scholarship she wasn't allowed to take. But she loves me all the same—in spite of everything—Adam, the baby brother, the only son, the boy. There's family life for you. You have a family?"

Jemima shook her head.

"How wise. To return to the sad story of this benighted building: at which point my late and lightsome friend, Miss Dollie Stover as was, quite coincidentally persuaded me to move in. From the street to the third floor. One of her reckless gestures, I suppose. Slipped me a key. She also seemed to dislike both the décor of the third floor—good thinking—and the woman who was responsible for it. A woman with a ridiculous name. Bunny something or other. I was her secret vengeance on this Bunny."

"Binnie," murmured Jemima.

"Nothing loath, I took the hint. I didn't reveal my connections. Nor for that matter did she reveal hers. We both as it were pulled the thickly woven expensive wool carpet of fantasy over each other's eyes. She, the mistress of the tycoon, posing as the skittish little-girl-loose; me, the brother of the tycoon's assistant posing as the squatter-in-danger-of-the-law." At this point Laura Barrymore attempted to put one long serpentine arm round Adam's neck. Laura *entière à sa proie attachée*, thought Jemima. But Adam disengaged himself with a brisk movement and said: "Not round the neck, I can't bear being strangled by women."

It did not sound as if he was altogether joking. Then he went on: "After I spoke to the police, Katy fixed it for me. Made it legitimate. That's her secret aim in life, I suppose, and this time I let her have her way. This is my flat now. The Lion's Den is now Adam's Garden of Eden: you see, Sir Richard did not care for the décor for some odd reason."

"Isn't it funny, Katy Aaronson and I were at school together?" Laura put in suddenly, with a return to her gracious manner. "Quite a coincidence."

But Jemima did not care to stay and examine the coincidence. She did not think Adam would linger very long in Miss Barrymore's snake-like embrace; she had probably served her purpose, as Katy Aaronson had in a sense served hers. Unlike Chloe Fontaine, née Dollie Stover, formerly of Folkstone, Adam Adamson née Aaronson, formerly of Highgate, was a survivor.

Back on the first floor, Jemima knew the first telephone call she had to make.

"Sir Richard," she began in her most formal manner. "This is Jemima Shore, Investigator." To her surprise he had answered the telephone himself. Perhaps by Sunday Sir Richard was bored in the country. It was certainly the impression given by his alacrity in answering her call.

"I would like you to talk to me; to come up to London and talk to me." Whatever the rival claims of the minister and Lady Manfred—or the Medea-like Lady Lionnel—Sir Richard showed no hesitation in accepting her invitation. Nor did he hesitate when she named Chloe's penthouse flat as their rendezvous.

"You have the keys?"

"Yes, the police gave them to me so I could pack up my things."

Jemima did not think it necessary to add that she had recently repossessed herself of them, having found them lying untouched in the gutter of Adelaide Square where they had fallen from on high, hurled by Kevin John.

With some strange feeling of the relentless pursuit of coincidence, Jemima found the rendezvous fixed for one o'clock. Or between one and two, depending on the traffic. Sunday. Eight days since Chloe had died.

She put down the receiver; she thought to make two other telephone calls. The first was to Stavros, already at "The Little Athens." The second call was to Isabelle Mancini.

She did not call Pompey.

Then she went for the last time onto the balcony of the first floor and gazed into the gardens. At this level the trees were more like barricades than floating galleons with the tops of their masts visible. The over-high parapet was like another barricade. It was odd how depopulated the gardens remained: in the other Bloomsbury gardens roundabout people desported themselves, lay on the dry and yellowing grass, looked upwards and imagined themselves on a perpetual bank holiday in the country. The bars which surrounded the gardens of Adelaide Square—a virtual cage with two gates, one at either end—constituted an effective discouragement. One could not readily imagine a passer-by climbing the railings.

Yet someone *had* climbed them—two people in fact. Chloe Fontaine had climbed them one hot summer's night, locked out without her keys including her own resident's key to the enclosure. And there she had on her own admission indulged in a carnal encounter with someone described by Pompey in his vein of wit, as a Sunday newspaper headline: The Lover in the Gardens. As Jemima gazed towards the forbidding railings and slightly depressing late summer shrubs, other memories floated back to her, not only Chloe's voice from the past—"Still it was an interesting experience . . . rather a surprise altogether"—but other murmurs, from the people linked to Chloe in her life, now cruelly linked to each other by her death—for as long as the identity of her own murderer should be unknown. Once it was known, then the links would be broken.

The identity of that lover—another lover in disguise as Adam had been her, Jemima's, lover, and also Chloe's lover, in disguise—had it perhaps been staring her in the face all along? An identity which gave not only motive but opportunity.

Certain things for the first time became clear to her. More than ever, Jemima needed to confront Sir Richard Lionnel.

Chapter Eighteen

That Fatal Saturday

As she re-entered the penthouse, Jemima felt all the old dread returning. Yet on this occasion it was tension for the role she knew she had to play rather than fear of the unknown which gripped her. For her, there were to be no more surprises in the short sad tale of the Chloe Mystery, only an unravelling which would also bring sorrow and a new form of tragedy in its wake. All the same, tension and a kind of nervous excitement would not be banished. It was almost as if the flat itself was aware of the strange concourse of people which Jemima, like Hagen in *Gotterdämmerung,* had summoned to the cause of revenge.

She herself was no longer the tunic-skirted, bare-footed goddess of the morning's flight. Immaculate in a plain navy-blue dress with white collar and short sleeves, she was deliberately presenting her most unruffled image, what Cy Fredericks of Megalith was apt to term "your Jemima of Arc bit." Golden bell of hair carefully controlled, dark stockings on her long legs above the high-heeled scarlet sandals, she smiled grimly at the irony of this single, unavoidable splash of red. Her gold sandals, thongless, were still in the penthouse flat. She did not wish to present herself as the avenging angel, not quite in that lurid light; but her television training had made her automatically select those elements in her small wardrobe which would make up the appropriate passionless appearance.

Already thus attired, she had called on Adam Adamson on her way up and invited him to attend some kind of mystery conference. Where he was concerned, mystery was, she knew, the right note to strike. Standing at the door of the third-floor flat—now his own domain—he was wearing the same clothes in which he had first waylaid her: white T-shirt, as pristine as Jemima's own dress, and jeans which looked newly washed. Should his cleanliness have made her more suspicious of his credentials as a squatter? On the other hand it had seemed logical that a revivifier should present a clean face to the world, and Adam himself had always rejected the label of squatter.

"You can bring Laura with you, too, if she's around. And Tiger, for that matter, who seems to have grown attached to you. Though I should warn you that Isabelle Mancini is due to arrive upstairs at any minute. And she's apt to be rather strong on the subject of disloyalty as she sees it."

Adam smiled and indicated the floor of the flat with that grandiose wave of the hand he generally used to indicate the works of Sir Richard Lionnel. It looked like a very expensive luggage boutique: suitcases of all shapes and sizes, burgundy-coloured Cartier, Gucci, Hermès, any brand of luggage where initials were apt to be strewn all over the cloth or leather or tapestry, including innumerable small dressing-cases, were spread about.

"I think I've discovered that for myself," he said. "These came round in a taxi with a letter which should by rights have ignited the paper it was written on. Laura tells me that Dollie—Chloe—wanted to make use of Isabelle's love letters. I can only suppose she had never received her written insults else she would have made use of them. This one was definitely worthy of inclusion in some anthology or novel."

His next words reminded Jemima that Adam, among his other qualities, had always been able to read her thoughts.

"Not very long, I think," he went on. "The luggage, I mean, its stay on this particular floor. Laura should really share a flat with Katy, don't you think? They both, in their different ways, need to strike out. Thank you for the invitation: Laura and Tiger and I will be happy to attend your mystery conference."

To Kevin John, Jemima merely said, much more briskly: "There's going to be a reception. A reception and an explanation. Are you up to it?"

"Who am I going to receive?" He had greeted her return with a cry of joy and the words: "I knew you would come back and rescue me." Then he gazed at her mesmerically with those vast blue eyes, which only the depth of their hue rescued from being cold and even calculating.

Otherwise her entry was something of an anticlimax after the dramas of her previous arrivals. It was a relief merely to find

Kevin John sitting in the white armchair, alive, and even fresh-looking. His hair, which was flopping over his forehead, gave the impression of being newly washed. Not much could be done about his crumpled white shirt and grey trousers, but his tie was fastened, and the jacket of his suit flung over his shoulders with some attempt at style.

Jemima's first thought was of relief that he was no longer drunk. He did not even smell of alcohol, but, Jemima noticed wryly, of her own Mary Chess sandalwood bath oil which he must have found in the bathroom and poured out in quantities. Her second thought was to be surprised all over again, now he was tidied up, by his amazing good looks, undiminished by Time's rough hand.

Kevin John had also done some kind of tidying-up job on the flat itself. The mess of sardines and biscuits had been eliminated—quite efficiently; but then Kevin John, who had boasted of being a good cook, was no doubt a good cleaner as well.

There was one further change. On the floor, Chloe's own novels had been turned over onto their backs. Now all there was to be seen was the title *Fallen Child, Fallen Child,* over and over again. Jemima wondered if Kevin John, rather than the police, had been responsible for the original montage of accusing helpless photographs which she had found when she re-entered the penthouse. If so, he had repented of the gesture.

"*You* are not going to receive anyone," she told him, "But through this door will come in a matter of time a small procession. Then we'll have a reception followed by an explanation. As for the guests—why not let their identity remain a surprise? But first I have to test something."

Jemima opened the cupboard in the corner of the sitting room, looked in then shut the door again, leaving Kevin John murmuring rather dazedly: "A party, does she mean there's going to be a party—here? Maybe I should ask Dixie—no, Dixie's a bastard, ask Croesus, Croesus is a good fellow." He found the word Croesus very difficult to pronounce clearly.

Shortly after Jemima returned, the door was pushed open and Adam Adamson stood in the doorway. Tiger, a golden familiar, crouched on his shoulder. Laura Barrymore, another golden familiar, followed him. She had obviously dug into her expensive suitcases, since she had changed the bright green cat-suit for a pair of scarlet and black printed tigerskin trousers and a transparent scarlet chiffon blouse; across this her numerous gold chains and red beads acted as a necessary breast plate. She no longer looked like a serpent, but with her spare curved body and hair now braided, she looked like some blonde Indian warrior.

Before Laura had time to construct one of her gracious greetings, there was a noise behind her as though of some vessel propelled forward by a series of noisy gusts of wind. Isabelle Mancini, when she appeared, puffing heavily from the effort of the stairs, did indeed resemble some kind of stalwart ship, a trireme perhaps, her flailing arms in their grey draperies representing the oars. She also retained a certain splendid dignity as, chin well forward, black hair strained back, she swept rather than pushed Laura out of the way, ignoring Adam altogether, and entered the penthouse flat.

Then and only then did Isabelle judge the moment right to give a scream, as though at some monstrous sight, a freak of nature: "Terr-r—rible child! Tr-r-raitor! What are you doing here? Tell me! Speak! I demand you speak at once! Speak! Talk to me of your disloyalty, your t-r-r-r-eachery . . ." It would never be known whether Laura Barrymore would indeed have spoken on these interesting topics, let alone whether Isabelle Mancini would have drawn breath for long enough for her to be allowed to do so. For at that moment there was a new, and in its own way more dramatic, arrival.

Sir Richard Lionnel, perhaps because he was the owner of the stairs, positively bounded up them. There was no trace in his energetic manner and fit stride of the gravity with which he had entered the flat a week ago, accompanied by Pompey. His tonsured ring of black curly hair sprang from his head in its devil's horns, and his black eyes snapped and glittered with something which looked very like anticipatory joy.

I am sorry, Sir Richard, thought Jemima, when she had received him, crossing her dark-stockinged knees discreetly and tugging at her short navy-blue skirt, these red shoes—which it was impossible to underplay—are not a portent. This is not a rendezvous. Nor do I wish to decorate the third-floor flat, or this flat, or any of your dwellings. Nor even live permanently in Montagu Square which no doubt you would offer me.

But Sir Richard, if disappointed or even quite simply amazed by the array of people he found before him in the white sitting room, now with its balcony windows drawn right back, remained imperturbable. He greeted each person in turn with great urbanity as though welcoming directors to a board meeting of uncertain temper. Isabelle Mancini found the article on his wife and Parrot Park in *Taffeta* enthusiastically recalled—"the best photographs of Francesca ever taken—what was the girl's name?" Laura Barrymore, who it transpired had acted as editorial assistant on this feature, got a polite salute but no more, which led Jemima to suppose that she was one of the few members of the female sex Sir Richard did not find personally fascinating. Laura, visibly pulling herself together after Isabelle's assault, managed a sketchy imitation of her former gracious manner.

The encounter which had caused Jemima the most anxiety in anticipation was that between Sir Richard and Kevin John. But once again a diversion robbed it of its full flavour. It had to be faced that the ugly look had returned to Kevin John's face, making him more bull-like and less overtly handsome in his decayed film-star fashion. Also he loosened the tie at his neck, an automatic gesture which Jemima did not like the look of, and there was a knotted vein beating at the corner of his temple. But at this moment Laura Barrymore, someone with an obvious gift for choosing the dramatic moment for her appearance—and in this case her disappearance—gave a shriek, and clutched her gilded throat.

"Isabelle—Adam—together?" she cried through a series of sobs in which her accent became more and more refined like that of the transformed Eliza Doolittle. "This is utterly intolerable." And throwing out her long arms, so that her tight golden bracelets flashed, she fled down the penthouse stairs and out of sight. This time, after an interval of slightly stunned silence during which the others present looked mainly at their toes or, in the case of Sir Richard Lionnel, out of the window, the front door was heard opening and shutting.

Isabelle was the first to break the silence. "Idiot gir-r-rl!" she exclaimed. "Where will she go? Dressed up like that at lunchtime, after all I have taught her." But there was a gleam of satisfaction in her eye. Isabelle smelt victory. Jemima thought the expensive suitcases would soon be making the return journey from Adelaide Square.

"Why don't the rest of you all sit down?" Jemima spoke with determination before the spell of their silence could be broken. At this, she was faintly amused to see that the four remaining participants in the mystery conference reacted exactly according to character. Kevin John relapsed rather than sat back into the large white armchair he had previously occupied.

Sir Richard Lionnel ushered Isabelle towards the white sofa, helped her to sit down with a certain solicitousness, and then, remarking politely: "Thank you, I myself prefer to stand," took up his station with his back to the balcony. He had already lit one of his black cigarettes, which he was smoking rapidly, flicking the ash in the direction of the grey and white plants. Whether by choice or chance, he was situated so that his expression could not be checked.

Adam Adamson, without saying a word, sat down exactly where he had been standing, not far from the doorway; he descended cross-legged as though he were a piece of furniture which had been neatly folded up to save space. Then he murmured *sotto voce:* "Speak, goddess."

Jemima seated herself beside the sitting-room cupboard, in an oatmeal swivel-backed office chair which she had never occupied. It was—had been—Chloe's writing chair. In her brief interlude of peace in the flat, Jemima had instinctively avoided it. Now it seemed the right place from which to speak in her capacity of recording, if not avenging, angel.

"First of all, this is a story of love," Jemima began, without further preamble. "Love and of course later on death. But primarily a story of love. I thought we were dealing with hatred, and all the time we were dealing with love. Until I got that emphasis right, thanks to a chance remark by one of you quite recently, I never began to understand the truth about the death of Chloe Fontaine. Oddly enough the police—Detective Chief Inspector Portsmouth—got that right from the first. All the stabs. He said to me: 'sign of a lover, more likely than not.'"

At this point Sir Richard Lionnel threw away his black Sobranie and immediately lit another one.

"Miss Shore, if I understand you right"—he spoke still with urbanity, but the impatience was not totally disguised; the drags on his cigarette were also faster—"you have asked us all here on a Saturday morning to tell us about the death of poor Chloe Fontaine. If that is so, aren't you rather preempting the work of the police? And possibly, if I may say so, rather embarrassing our friend here?"

"I'm not your friend, you bastard," said Kevin John thickly. "*She's* my friend and my darling, Jemima Shore, Investigator. I asked her to solve the mystery of the universe and she has. As for the police"—he made an extremely rude gesture—"that's for them, all of them, the long and the short and the tall of them. I need a drink." He rose heavily to his feet and shambled off to the kitchen, returning with a bottle of wine and one glass which he proceeded to fill, drink down and fill again. No invitations to share the wine were given, and no one present appeared to regret this fact.

"A story of love," resumed Jemima as though none of these interruptions had taken place. "And all of you here, in your different ways, loved Chloe. It's what you properly have in common, it's what links you together, much more than your common implication in her death."

Isabelle frowned. "But Jemima, my darling," she began in a puzzled voice, " 'e did it. Ver-r-ry sad. A cr-r-rime of passion— 'oo does not understand it? But 'e did it." She indicated Kevin John, proceeding at that moment relentlessly to his third glass of wine. " 'E was drunk, of course; *mais quand même*." Isabelle shrugged her shoulders.

Jemima ignored her. "That's why it's as well that Laura has left us. Because Laura Barrymore certainly did not love Chloe Fontaine. She would have been the odd one out in our chain, broken the links. But for the rest of you: let us take you first, Sir Richard. No, Isabelle, let me speak. You, Sir Richard, loved her. She fascinated you; she was your romantic type, as you told me yourself, wayward, emotional, unpredictable as she was in everything except her work, the exact opposite to those strong sensible women with whom you take care to surround yourself on the domestic front, your wife, his sister"—she pointed to Adam. "No, Isabelle, let me go on."

"She, Chloe, represented danger, didn't she? That was half the point of it all. The penthouse flat in your own building, the secret holiday. Unfortunately Chloe saw things from exactly the other angle. When Chloe decided that you represented for her security, money, protection and the abandoning of the endless struggle to support herself in the world's most precarious livelihood, novel-writing, in favour of ease and luxury, including luxury to write if she so wished—well, you weren't interested were you?"

"You're right about one thing, Miss Shore," Sir Richard spoke without emotion. "In my own way, I did love her. Having said that, as far as I'm concerned there's really no more to be said on this rather distasteful subject, so if you will excuse me—"

"Ah, but forgive me, there is. Quite a lot more to be said. You see, Chloe—in her own way a very determined woman even if her objectives were sometimes a little ill-defined—had decided that nothing would satisfy her but security, the security of marriage. And that meant obliging you to leave your wife, something you were manifestly loath to do. For one thing, Lady Lionnel is an extremely jealous woman not likely to relinquish her husband of many years' standing without a struggle. Then you, particularly at the present time, had a great deal to fear from scandal, with a grand new job coming up.

"No, Sir Richard, it was a delicate operation to make you get a divorce. Chloe knew that. Then, when fate dealt her an unexpected card in the shape of pregnancy, she made the mistake of thinking it was an ace. She thought she could persuade you into marriage by the lever of the child. Whereas in fact the card was not an ace, but the most diabolical kind of joker—for not only was the child *not* yours, as she herself was well aware, but it also *never could have been* yours—"

From Adam's startled expression, Jemima realized that he had not known Chloe had been pregnant. He looked rather white.

"She was a liar," said Lionnel rather gruffly. "And—well, that's enough. I still loved her."

"Yes, you loved her. You loved her enough to come round to Adelaide Square, hot foot, that fatal Saturday. You came to warn her about your wife, didn't you, Sir Richard?"

"Don't deny it! I saw you, you murdering bastard."

For a moment it looked as if Kevin John, having interrupted, might spring at Lionnel. But Jemima went relentlessly on. "You worried that Lady Lionnel, who had come up from Sussex to 'The Little Athens' to confront you, would come here to Adelaide Square and find Chloe. So you hurried round, on the pretence of getting a taxi, hurried round—it's not far, and you had the alibi, it's always difficult to get taxis in the Tottenham Court Road, especially on a Saturday."

"Clever of you to work that out, Miss Shore. Stavros, I suppose. I should never have taken the risk of taking a woman of your intelligence to the same restaurant. Do the police know?"

"Not yet."

"But I'm going to tell them," Kevin John threw in belligerently.

"On the contrary," interrupted Jemima. "Even at the end of this mystery conference, you have nothing to tell them about him. Nothing at all. Because you see, Sir Richard Lionnel did not kill Chloe Fontaine. Shall we say he did not love her enough to kill her?"

There was a silence while Jemima watched the vein beating in Kevin John's temple.

"For having reached seventy-three Adelaide Square so rapidly, he veered away," she continued. "Yes, Kevin John, he veered away as though he had seen someone he knew. Your own words to me last night—or was it this morning? Having come round to warn her about his wife, having telephoned her first but got no answer (you told the truth about that telephone call to the police, Sir Richard, if not the whole truth), you saw someone you knew, someone dangerous to you, outside the building. At that sight, you veered away. You rushed back to 'The Little Athens,' getting a taxi on the way. Chloe was never warned, and Lady Lionnel, for all her threats, satisfied with the scene she had made, went back to Sussex. No, Sir Richard, it was not you who came back."

"True. All perfectly true." Sir Richard extended the immaculate white cuffs from his tweed jacket and inspected them gravely, as though confirming them rather than Jemima Shore in the truth of their remarks.

"Then who did the bastard see?" enquired Kevin John truculently. "Who are we talking about? Me, by any chance?"

"No, not you, Kevin John. You didn't kill Chloe Fontaine: a point you've made over and over again—to the police, to me, and to anyone else who would listen, and it's true. Perhaps in the end you didn't love her enough, or desire her enough, to pursue her through to the end. You could have a new happy life in Devon—Cornwall? sorry—with a new young happy girl, whom Chloe called 'submissive,' and come up to London on a bender, try and seek her out, the ever elusive she, Chloe, the one that got away, the unsubmissive one.

"But in the end, when all that was over, when you'd delivered a few blows, when you'd drunk more than a few drinks, you were prepared to go back to Cornwall, weren't you, into the embraces of another, and forget her. In short, when she delivered her final ultimatum—that fatal Saturday—"

" 'Get out of my life, you drunken slob!' That's what she said.

She never had a lover as good as me, she knew that." Kevin John sounded both childish and indignant. "And now: you drunken slob, that's all I was to her. There's gratitude for you, there's women for you. I used to screw her all night, and at the end of it all—you drunken slob."

There was a change of tone. "Added to which, she'd got away with my best picture, the best damn picture I ever painted."

"And you went. The police didn't believe it. But I did. You went. No, Kevin John, you didn't love her enough to kill her."

Isabelle Mancini rose and, as though about to sing, settled her flowing grey veilings round her, then clasped her fine strong hands together. Silver bracelets, looser, heavier than the constricting golden serpents which adorned Laura Barrymore, clanked down her arms as she did so and gradually settled like hoops over a fat peg at a fair.

"Thees is absur-r-rd, dulling." She sounded hysterical, and there were tears in her eyes. But Adam's swift uprising from the floor forestalled whatever metaphorical aria she would have sung.

"In case there's any doubt in your mind," he said in a careful voice, very different from the usual carefree richly embroidered tone he affected, "I did love her—a little. I find it very easy to love people a little. I love you a little, Jemima Shore, Investigator, for that matter. But more than that at the present time is outside my present capacity." He spoke as though he had measured himself out like a medicine, and found the vessel destined to receive it not large enough. "In theory I regret her death, and the death of her unborn child, quite as much as the destruction of the buildings Sir Richard Lionnel has murdered. Whether or not it was anything to do with me, is immaterial since it was a life. In practice I can express myself much more freely about the buildings. You can take it from that, Pallas Athena, that I did not kill Chloe Fontaine."

"I know that, Adam." Jemima thought it unnecessary to add that she also knew, had in a sense witnessed first hand, the exact nature of his alibi. "No, be quiet, Kevin John, let me continue." She turned to Isabelle, down whose cheeks tears were now freely flowing.

"The fourth person who loved Chloe, was you, Isabelle. Yes, you did love her. I suspect in your heart of hearts you love her still, for all her disloyalty, her treachery in using your letters in her novel, her cruel threat to publish those letters in the anthology

Valentine Brighton commissioned. That's because you, with all your concentration on disloyalty, are loyalty itself—I think you gave your warm heart to her and never quite managed to withdraw it.

"For it was you, Isabelle, who gave me the clue to the true killer of Chloe Fontaine. That day in 'The Little Athens,' when we talked about Chloe's need for violence, even from those she loved. There was someone you mentioned—do you remember; a fifth person who loved her, but could not by temperament provide that violence? If only he had been able to give her something like that—the violence she craved, you said, 'life would have taken a different turn for Chloe.' Isabelle, do you remember? You were right. For that person, that lover, did in the end, provoked beyond all endurance, find the violence in him to proceed, the violence she wanted. And in so doing he killed her."

"Valentine," said Isabelle in a sad far-off voice, "Valentine Brighton. Poor boy."

Chapter Nineteen

"Tell Me Who to Kill"

"Yes, Valentine Brighton. Valentine: the lover in the gardens."
Peace, a strange resigned calm, had been restored. Jemima and Sir
Richard between them had had to restrain Kevin John, who at her
words had bounded out of his chair with surprising force considering his condition, fists doubled, his attitude expressing what he
scarcely needed to put into words: "Tell me who to kill."

The knowledge, when it penetrated, that Chloe's murderer was
beyond his personal vengeance, caused him further furiously
expressed anguish. It was some time before all this turmoil
subsided.

"I told you that this was a story of love. Love unrequited, love
exploited. Valentine Brighton, inhibited, repressed, the only child
of a dominating mother, fatherless from an early age, a classic
text-book case perhaps; with a very low sex drive indeed, if any
drive at all—that fact was far more important than whatever
direction it took—from the first he was utterly fascinated by Chloe
Fontaine. You saw the truth of that, Isabelle, with your own
knowledge of love.

"Never mind all his little throwaway pretend-snobbish jokes,
the ones that made us all wonder secretly whether they weren't for
real, whether he wasn't at heart a great deal more snobbish than he
admitted: 'Mummy wouldn't like it, Chloe wouldn't go down well
with the neighbors' and so forth. Mere persiflage to disguise
feelings which were all the more violent because he couldn't
express them—physically, that is.

"In the meantime he makes do with his double role of confidant
and publisher: confidant while Chloe goes to bed with half
London, or so it seems to him, the outsider, the observer. But still
in a sense he still possesses her, doesn't he? He's the only one, for

example, who knows the truth about her liaison with you, Sir Richard, because he's so safe, or rather Chloe thinks he's so safe, which is rather a different matter.

"Chloe-watching, for that is what it was, became an obsession with him. And then a mania. For Chloe, courtesy of Sir Richard Lionnel and Lionnel Estates, actually came to live in Bloomsbury, the next-door square to his office, the actual square where he had his own small London flat. And this square, Adelaide Square, has gardens, thick shrubby deserted gardens, to which only residents have the key.

"Chloe's move to Bloomsbury gives new life to Valentine's passion. It brings death to Chloe.

"To begin with, Valentine can see so much more of her comings and goings; it's easy for example to observe the entrance to seventy-three Adelaide Square from the gardens; I know, I've done it—I saw you, Adam, on the afternoon of her murder . . . As an occupation, Chloe-watching was probably often difficult to resist for a lonely man on a hot summer's evening. I expect he always swore to himself he'd never do it again. We all plan, don't we, to resist our secret self-destructive pleasures the next time?" Jemima thought back to past loves of her own, married loves, telephone numbers dialled without hope or reason and answered, predictably, by wives; houses with lighted windows, and other windows even more hauntingly unlighted, hopelessly regarded from a taxi at night . . .

Jemima went on, wrenching her thoughts back: "But Chloe too had the right to use these same gardens. A right on the whole, she didn't exercise—too busy elsewhere, a cynic might say. Until one fine day, one fine night rather, Chloe forgot the keys to number seventy-three . . . We shall never know the circumstances under which she forgot them, as a result of which she climbed into the square gardens (the key to the square was with the flat keys). She had the idea of sleeping out there, it was after all summer, and it was very hot. But it is tempting, is it not, to think she sought her own fate? Perhaps her story to me afterwards wasn't true; perhaps she didn't forget her keys—Chloe in that respect was the reverse of careless; perhaps after a dull evening out, she glimpsed Valentine lurking and the spirit of devilry took over; it's not important—and, I repeat, we shall never know. They're both dead now.

"What is important is the fact that that night, that fine wild summer's night, evidently inspired something new in Valentine, extinguished some long-held fear, conquered some inhibition, lit the vital fire so long laid. And Valentine—the resident lover, the lover with the key, became the lover in the gardens.

"They had what Chloe afterwards called 'a casual encounter'— a surprising one, short-lived, because she by this time was utterly determined to marry you, Sir Richard. It was also a carnal encounter. A very brief one. That short duration must have caused Valentine enough pain in itself, but cruellest of all was the fact that Chloe continued to tell him, her erstwhile lover for at least one passionate night, all about her plans for Richard Lionnel.

"It was at this point that Valentine's Chloe-watching took a desperate turn. First he discovered a route up to this flat by the fire escape, at the back of the building. Again, was this discovery choice or chance? He told me the latter. But it's not important. What is important is that he also found a loose brick in the back wall, or loose enough, Sir Richard, with due respect to Lionnel Estates, for him to prise it away.

"He did so. He probed further. He was confronted by a picture. Or rather the back of a picture whose front he knew well. This picture was called 'A Splash of Red.'" Kevin John gave a kind of groan.

"It hung in her bedroom. He'd often seen it, as we see it now." Jemima uncrossed her dark legs in their scarlet sandals and walked unhurriedly towards the bedroom doors. She opened them in the same deliberate fashion. The painting stared down at them, the violence of the subject matter made more shocking by the fact that the bedroom itself was now empty—clean, white, virginal— except for the white-shrouded bed.

Isabelle shuddered. She said something which sounded like: "R-r-repulsive." She might have been referring to Valentine's behaviour.

Jemima continued: "In this picture Valentine cut a hole. To put it bluntly, a spy-hole." She did not look to see if Kevin John, or for that matter Richard Lionnel, winced. "And so Chloe-watching took on another dimension. Did she know? In this case I think it unlikely, but once again, we'll never know.

"I'll pass over speculation and cut to Saturday, the fatal Saturday of her death. Several things happened on and around that day, leading up to her murder, and I'll try and put them in order, so that you, like me, can understand the tragic progression. On Friday evening Chloe installed me in the penthouse flat as caretaker and cat-sitter in her absence; this was primarily because Lionnel was worried that the Press would pick up his affair with Chloe, and she had the brilliant idea that I, of all people, being a member of the media, would be able to fend them off. I was of course quite innocent myself as to the true nature of her holiday. Then Chloe herself departed to spend the weekend—the weekend only—on the first floor while you, Sir Richard, took in your Downing Street meetings.

"In the meantime I received two telephone calls, or rather two *types* of telephone calls: the first came from Chloe's parents, who had expected to see her in Folkestone and never received the letter putting off the visit. The second came from Valentine and I think were obsessional calls no longer directed necessarily towards Chloe, or even towards me who received them; they were the measure of the madness which was now enveloping him.

"Because, you see, Valentine had taken vengeance into his own hands and had tipped off Lady Lionnel in Sussex about her husband's secret little holiday with the pretty lady writer. There can be no question that that information was passed on deliberately. Whereupon Lady Lionnel insisted on coming up to London to confront her husband. And Valentine, he too was in London. He was here, not to warn Chloe as he pretended to me, but to gloat. You, Sir Richard, tried to warn her. But Valentine, the watcher, wanted to observe in his twisted way, his darling, his loved one, receiving her come-uppance at the hands of the woman he had deliberately set upon her.

"Unfortunately it is now, quite independently, that Chloe has her inspiration about her parents. If the wife can stage a scene, so can the mistress. She's pinning everything on this holiday, but so far Sir Richard isn't rising to the bait—just invoking the name of his notoriously jealous wife. However, Chloe knows that her stepfather is still quite strongminded enough in his late seventies to express himself forcibly on the subject of pregnancy and marriage to the highest in the land—in this case exemplified by you, Sir Richard. She had planned to tell you about her pregnancy while you're both abroad, but now this seems a better way to do it, more difficult for you to back out, a gambler's throw, perhaps, but then Chloe in her personal life was ever a gambler."

Sir Richard did not react, merely drew on his black cigarette.

Against the light his expression remained unreadable. Jemima passed swiftly on: "Chloe has written to her parents with a view to a visit and breaking the news to them personally. But Sir Richard's weekend session at number ten changes all that. She puts off her trip to Folkestone. Then she telephones her parents to invite them to London instead and discovers to her horror that her second letter putting off her visit hasn't arrived. In fact her first letter, confirming her visit, has arrived only that morning. She hasn't thought about them for so long, or written or visited them—hasn't needed them, you might say—that the normally careful Chloe has failed to note their change of postal address. They're so worried that they've already telephoned me to check up. Still, the dramatic news that Chloe is pregnant overrides everything. Her mother's too frail, but her stepfather agrees to come up on Saturday afternoon."

Isabelle gave a gasp.

"Mais c'est incroyable," she exclaimed. "She 'ated babies. Books not babies, 'ow many times 'ave I 'eard 'er say it?"

"Not this baby, Isabelle. Because she thought it would help her in her plan. But it's now that there's a hitch. One thing she doesn't know about—you, Kevin John, you who have erupted back into her life like the splash of red you are—only she doesn't know it yet.

"Kevin John, quite unknown to Chloe, had made an early-morning appearance in the penthouse and found me there. We'll draw a veil over that. He came back again at lunchtime. This was the fatal return. For this was the return which Valentine unexpectedly witnessed. Yes, Kevin John, he saw you. Through the hole in the picture. The hole he had made to spy on Chloe."

A reference to his own picture did at least penetrate Kevin John's consciousness. His fists clenched again and he swivelled his blue eyes in that direction. Then he delivered a stream of obscenities about the late Lord Brighton, which left Sir Richard unmoved, caused Adam to yawn, and provoked Isabelle to murmur something Gallic and disgusted.

"You, Kevin John," went on Jemima, "the force of sexuality, of violence, all he could never be, all of which he confidently believed had been rejected from Chloe's life; Sir Richard—security—that he could understand. But your kind of rampant sexuality, never. It cracked something in him, to see you there, sent him mad. It was you who came back, Kevin John, just as the police thought, except you didn't kill her. You're so fatally at home, aren't you, or so he thought, with a razor in your hand. So she'd lied, lied all along, the one thing she never did to him, swore she never did. 'I always tell the truth to Valentine, he can't resist that'—her own words to me.

"Never mind that Valentine wrongs Chloe. It's actually *your* razor, Sir Richard. She hasn't gone back to you, Kevin John. Far from it. She's not even present. Later, when she does return, she calls you a drunken slob, in effect throws you out. Valentine doesn't know that, for at this point he leaves, goes away, back into the gardens where you, Sir Richard, later spot him watching the house. Yes, it's Valentine Brighton you saw, Sir Richard, your country neighbour, the friend of your wife, the trouble-maker. From him, and his gossiping malicious mother, you flinch away.

"Valentine Brighton waits in the square gardens until he sees you, Kevin John, leaving. From something you said to me earlier, I think you may also have glimpsed him. But you thought he was harmless, 'that's impossible' you told me—"

"Bloody harmless, was he?" exploded Kevin John. "If I hadn't been such a"—more obscenities followed, applied equally to Kevin John himself and to Valentine Brighton—"I'd have spotted what he was up to. Yes, I saw him in the gardens, lurking in the bushes, he was just the type, wasn't he? Not even a pansy, just a neuter. Impossible, yes I damn well did think it was impossible that *he* should be anybody's lover let alone banging away like that in the middle of central London—"

"Then Valentine can't bear it any longer," continued Jemima, thinking it prudent to cut short this tirade. "He rushes back into the building. Runs up the front staircase this time. The front door of the penthouse is still open. Chloe's surprised. She's still in her white petticoat. Why?

"Now the answer to that one is in fact very simple, although for a long time I didn't spot it. Like you, Kevin John, like Valentine himself, I thought she must be having a rendezvous in the penthouse with a lover, and that baffled me. The police of course thought she indulged in some kind of love scene with you, Kevin John. Or at least the preliminaries to it.

"Then suddenly it came to me. When does a woman take off her clothes? Down to her petticoat. In the daytime. The reason is obvious. Not to receive a lover but to change them! She was in her own flat, wasn't she? She knew I was out. She'd come up to the flat simply to *change* her clothes. And why did she change? Why, quite simply to receive her stepfather suitably dressed for the occasion, for the confrontation. You all remember how meticulous Chloe was about that kind of thing—neat, the right clothes for the occasion.

"You see, she only had holiday clothes downstairs with her. She wouldn't have wandered up the staircase in her petticoat. She came up here and merely took off her dress beside the sitting-room cupboard, where she stored her London clothes to make room for mine in the bedroom.

"At this point, before she has a chance to choose a dress the cat escapes and, frightened of the traffic outside, she dashes after it, all the way down to the basement, just as she told you, Kevin John. Which means she misses you coming up the stairs; you're by now in the bedroom; she returns, is about to put on another dress, when you, Kevin John, surprise her. Being Chloe she has already hung up the dress she has removed. But the cupboard, which she had locked the previous evening in my presence, is still open.

"After your departure, Valentine rushes in. We'll never know exactly what happened then, since they're both dead. Perhaps she taunted him, teased him, flirted with him a little in her provocative way, not realizing the seriousness of the situation, of his madness. I think it more than likely she taunted him with her pregnancy: babies, as he once told me, horrified him. It was her, Chloe, that he wanted.

"And so he killed her, killed her with one of your long sharp knives, Isabelle." Isabelle gave a gasp and the tears started to flow again. "The knives you gave her, before she cut your friendship to pieces."

"Cruel, poor little Chloe," whispered Isabelle.

"One stroke killed her: he was strong, expert, a sportsman, brought up in the country even though he had rejected it. The other stabs were for passion and love, and pain and frustration, and perhaps for all the other people she had loved and, in his tortured mind, betrayed him with.

"He left her. He left her dead in the bedroom, so that we know she must have led him in there, gone willingly. But it was no part of his plan to be discovered. No, it was now that the cold, detached, clever part of his mind took over. No scandal for Valentine Brighton—above all, no scandal which would break his mother's heart. Those last words of his to me in the Reading Room—'Poor Mummy, how will she bear it?'—not about his voyeurism after all, but the horror of her only son being a murderer. So away with the prints, the evidence, and even when you, Kevin John, are arrested, he still feels no compunction, no desire to protect you from the consequences of his own deed. For he summons me to the Reading Room again explicitly to reveal your presence at the scene of her death.

"But I'm jumping ahead. After he's killed her, the madness leaves him, he has to establish an alibi and fast. So he goes to the British Library, where he knows he'll find me. In fact he strikes lucky, sees me in the street on the way from the Pizza Perfecta, and tails me. It's easy then to sit down, deliberately clear the seat next to his (despite the fact it's officially occupied) and rely on me discovering him, theoretically asleep. Then he talks of Lady Lionnel, of warning Chloe. He looked terrible then, ghastly. No wonder. He had just killed the one person—other than his mother—that he felt anything for in the world, and he knew he was sending me back to find her lacerated corpse."

"So that bastard set me up!" shouted Kevin John, brandishing a bottle which was nearly empty. "He would have testified against me. And all the time he knew I hadn't killed her, because he'd fucking well done her in himself." There was bewilderment as well as rage in his voice, as though he found such diabolical adult villainy directed towards himself hard to comprehend.

Why pretend, thought Jemima. "Yes, Valentine hated you," she said directly to him. "He was also deranged where you were concerned. He loved her but he hated you. Afterwards it was you he wanted to kill, extinguish, punish, as he had already punished her."

"May one enquire how you are going to prove all this?" asked Sir Richard coolly. Of them all he remained the most detached. Adam still looked white, shocked, and as a result, even younger. But Sir Richard was once more inspecting his splendid cuffs with their agate links. "That policeman of yours, Inspector Portsmouth, isn't it? Is he going to be much impressed by all this analysis. What proof do you have after all? The man's dead. I did see him in the gardens—fair enough—but that's no evidence that he was about to commit a particularly revolting crime."

"The police *have* to believe her: she's Jemima Shore, Investigator!" Kevin John put the bottle to his lips and drained it, then leaping up, he rushed over to Lionnel. The latter stepped calmly backwards and sideways onto the balcony to avoid his rush.

Kevin John took him by his tweed lapels.

"You adulterous fascist shit. They have to believe her. I'm innocent, innocent, can't you understand that?"

Lionnel, with continuing aplomb, merely plucked Kevin John's fingers from his coat, and stepped further away. He acted sharply but not violently: Jemima was reminded of his treatment of Tiger that Saturday evening—"cats in their place." Artists too, it seemed.

"He's not guilty. That's clear," said Isabelle reprovingly as though Sir Richard had somehow suggested that he was.

"I believe you. It figures. But I hope you can prove it, because—otherwise, well—a dead man. A dead Lord. A dead Lord with, I take it, a live mother. Will the fuzz buy that one? I doubt it." Adam spoke, not very loudly, but loud enough for Jemima to hear.

"But you saw him there—in the gardens." Kevin John, wielding the now empty bottle, was still menacing Lionnel; on the balcony, shouting at him, his face red, almost purple, his voice roaring; he looked quite out of control. "You'll tell the police you saw him."

"Will I, indeed?" Sir Richard, moving one more pace away, sounded highly remote from the whole affair. "I'll have to talk to my lawyers about that. Naturally I shall cooperate as and when may be necessary; but otherwise I see no need to be mixed up further in this filthy business."

He paused. "Besides, I'm not at all sure that you're *not* guilty—please forgive me, Miss Shore, but I knew poor Valentine Brighton well, and of course Hope Brighton is one of Francesca's closest friends. We're country neighbours, you know what that means, one really gets to know people well, doesn't one, in the country, quite unlike these rather intense *urban* relationships."

Another pause. Sir Richard had moved; he no longer had his back to the light, so that the expression on his face was once more visible. Afterwards Jemima would always remember that there had been something mocking, malicious, cruel about that expression, as though he were the controlled matador to Kevin John's maddened, helpless bull. For the first time she saw the ruthless tycoon who had torn down the beautiful houses of Adelaide Square and built for profit, the modern horror which had become

Chloe's tomb, and might become the tomb of Lionnel's own reputation, were he to weaken.

"Charming fellow, Brighton, in my opinion very much one of us," he went on. "Wouldn't hurt a fly, hated shooting, any kind of blood sport; Francesca, who's much to that way of thinking herself, used to have wonderful talks with him about it. And Chloe, herself, she used to laugh about him. My tame tabby, my other pussy-cat, she used to call him. Whereas our friend here—"

"Is that me you mean?" Kevin John was bellowing.

"Yes, my good man, indeed I mean you. Quite the brute, aren't you, with your great fists and muscles, and your obscenities, quite the murdering type, I would have said myself. Do you really think she found that kind of thing attractive just because you're some kind of stud, she, Chloe? Why she loathed it, loathed the memory of all your repulsive violence, the beatings, to say nothing of your endless sexual boasting, she used to tell me about it—"

The virulence with which Sir Richard Lionnel spoke was so unexpected, so outside his usual calm diction, that Jemima was still too startled to react, while Sir Richard continued in the same tone of rising venom: "I wouldn't be a bit surprised if you didn't do her in after all, poor little thing; anyway it's clear she wouldn't have died, we wouldn't all be in this appalling mess, if it wasn't for your blundering return, you disgusting drunken oaf—take your hands off me—"

Isabelle screamed loudly, but stood immobile in the sitting room wringing her hands. Adam leapt lithely off the floor and darted forward, but even so did not reach the balcony until too late. Jemima too rushed forward. She also was too late.

For Kevin John, at Sir Richard's last words, first hurled the bottle over the balcony, its crash only just audible over the fracas which followed, and then flung himself at the tycoon.

"Murdering type, am I? We'll see about that." The rest of his words were more or less lost, although afterwards Isabelle was prepared to swear that he had said something like: "I didn't kill her but I will kill you." Jemima was less certain.

In the end all any of them knew for certain was that Sir Richard, taken off guard, standing against the concrete parapet which fronted the balcony—that Lionnel fancy, the parapet just slightly too low for safety—was forced back against it, onto it, over it, still with Kevin John shouting and shouting while at his throat. And quite suddenly Lionnel was no longer there. Kevin John was there. Standing, panting, great fists now hanging at his sides. But the substantial figure of Sir Richard Lionnel had vanished.

A strange sound reached their ears as he disappeared, not so much a scream, as a huge sigh or a cry, perhaps merely the sound of his body rushing through the air. The noise of its landing far below was almost extinguished by the hysterical screams of Isabelle Mancini. Nevertheless the disseminated thud indicated that, far below, something heavy had met its end.

Chapter Twenty

The Last Word

"A murdering type," commented Pompey with satisfaction afterwards, when Kevin John Athlone had been charged with the willful murder of Sir Richard Lionnel—this time there was to be no bail. Even Punch Fredericks did not suggest it. In view of this Pompey was really quite restrained in his private comments on solicitors, who believed in bail-for-everyone—even murderers, and the consequences of their rashness.

"A murdering type. Didn't I say so all along?" It was an echo of the dead man's last—fatally provoking—words.

"But he didn't kill Chloe Fontaine," retorted Jemima. "Didn't I say that all along?" Charges against Kevin John for this crime had been withdrawn, a fact which had passed almost unnoticed in the Press, in view of the welter of publicity which had surrounded the death of Sir Richard Lionnel, the Lion of Bloomsbury, hurled—as the Press liked to put it—from the top of his own notorious building.

"How about that for a victory for the feminine instinct?" Jemima added.

"Ah, my dear, always let a woman have the last word." Pompey shook his head sagely. "That's what twenty happy years with Mrs. Portsmouth has taught me. Above all, never argue about her instincts. Shall we settle for the fact that we were both right?"

"You do have your murderer," Jemima pointed out. "Or rather, your alleged murderer. If not precisely for the crime you were investigating."

"Very true. And I must tell you that sometimes in the watches of the night I wish we did not—or rather I wish we did not have this particular crime. What with enquiries from number ten, very polite mind you, just interested, and Lady Lionnel, now *there's* a terror for you, and the dead man's secretary or whatever she calls herself, another terror, and sister, by the way, of your friend the squatter—I don't know what the world is coming to. Give me the Dowager Lady Brighton every time. She may be a terror, but she's a lady too."

It seemed doubtful, at the time of Pompey's chat with Jemima, whether the murder of Chloe Fontaine would ever receive an official solution. This was partly due to the activities of Lady Hope Brighton, who on the one hand threatened dire penalties if her dead son's name was blackened on such slender evidence, and on the other made a series of heart-rending appeals as a grief-stricken mother. It was also due to the extreme reluctance of Mr. Stover, on behalf of his wife, the dead woman's next of kin, to press for any form of revenge. The attitude of Valentine Brighton's mother, in which despair and authoritarianism were mingled in roughly equal parts, found an answering echo in Mr. Stover's own breast.

There was a last interview with Jemima Shore, in which Mr. Stover, grown suddenly much older and even smaller, began by sounding more bewildered than aggressive. But on the subject of the Press, for whom his full hatred was reserved, he still managed to express himself with something of his old strength. He for one was clearly immensely relieved that there would be no murder trial centred exclusively round the lives and loves of his stepdaughter.

"The things they wrote about Dollie!" he exclaimed to Jemima. "Did they not think of her mother, her mother and me?" He broke down a little. "Despite her change of name. Always made it quite clear who she was, when she was on television, and so forth, the relationship, told the neighbours, and now—"

"At least her books are selling well. At long last. And they're thinking of televising *Fallen Child*. She would have liked that," put in Jemima.

It was a bald statement but true. Chloe's premature death, under hideous circumstances, had in a strange way bumped up her literary reputation. Dr. Marigold Milton, whose moral enthusiasm in a good cause terrified her intellectual inferiors, pointed triumphantly to her long advocacy of Chloe's novels in a major piece in *Literature*. Other critics, honorably determined not to consider the scandal which surrounded her name, but their attention drawn to it nonetheless, found themselves pondering on Chloe's books as a whole for the first time. After all, her work, as well as her life, was over. In all this, the avidity of the public for further details concerning Chloe Fontaine was no disadvantage. In future, while her frozen body was freed at last into the obliteration of burial, her work would flourish.

"And we've got to know you," Mr. Stover spoke with perfect confidence. "Her mother said that this morning before I left. The last thing she said—'We've got to know Jemima Shore, haven't we, Dad?' She'd like to give you that picture, the wife, not sell it back to them as the gallery suggested. 'Why don't we give it to Miss Shore,' she said, 'to remind her of Dollie?'"

"No, no," Jemima interrupted hastily. "The gallery is quite right. Sell it." She had no wish to introduce "A Splash of Red" into her own life.

"You'll visit us, I expect," Mr. Stover continued remorselessly. "When you're our way. We'll talk about memories—Dollie—Chloe, I mean." It was one of the touching things about Mr. Stover that latterly he had made a determined effort to refer to his stepdaughter by her literary name. "You can tell us about what goes on in television, books, well it's all the same thing isn't it? She knew all about it, Chloe, our girl."

Mr. Stover went on: "And if you ever wanted to make a programme about Dollie, Chloe, all of this, well, you would need us, wouldn't you?"

"I'll visit you," said Jemima Shore gently. She said it with a slightly heavy heart because she knew she would keep her word. Dollie Stover might have left her parents coldly unvisited, but she, Jemima Shore, would keep in touch with them. A sense of duty and sadness would not let her neglect them.

In the meantime Tiger, the golden Lion of Bloomsbury transplanted to Holland Park, graceful, wild and ultimately unknowable, would remind her of Chloe Fontaine.

ABOUT THE AUTHOR

ANTONIA FRASER is the acclaimed author of several historical biographies, among them *Mary, Queen of Scots*, *Cromwell*, and *Royal Charles*. The Jemima Shore mysteries include the full-length *Oxford Blood*, *Cool Repentance*, *A Splash of Red*, *Quiet as a Nun*, *The Wild Island*, and *Your Royal Hostage*, and a collection of short stories, *Jemima Shore's First Case*. A television series based on the Jemima Shore mysteries was aired nationwide in 1983. In 1986 Antonia Fraser was chairman of the Crime Writers' Association.

She lives in London with her husband, the dramatist Harold Pinter.

• A JEMIMA SHORE MYSTERY •

QUIET AS A NUN

Here is a special preview of Jemima Shore's first case,
QUIET AS A NUN, by Antonia Fraser, which will be
available as a Bantam paperback in April 1990, at your
local bestseller.

1
Out of the past

Sometimes when I feel low, I study the *Evening Standard* as though for an examination. It was in that way I found the small item on the Home News page: NUN FOUND DEAD. It was not a very promising headline. Nevertheless I conscientiously read the few lines of print below. It staved off the moment when I would look round the empty flat resolving to cook myself a proper meal for once, and knowing that I would not do so.

"Sister Rosabelle Mary Powerstock," the story continued, "of Blessed Eleanor's Convent, Churne, Sussex, was found dead today in a locked building on the outskirts of the convent grounds. It is believed that the forty-one-year-old nun, known as Sister Miriam at the convent where she had lived for eighteen years, had taken ill and was unable to raise the alarm. Reverend Mother Ancilla Curtis said today that Sister Miriam would be a great loss to the community of the Order of the Tower of Ivory, and would be sadly missed by her many pupils, past and present.

"Sister Miriam was the daughter of a former Lord Mayor of London."

Before I had finished reading the short item, I had been transported back a whole generation. I knew that ruined building. It was in fact a tower. Blessed Eleanor's Retreat, as the nuns called it, in memory of the foundress of the Order of the Tower of Ivory. Sometimes irreverently referred to by the girls as Nelly's Nest.

For that matter I knew Sister Miriam. Or I had known Rosabelle Powerstock? Rosa. Had I known Sister Miriam? On consideration, no. But for a short while, long ago, I had known Rosabelle Powerstock very well indeed. For a few moments the cold elegant surroundings of affluent London in the seventies dissolved. It was wartime. A little Protestant day-girl sent by the vagaries of her father's career to a smart Catholic boarding convent conveniently next door. Bewildered and rather excited by the mysterious world in which she found herself. The resolute kindness of the nuns—was there any kindness like it for the undaunted firmness of its warmth whatever the reaction of its recipient? Reaching its final expression in Reverend Mother Ancilla.

I learnt that the nuns in their religious life adopted a name, Latin or otherwise, for some virtue or religious attitude they particularly admired; failing that, the name of some especially inspiring saint. Ancilla meant Handmaid of the Lord—echoing the great submissive answer of the Virgin Mary to the angel's unexpected announcement of her coming motherhood, "Behold the handmaid of the Lord." No doubt the Lord had been happy with his handmaid, Ancilla Curtis: but it was difficult even now to envisage any relationship in which Mother Ancilla was not the dominant partner.

And Rosa—the late Sister Miriam. So she had taken that name in religion. She had always declared her intention of doing so—if she became a nun. It had been a fashionable topic of conversation at Blessed Eleanor's.

"If I become a nun, and of course I wouldn't dream of doing such a thing, I'm going to marry and have six children, then I'll be Sister Hugh. After little St. Hugh of Lincoln."

"I'll be Sister Elizabeth. After St. Elizabeth of Hungary who gave bread to the poor and it turned to roses when her husband tried to stop her."

"Did the poor eat the roses?" I enquired. I was not trying to mock. I was fascinated by the whole concept. To cover up, I said quickly: "If I become a nun, that is to say if I become a Catholic first, and then become a nun, I'll be Sister Francis."

How lovely. The birds. The dear little animals. That met with general approval.

"No, not St. Francis of Assisi." Honesty—or cussedness—compelled me to add, "St. Francis Xavier." I had just been reading about the origins of the Society of Jesus, and the heroic struggles of that St. Francis to convert the Japanese, dying in the attempt. Like many non-Catholics I was morbidly intrigued by the Jesuits. Secretly, the one I would really like to have chosen was St. Ignatius.

"Jemima should be Sister Thomas," said Rosa sweetly. "Doubting Thomas."

"Isn't Miriam rather an Old Testament sort of name?" I countered. I meant rather Jewish.

"It's one of the titles of Our Lady. Our Lady Star of the Sea." Rosa loved to snub and enlighten me at the same time about the intricacies of her religion. Humbly, I loved to listen to her. I thought of the other titles in that great litany. Star of the Sea, pray for us. Mystical Rose, pray for us. Tower of Ivory, pray for us.

Like most Protestants, I knew the Bible much better than my Catholic friends. Besides, my terrifying nonconformist grandfather had been fond of reading it aloud. He was particularly fond of the Song of Solomon. "Thy neck is as a tower of ivory," sang Solomon—and thus my grandfather in his booming voice, "Thine eyes like the fishpools in Heshbon by the gate of Bath-rabbim . . ." Fish pools. Not very pretty to modern ears. But thinking about fish pools, dark, with swirling depths, the phrase was not inapt to Rosa's eyes in certain moods.

Mysterious Rosa, once my Star of the Sea, was now dead—in her ruined Tower of Ivory.

I shook myself, to remove the touch of memories long buried. Wartime had brought strange schooling to many, and quick changes. After the war my parents had decided to go back to their original Lincolnshire and make their home there.

"Goodbye, Jemima," Reverend Mother Ancilla said in our final interview. She combined the roles of Reverend Mother of the convent and headmistress of the school, an awesome conglomerate of power. This time it was very much the headmistress who was to the fore.

"What a clever girl you have been. Top of your form.

The nuns all say they will really miss teaching you. A very nice impression to leave behind. Don't forget us."

"Oh Mother, I couldn't," I gushed. That was one thing the convent taught you—how to return a soft answer. Mother Ancilla paused. I knew quite enough about nuns by this time to know that they never left you with the last word.

"This cleverness, Jemima. A wonderful gift from Our Lord. You must develop it of course. Go to university perhaps?"

A mutter. "I hope to, Mother."

"But there is the spirit too as well as the intelligence. The spirit which bows itself and in doing so finds its true happiness. Self-abnegation, Jemima." She paused again. At no point had the nuns ever tried to convert me from the thin Protestantism spread upon me by my parents. It would have been quite outside their philosophy to attempt by words what example could not do. I felt her pause was a delicate acknowledgement of that restraint.

"St. John of the Cross, one of our great mystics, once wrote that unless I find the way of total self-abnegation, I shall not find myself."

"Yes, Mother." I bobbed a curtsey.

At the time her parting words had seemed singularly inappropriate. And later even more so to a successful career, carved, sometimes clawed out, by methods which always contained a great remembrance of self. Ironically enough, it now occurred to me that in my relationship with Tom I had probably realised self-abnegation at last.

The thought of Tom brought me back sharply to the empty flat, as it always did. He had said that he might telephone about ten.

"If I can get to my study and she has a bath so that she doesn't hear the click of the telephone as I pick it up."

It was a proviso which had been made before.

I once said: "Tom, why don't you get a telephone which doesn't click?" He said nothing, but kissed me gently. So it was the way of total self-abnegation. It was now eight o'clock. There were two hours to wait. I turned on the television and turned it off irritably, deciding that the critic who said in this week's *Listener* that my own programme was really the only thing worth watching these days had after all a great deal to be said for him. I picked up the autobiography of the children's doctor from Nigeria I would interview on Friday. I forgot Mother Ancilla. I had long forgotten Rosa. Sister Miriam I did not know. I even forgot Tom for an hour and a half, and the last half-hour passed not too slowly, considering it was actually an hour, and nearly half-past ten before he managed to ring.

The letter from Mother Ancilla arrived about a fortnight later. The small convent writing paper, covered clearly and carefully in a still familiar handwriting, unlocked its own memories. Nuns did not waste writing paper: waste was not only extravagant, but also displeasing to God. I was curiously unsurprised by the arrival of the letter. It was as though I had been expecting it. The previous memories had warned me: we are after you, out of the past.

Mother Ancilla's letter was complimentary on its first page, sad on its second page and astonishing on its third. The compliments referred to my own career, "which although we did not play, I fear, the whole part in your education, we have nevertheless followed with interest. And of course like all our old girls, you have always had the prayers of the community. Our girls nowadays regularly watch your programme on television— yes, we have colour television in St. Joseph's Sitting Room, the gift of an old girl. Your programme is one of the few we can safely trust to be both entertaining and instructive. Sister Hippolytus often tells the girls about your earlier triumphs in the debating society, and how she predicted a public career for you."

It was a surprise to me that Sister Hippolytus had predicted anything so favourable in my future as a public career. Famous for her sharp tongue, Sister Hippo was one of the few—no, the only nun who had made me conscious of my alien status. Then I remembered that "a public career" on the lips of certain Catholics was not necessarily the golden prospect it would seem to the rest of the world. Motherhood, sanctity, those were the true ideals. Neither of them had I satisfied.

The sadness referred to the death of Rosa. "You will perhaps have read in the papers of the death of Sister Miriam, whom you knew as Rosabelle Powerstock. Perhaps like us, you felt that the coroner's remarks were a little unfortunate." In fact I had not actually seen a report of the inquest. My newspaper-combing phase had passed. I had been busy, and besides, Tom's wife had gone to stay with her mother. Later in the month, there was the prospect of a really long trip to Yugoslavia for the two of us.

"But even in these enlightened days," Mother Ancilla's measured letter continued, "I suppose we must remember that the Catholic faith was once persecuted in this country. There is still a great deal of prejudice about. Poor Sister Miriam, she did not have a very happy life latterly, she had been ill, and although the manner of her death was tragic—Sister Edward blames herself dreadfully and of course unnecessarily—one cannot altogether regret the passing of her life on this earth. R.I.P."

The third page astonished me by containing a remarkably pressing invitation to visit the convent as soon as possible. It was couched in language which, even disguised by Mother Ancilla's precise calligraphy, sounded remarkably like a plea.

"In fact, in general, these have not been very happy times for the community as a whole. I want to ask your help, dear Jemima, in a certain very delicate matter, which I cannot explain in a letter. Will you make time in a busy life to come down and see us? After all these years. As soon as possible . . ."

"*My* help," I thought lightly. "Mother Ancilla must be desperate to want *my* help." But as it turned out, that was quite a sensible reaction to her letter.

2
"I want to find myself"

I arranged to drive down to the convent the following
Saturday. My work would be over for the week—my
programme was recorded—and by Friday I was generally filled by a post-programme adrenalin in which all
things were possible, whether the programme had gone
well or badly. In this case it had gone well, and on
Friday night I was going to have dinner with Tom. He
also said that he would be able to spend the whole
night with me, in my flat.

"What if—she—telephones you at home?" I did not
particularly like saying Carrie's name, or introducing
her into the conversation. But the question had to be
asked. In the past we had both endured some unsuc-
cessful stolen nights, when Tom lay sleepless in my
bed, wretchedly imagining the unanswered telephone
and Carrie's subsequent anguish.

"She won't," said Tom cheerfully. "Mother-in-law's
telephone has broken. She chatted the wire through.
Thank God. Long may it stay that way."

I thanked God too. The Almighty suddenly seemed
to be taking a more friendly interest in my affairs.
Perhaps it was the influence of Mother Ancilla and the
prayers of the community? That reminded me to tell
Tom that I had to be off early the next morning. For a
moment I was almost tempted to postpone—no. It would
do Tom no harm to find that I too had some personal
commitments beyond the vicarious ones imposed on
me at second hand by Carrie. Though Tom might frown.

Later, Tom did frown. After all he loved me. We were
in love. He pushed back his hair off his forehead. It was
a gesture almost as familiar to me as his kiss. Tom's hair,
straight, floppy, unmanageable, was another of the persistent problems in his life. Still frowning, he said:

"Blessed Eleanor's Convent. Wasn't that the awful
place where the nun starved herself to death? Quite
mediaeval, the whole business. Nobody knows what

goes on beyond convent bars, you know. It was pure chance this case got out in the open because the nun actually died. I think the coroner was quite right."

"Oh Tom," I burst out. "Don't be so ridiculous. There aren't bars. It's a school. I was there in the war and afterwards. I must have told you. As for the coroner, I thought it was disgraceful what he said. Now Popery rides again." (I had since looked up the clippings.) "It was accidental death, no-one denied that, and he had no business blaming that poor young nun who gave evidence. Nuns have feelings just like anybody else."

"Well they don't look like anybody else," said Tom.

"Really—" Mother Ancilla's letter had made me feel curiously protective, even in the face of Tom.

"Or rather they all look just like each other. I saw a couple on the tube today. Couldn't possibly have told one from the other, even if one had been my sister. Two identical black crows."

"What extraordinary prejudice from Tom Amyas, M.P., that well-known hero of liberal causes."

Tom grinned. "Sorry. Some rooted anti-Papist prejudice in me somewhere. Relic of my childhood I think. The Inquisition and all that. I remember reading *Westward Ho!*—connections with my name—and being full of British indignation about it all. It still horrifies me: the idea of the imposition of *belief* upon others . . . you should know that."

"I hardly think that an obscure convent in Sussex full of harmless middle-aged women can be blamed for the horrors of the Spanish Inquisition four centuries ago," I said coldly. I was oddly narked by Tom's remarks. I tried to tell myself that at the first hint of Catholic persecution returning to this country—perish the unlikely thought—Tom would be the first to throw himself into the cause of quelling it. Save The Nuns: I could see him marching now with his banner. It was one of the things for which I loved him. But we had never discussed Catholicism before—why should we—and I hated to find even this corner of prejudice in my kind and gallant Tom, the champion of all those in trouble.

I thought of telling him that Mother Ancilla too was

in trouble, or thought she was. I decided not to. We dropped the subject.

But I remembered Tom's remark the next day as I drove up the long gravel drive to the convent. It was autumn. In the sunshine the convent grounds were immaculate. It was the season in which I had first arrived at Blessed Eleanor's as a day-girl. I walked with my mother from my parents' leaf-strewn autumnal garden, which had a kind of rich self-made compost underfoot throughout at this season, through to gardens where evidently no leaf was permitted to rest for very long before being tidied away.

"The nuns must catch the leaves before they fall," said my mother jokingly, to leaven the slightly tense atmosphere of a new school. She paused and gulped.

"My God, look at that." We both stopped and observed a nun—young? old? who could tell?—carefully catching a leaf long before it fluttered to the ground. She put it carefully away in a pocket, or anyway somewhere in the recesses of her black habit.

"Catching leaves is lucky." My mother was quick to seize on an occasion for optimism. "We'll find out who the lucky nun is, and you can make friends with her." I assented rather dubiously. But we never did find out who the lucky nun was. As Tom observed thirty years later, from a distance they really did all look exactly the same.

At that moment two nuns pulled a crocodile of small girls into the side of the drive as I passed. Identical. Two black crows. The children's uniform, a blur of maroon blazers and pink shirts, seemed singularly unchanged from my own day. I smiled. The children smiled amiably back. Both nuns smiled. The autumnal sun continued to shine, mellowing the rather fierce red brick of the convent façade. That too seemed much as I remembered it. Peaceful. Tidy. Even the creeper on the walls did not romp but climbed up in an orderly fashion. It was difficult to imagine what possible troubles could lie behind that calm exterior—troubles, that is to say, that could not be solved without recourse to the prying outside world. That was after all the world that I represented: Jemima Shore, Investigator, was how I was billed on television. It was a deliberate parody of the idea of the American detective, a piece of levity considering the serious nature of my programme. I was nevertheless an alien to the convent world. But Mother Ancilla had deliberately sent for Jemima Shore.

I stopped feeling an alien when a nun answered the door. She was very small. Ageless, as all nuns tended to be, with their foreheads and throats covered, so that the tell-tale signs of age were hidden. The short black cape covering the upper part of her body, whatever it was called, part of the nuns' uniform, also partially hid her waist. It had the effect of making her figure into a sort of bundle. She looked a bit like Mrs. Tiggy-Winkle—hadn't there been one nun we named Tiggy? Perhaps all small nuns looked like Mrs. Tiggy-Winkle. I gave my Christian name just in case.

"It's Jemima Shore to see Reverend Mother Ancilla."

"Ah Miss Shore," she beamed. So I didn't know her. "We've been expecting you." Into the reception room, a large room just by the front door, known for some reason as the Nuns' Parlour—although it was very much not part of the nuns' accommodation, being used exclusively for confrontations between secular and religious worlds. Here parents bringing quivering offspring to the convent for the first time were welcomed, smoothed down by Mother Ancilla, and made to feel—so my mother told me—that they themselves were about to enter a disciplined but friendly institution.

The Nuns' Parlour really was exactly the same. The reproduction holy pictures in their dark frames, with their dully gold backgrounds. Fra Angelico seemed the prime favourite. On the table lay the familiar pile of wedding photographs, still surely dating from the forties. At any rate they were still mainly by Lenare and not by Lichfield. Perhaps the old girls of Blessed Eleanor's had abandoned their propensity for lavish white weddings, like the rest of the world? These wedding photographs, when I was at school, had exercised the same secret fascination over me as the Jesuits. I used to gaze at them covertly when my father was discussing my need for better science instruction with Mother Ancilla.

"But Mother Curtis," he would say at the beginning of every term, finding the name Ancilla evidently too much to stomach: "Science instruction by *post* is really not enough to equip your girls for the modern world."

"Oh Captain Shore," Mother Ancilla would regularly reply with a tinkling laugh. "I keep asking Our Blessed Lord to send a vocation to a good young science mistress to help us out, but so far, He, in His infinite wisdom, has not seen fit to do so."

"I seem to remember a saying about God helping those who help themselves," began my father. No doubt he intended to refer to such unsupernatural expedients as advertisements and educational agencies. But no-one bandied words with Mother Ancilla and stood much chance of emerging the victor. Especially about Almighty God, someone whose intentions, mysterious as they were to the whole world, were somehow less mysterious to Mother Ancilla than to the rest of us. In the language of today, one would have referred to Mother Ancilla as having a hot line to God: or perhaps an open line was the correct term.

"Exactly, Captain Shore. Helping ourselves. That's exactly what we're doing with our postal science lessons. Just as Our dear Lord wants us to do."

My father gave up: till the beginning of the next term. I stopped gazing at the brides. Even then I suspected that I should never make that honorific folder. God might help those who helped themselves, but he did have a habit of not marrying them off. At least not in white.

As I turned over one photograph—the face was vaguely familiar—I heard a single sonorous bell ring somewhere in the convent. I recognised the signal. All the nuns had their own calling signal, like a kind of cacophonous morse code. One ring, then another for the Infirmary Sister, two then one for the Refectory Sister and so forth. One bell on its own called for the Reverend Mother.

Silence.

A pattering of feet on the heavily polished floor. The swish of robes outside the door, the slight jangle of a rosary that always presaged the arrival of a nun, and then—

"Jemima, my dear child." Reverend Mother Ancilla kissed me warmly on both cheeks. I reflected ruefully that probably to no-one else in the world these days was I, at nearly forty, still a child. My parents were both dead. Tom? I could not remember him using the term even in our most intimate moments. Besides Tom, as a crusader, liked to see in me a fellow crusader. He had his own rather demanding child in Carrie and, for Tom, to be childlike or childish was not necessarily a term of endearment.

I studied Mother Ancilla's face as we talked, and I answered her preliminary polite enquiries. Nuns' faces might not show age but they did show strain. On close inspection, I was faintly horrified by the signs of tension in her mouth. Her eyes beneath the white wimple were no longer the eyes of a fierce but benevolent hawk as they had been in my youth. They reminded me of some softer and more palpitating bird, the look of a bird caught in the hand, frightened, wondering.

"You never married, my child?" Mother Ancilla was asking.

I hesitated how to reply. There was still something compelling about Mother Ancilla. "Too much involved perhaps in your work," she said tactfully, after a minute's silence between us.

I nodded, relieved and disappointed at the same time. That would do. Besides, it was true. Until I met Tom I had been too much involved in my work—for marriage, if not for love.

"We here, of course," continued Mother Ancilla smoothly, "understand a life of devotion, for which the ideal of home and family is sacrificed. We too have made that sacrifice, in honour of Our Blessed Lord." She fell into silence again. "It can be very hard. Even at times too hard, unless the grace of God comes to our aid. Sister Miriam—"

"Yes, Mother?" I said as helpfully as possible.

"Perhaps the sacrifice was a little too much for her? Who can tell? Perhaps Sister Miriam should never have become a nun in the first place. I wondered so much about her vocation."

This was surprising. I had anticipated some more religious bromides, as I described them to myself, about the value of the sacrifice.

Mother Ancilla took my hand and said suddenly and urgently:

"Jemima, we must talk." This time she did not call me her child. "We don't have much time."

"I'm not all that busy," I began. I realised with a faint chill that she was talking about herself.

"I'll begin with Sister Miriam; Rosabelle as you knew her." It was a pathetic story, not uncommon perhaps in a single woman these days, a spinster. But I was conventional enough to be shocked by its happening to a nun. A decline in health. A form of nervous breakdown, culminating in a hysterical outburst in the middle of teaching. Sister Miriam was whisked away to a sister house of the convent in Dorset by the sea, a convalescent home. There she found the greatest difficulty in eating, although with the help of tranquillizers her composure returned. After six months Sister Miriam was adjudged ready to return to Blessed Eleanor's. But she was given light duties, French conversation with the Junior school—

I gave an involuntary smile. "That wouldn't have been a light duty in my day," I explained hastily.

"We have a language laboratory nowadays. The gift of an old girl."

A laboratory. That reminded me of the old days of my father's arguments. I wondered if God had ever sent Mother Ancilla that experienced science mistress. And was it too much to hope that God would also have inspired an old girl to endow a science laboratory?

"And the most beautiful science laboratory, by the way. How pleased Captain Shore would have been to hear that, wouldn't he, Jemima?" So she had not forgotten. Mother Ancilla never forgot an adversary.

"Did you get the science mistress too?" I couldn't resist asking.

Mother Ancilla opened her eyes wide.

"Why, of course. They both came together. Sallie Lund, an American girl. When she joined the Order in

1960 she was already a trained scientist, so naturally she could teach science here. And as her father pointed out, she could hardly teach science without a laboratory. A very dear man, and most practical about money, as Americans generally are. So he gave us it."

I was only surprised that it had taken Mother Ancilla till 1960 to iron this matter out.

We had been distracted. Mother Ancilla returned to a sadder topic than her scientific victories.

"As I was saying, Sister Miriam appeared to return to normal, although she still found great difficulty in eating. Difficulty that persisted for all her valiant efforts to overcome it. She told me once that strange visions seized her, that God wanted her to die, to go to Him, so that it was His will that she should not feed the flesh. . . ."

For a moment, I felt a strong distaste for the whole convent and all its works expressed in such language.

"I told her that it was God's will that she should make a good nun and eat up her supper. Such as it was," said Mother Ancilla sharply. I remembered that uncanny attribute she had of seeming to read one's thoughts.

"A form of anorexia nervosa, I suppose."

But the story got worse. Rosabelle began to talk of her visions, eat less, hide her food, got thinner, a doctor was called, more doctors. She got fatter again. She seemed more cheerful. She took more interest in life around her. One day when attention was no longer focused on her and her affairs she disappeared. A typed note was found: "I can no longer hide from the community that I have lost my vocation. I have gone to London to stay with my relations. Please don't try to find me. I want to find myself."

"I want to find myself!" I echoed. It was the phrase Rosa had used to me years ago in our teenage discussions about our future, lasting half the night.

"But of course she never went," I said.

"No, poor unhappy Sister Miriam. She went to Blessed Eleanor's Tower and locked herself in and—well, you probably know the rest. You probably read the newspapers." I nodded.

"What's her name? The nun who knew all the time where she was and never told."

"Sister Edward."

Sister Edward. She was the one I felt sorry for. But how she could have been such an idiot—"She is young, young in religion, she has only just stopped her postulancy. I think she really believed Sister Miriam when she spoke of her vision and the need to undergo a period of trial and purgation. And then when she realised that all along Sister Miriam had lain there, that the old key had snapped off, that she had tried to escape and been too weak, the door locked, growing gradually weaker, she nearly broke down herself."

"It might have been better not to go into the court with that story all the same."

Mother Ancilla opened her eyes wide. "That would have been against the law, Jemima." I was reminded of the formidable rectitude of the convent.

"All the same, to give the coroner the opportunity to refer to the centuries-long tradition of perverse practices and cruelty of the Church of Rome, and the suggestion that Sister Edward *gloried* in Sister Miriam's death."

"Our reputation is very low around here now I fear. They are simple people. It's quite deep country you know. Churne village has people in it who have never been to London, for all the short distance. The nuns hate to go shopping alone at the moment. Some very hurting remarks are made."

At last I perceived why Mother Ancilla had sent for me. It was, I assumed, to rectify the convent's "image" in the national, or at any rate, the local mind. With the touching faith of ordinary people in television, Mother Ancilla obviously thought her former pupil could do it for her.

"Jemima," said Mother Ancilla sharply, interrupting this train of thought. "You've got to tell us. Why did she die?"

Kinsey Millhone is...

"The best new private eye."   *—The Detroit News*

"A tough-cookie with a soft center."   *—Newsweek*

"A stand-out specimen of the new female operatives."
    —Philadelphia Inquirer

Sue Grafton is...

The Shamus and Anthony Award winning creator of Kinsey Millhone and quite simply one of the hottest new mystery writers around.

Bantam is...

The proud publisher of Sue Grafton's Kinsey Millhone mysteries:

☐	27991	"A" IS FOR ALIBI	$3.95
☐	28034	"B" IS FOR BURGLAR	$3.95
☐	28036	"C" IS FOR CORPSE	$3.95
☐	27163	"D" IS FOR DEADBEAT	$3.95
☐	27955	"E" IS FOR EVIDENCE	$3.95

BANTAM MYSTERY COLLECTION

- 27121 **APRIL WHEN THEY WOO** Adamson $3.50
- 27000 **DEAD ON ARRIVAL** Simpson $3.50
- 28175 **ELEMENT OF DOUBT** Simpson $3.50
- 28073 **JEMIMA SHORE'S FIRST CASE** Fraser $3.95
- 28213 **JUST ENOUGH LIGHT TO KILL** Maxwell $3.95
- 27773 **LAST SEEN ALIVE** Simpson $3.50
- 27908 **MAY'S NEW-FANGLED MIRTH** Adamson ... $3.50
- 27723 **MURDER MYSTERY TOUR** Babson $3.50
- 27470 **MURDER, MURDER, LITTLE STAR** Babson $3.50
- 28096 **MURDER SAILS AT MIDNIGHT** Babson $3.50
- 27772 **NIGHT SHE DIED** Simpson $3.50
- 28070 **OXFORD BLOOD** Fraser $3.95
- 27774 **PUPPET FOR A CORPSE** Simpson $3.50
- 27361 **REEL MURDER** Babson $3.50
- 27269 **THERE FELL A SHADOW** Peterson $3.50
- 27073 **THE TRAPDOOR** Peterson $3.50
- 28019 **YOUR ROYAL HOSTAGE** Fraser $3.95